HEARTS DECEIVED

THE DIVIDED HEARTS SERIES
BOOK THREE

MICHELLE BOLANGER

Author's Note

When I wrote *The Kiss* in 2015, I intended it to be a standalone novel. But when Alexander Koch marched onto the pages as a villain who was only supposed to have a single chapter as the creepy, entitled heir to a fortune, he became much more.

He was so unexpected that I simply HAD to give him his own story in *The Touch*, which was published a year later in 2016. His character growth taught me more than I understood then about my writing style, and how characters tell me their stories.

I'm still learning from him. I sincerely hope you enjoy him as much as I do. His massive personality continues to live rent free in my head even 10 years later!

PROLOGUE

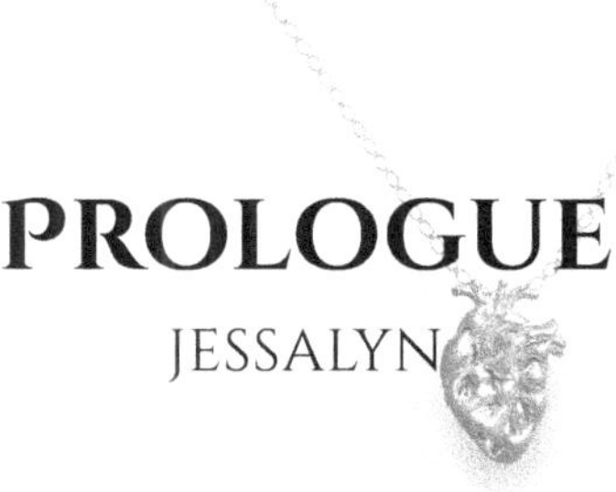

JESSALYN

(FIVE YEARS AGO)

Lyn's father walked behind her, surveying the fit of her royal blue suit. The tri-fold mirror allowed her to track his movements, and she tensed when he shook his head in frustration. He hovered over the trembling seamstress feverishly stitching the hem of her jacket.

"The sleeves are still too long," he said, his voice deceptively mild.

"I am sorry, Mr. Vogt. I apologize for the mistake." The woman's voice trembled.

"I paid you to do this job correctly the first time." He growled in frustration when the phone in his hand rang. "Excuse me." He swiped a finger across the screen as he left the room. "This is Marcus."

The door closed behind him, and the tailor's shoulders dropped. Lyn fidgeted with the hem of the jacket as the tailor adjusted the offending sleeve.

Her Mother sat across the dressing room; her pale blue-gray eyes moved between the tailor and the door as her thin hands twisted together in her lap.

Without the constant criticism, the young woman finished quickly. She didn't make eye contact with either of the other two women as she tidied up her supplies.

Lyn frowned. She was used to her father's temper and ached to reach out to the woman. But fear of her father held her back. There was no telling what he would do if he caught her consoling the help.

Unwilling to stay silent, Lyn dipped her head and spoke softly, "Thank you, Melinda. The suit fits perfectly."

The tailor's small smile vanished when her father opened the door. The bitter scent of his anger filled the room.

"That will be all." He moved quickly, and Lyn choked back a cry as his hand connected with her cheek. "You do not address the help by their first names. Have I taught you nothing?"

Fighting the urge to cover the stinging skin, she stared at the floor and pinched back tears. The tailor gathered the rest of her things and backed quickly out the door.

"Look at me when I'm speaking to you, Lyn."

Smoothing her features into an emotionless mask, she did as he asked. Staring back at her from his livid face were hazel eyes like hers. His were hard and cold, but she refused to show fear as his gaze slid over her face, examining her hair and makeup.

"You're as weak as your mother," he finally said. "Pretty will only get you so far. The Kochs won't put up with your weaknesses like I do."

Anger darkened her cheeks, but she pushed down. She did what she had seen her mother do so many times and wiped all traces of emotion from her face. Her next response would either diffuse him or set him off like a powder keg.

All her life, she had watched her mother pick herself up off the floor after arguments. Cowering, she would wait for him to leave the room, his anger spent, before cleaning up the mess of blood, or more often, broken glass.

Lyn couldn't understand why she took his abuse without complaint, or why she stayed with him at all. She had tried many times to get her mother to leave, but she always refused.

She was ten the last time she brought it up.

"I can't leave, Lyn. Your father and I are bonded. I can't break it no matter how much I might want to."

"Who cares about the bond! Let's just leave. We can hide somewhere. He doesn't have to know where." Lyn pleaded.

"Don't talk about what you don't understand. Get leaving out of your head. It's not the way we're made. When I took your father's blood, I committed my life to his. The choices we've made since then don't change the fact that he is my intended." Her mother's tone hardened. "There are some things you aren't ready to hear. Don't ask me again."

She didn't. Instead, she watched, listened, and learned, swearing she would never live with a man like her father. On a regular basis, he brought home human women, crushing her heart every time. She listened to the way he belittled her mother, hating him more every day. As she grew older, she learned how to hide her echo, and how to avoid his wrath.

Most of the time, she and her mother could avoid the worst of his outbursts by leaving the room. But on days like today, when it was impossible to avoid him, complete submission to his demands was the only way to prevent a confrontation. That, and hiding their own emotions.

Despite enduring a lifetime of his angry outbursts and hateful words, this was the first time he ever struck her. She didn't trust her voice.

When she didn't react further, he turned on his heel. "Wait here."

The door shut behind him, and her mother's gray eyes closed in sympathy.

"Oh, Lyn," her mother sighed. "Marcus only wants the best for you and from you."

"You keep telling me that, Mother." Angry and frustrated, Lyn's hands shook as she touched up her makeup. Minutes later, the dressing room door opened. The bite of anger in his scent had calmed a little.

"Today you will take your place as a pledged female in the Clan," he said.

There was nothing in his statement to indicate he was pleased. Instead, it sounded more like he was passing her off to someone else and was glad to do it.

"The Kochs are a powerful family, and the Elder honored us by allowing me to present you as their son's mate." His eyes fixed on her. "I expect you to show him the respect he deserves."

"Yes, Father." Remembering her mother's lessons, she suppressed the echo of her voice, dropping her eyes in what she hoped would be interpreted as respect. The pungent scent of his rage simmered just below the surface of his control. One wrong word would set him off again. She froze when he stepped closer and placed a kiss on top of her head.

"I'll do my best not to disappoint you, Sir."

He presented her with a brown bag emblazoned with the familiar white Louboutin script on the front. "Wear these. You won't look so diminutive and fragile in a proper pair of stilettos."

"Thank you, Father." She took the bag with barely trembling fingers and lowered to the bench beside her mother to slip into the new shoes.

Less than an hour later, she followed her parents up the impressive front stairs to the Koch mansion. She faintly heard the butler, Rosston, move the town car out of the way where would wait until the meeting was over. She wished she could stay out here and talk to him. Rosston was more like a father to her than a servant.

When she'd been younger, she would slip away and find him working in the barns. They would talk for hours, but now she rarely got to see him at all.

"Stop picking at the jacket, Lyn." Her mother's German accent was strong with warning.

"Yes, Mother." Lyn glanced up to make sure her father wasn't paying attention.

The broad shoulders of his hand-tailored suit of charcoal merino wool blocked her view. The stairs leading up to the mansion were roughhewn, and she watched her steps carefully to keep from scuffing the expensive blue suede. Damaging them would earn her lecture, or worse, when they returned home.

The door opened, but she was unable to see butler who greeted them.

"Mr. and Mrs. Vogt." The man's voice was soft yet firm, giving the impression they were expected, but not entirely welcome.

Her mother laid a hand on her father's lifted forearm, allowing him to escort her inside. Her parents entered the wide foyer as the butler half bowed and gestured with a white-gloved hand, indicating she should follow them inside.

"Miss Vogt." His gray hair was neatly slicked to one side, and his crisp black tuxedo made her feel as though she'd stepped back in time. Back when horse-drawn carriages dispensed people in front of mansions like this one, and perfectly written calling cards announced the identity of the visitor.

When the butler briefly met her eyes Lyn thought she saw a flash of pity in their brown depths before he turned away and closed the large door behind them.

"The Kochs will meet you in the parlor. This way please," he said, stepping past them into the room.

The foyer floor stretched out in large flagstone pieces that carried the feel of the outdoors inside. Curved walls rose around them, ending two stories above at the point of a wood-beamed roof where gleaming windows let in the fading red light of the Arizona evening. The entire mansion looked like an odd mix of middle age castle and southwestern style that somehow worked.

"I am proud of you, Jessalyn." Her father cleared his throat, and Lyn blinked at the pride in his normally impassive hazel eyes.

Whether the pride was in her, or for her good fortune at being pledged to such a wealthy man, she couldn't tell, but the compliment was so rare, Lyn found herself smiling slightly.

She drew a deep breath, and the thick citrus smell of a powerful Vampir male filled her sinuses with an ache she wasn't prepared for. The weight of his scent rode through the air of the mansion, swimming though her body and catching in her lungs.

He's in pain. Her chest hurt at the weight of it, and her heart surged in sympathy. The longer she breathed it, the more the burning sensation crushed down on her. She cleared her throat to hide a whimper and earned a stern look from her mother. As they walked, the smell of pain grew almost unbearably, tightening her hands into fists. Raised voices filtered down the hall.

"Another one? Really, Father?" The voice was a deep baritone. "Do you honestly think she will be any different than the others?" He sneered the last word, and Lyn flinched.

As an urge to rush to his side and comfort him crested over her, a sudden change in the male's scent froze her in place. The sharp spike of clove speared through the sweetness of orange. In it was the same bitter frustration and undercurrent of anger that rolled off her father.

Lyn's heart raced in fear as her parents continued to follow the butler toward the argument. Dread settled as reality sank in. Her nightmare was coming true.

"The difference no longer matters. The Clan has been gracious, but they are reaching the end of their patience with you. Miss Vogt's family is willing to overlook your behavior, and you should be grateful!"

Overlook what behavior? Helplessness set her hands trembling, and she was unable to make her feet move. Her father noticed she was not following, and his eyes snapped at her, demanding she move. But her feet were leaded with weights as the rest of their conversation chilled her blood.

"Grateful?" The first voice rose in a growl. "For what? Making me meet yet another female I will never be able to touch?"

"Alexander!" the second voice snapped. "You know that is not a condition the Clan is concerned with."

By now her parents and the butler had also stopped. Her mother's sympathetic eyes locked with hers while the argument continued.

The voice she now knew to be Alexander's gritted out. "They've given me until I am twenty-four. Wasn't that the arrangement?" There was a pause and what must have been an affirmative answer. "Then send her away. I still have three years to enjoy what little pleasure the humans provide before taking the oath of celibacy a Bond Mate will force on me." Heavy footsteps resounded on wood floors, and Lyn flinched at each one.

"Four years, Alexander." The steps paused. "Then you will claim her. It has already been agreed to."

"Fine." More steps, then a slamming door.

Lyn stared sightlessly at her mother. When she refocused, she was jolted to see tears wetting her mother's cheeks. The anger in the air soured into the violent stench that often filled the room just before her father lashed out.

Lyn's eyes widened with fear as her father's shoulders stiffened and the veins in his neck pulsed heavily under his skin. He never lost his temper in public, but she could smell how close he was to it and shivered.

Voices from the room just a few strides ahead were hushed, and she heard a female's gentle tones attempting to soothe the man. After few more seconds, heavy footsteps, less hurried than the others, approached.

Out of a large doorway on the left stepped Gregor Koch, Alexander's father. Taller and broader than her father, the expression on his face was murderous. Lyn's stomach twisted so painfully she took a step back. Bright red hair was cropped closely to the man's head, and he was swiftly buttoning his suit coat as though he had just risen from a chair.

His eyes widened when he saw the four of them standing in shocked silence in the hallway, but he recovered quickly.

"My sincere apologies for my son's absence." His lips thinned, and chillingly brilliant green eyes fell on her. Lyn squared her shoulders as she'd been taught and lowered her chin, waiting for his dismissal. "Miss Vogt, I must regretfully inform you that Alexander will not be available to meet you tonight. He has gone back to school earlier than expected. We will contact you when he has returned."

Alexander
(Six months later)

THE BITING smell of the pine boughs strung across the wide mantel of the dining room stung Alexander's nostrils, and the string quartet he hired for his parents' memorial service aggravated his headache. He debated sending them home early, though neither the smell nor the music was the root cause of the ache. It was the constant touch of the females trying to console him that were the real problem.

Throughout the service, he did his best to be gracious to those who either forgot or chose to ignore the pain their touch caused him.

Shaking the hand of another male and attempting to avoid his mate, Alexander suppressed painful tremors when she laid her hand on his forearm.

"We were so sorry to hear about your father's fall," the female said. "I sat with your mother for a few hours that day. She accepted death well."

"Thank you for being there for her, Mrs..." He disengaged from her and took a step back.

"Kristopher. Danielle Kristopher." The woman gestured to her mate. "I don't think I could accept my death so easily if something happened to Jackson."

Alexander reminded himself she meant well and inclined his head. "We never know what we're capable of until the moment comes."

He excused himself and turned to look for a servant with a drink tray. When he did, he lifted a glass of wine and sipped the cool liquid.

Gregor Koch fell to his death while scaling the rock face of a potential building site here in Arizona. Less than a day later, his mother succumbed to the agony of the broken connection. Unable to survive without his father's blood to sustain her, the blood need poisoned her.

The blood need made double funerals the standard for Vampir. Death to either member of a bonded pair meant death for the other, usually within days, sometimes sooner.

He sighed and glanced at his watch. Everyone here had known about his parent's death before he did. He'd been in Cancun after a memorable excursion with his father's secretary; the news reaching him several days after their deaths. Then, at twenty-one, he became the heir apparent for all things Koch.

Taking another swallow of the wine, he surveyed the room. His eyes landed on a young boy, probably thirteen or fourteen, intently watching a pair of girls much older than himself. The females actually looked closer to Alexander's age. His gaze went back to the boy.

He'd been about this boy's age when he'd suddenly become unable to touch a Vampir female without excruciating pain. The slightest touch from burned like hot oil. The longer or stronger the touch, the more intense the pain.

Repeated contact from those who only wanted to offer condolences meant his hand and arm prickled like thousands of needles were being driven into his skin.

He knew he should go introduce himself to the girls, but willingly adding to his pain wasn't something he intended to do. He's endured enough pain.

It seemed he was always enduring pain. The pain of touch, the pain of pitying looks from those who believed his pain made him weak, and now, the pain of loss. Through it all, Alexander's reliance on his closest advisor's training had enabled him to avoid the damage he knew he would cause if he ever let the anger get the best of him. Through Peter's physical training, his hard-won discipline of body and mind was the only thing that kept him from beating the life out of someone. He nodded to Peter who stood across the room talking to the Clan Elder, Res, and her mate, Samuel.

The burning of his skin should have been the worst he would have to endure during the service, but his older brother, Benjamin, arrived. Cursing as he came through the door, Benjamin's slurred voice cutting through the subdued chatter of the room like a knife.

"Finally dead are they, Alex? You must be delighted."

A hush fell over the room, the fading notes of a melancholy violin the only sound. Benjamin paused, his face drawing into a scowl.

"Am I the only one willing to say what you are all thinking?" he asked.

"Let's talk about this in private," Alexander suggested.

Benjamin wouldn't be silenced. He raised an arm to gesture sweepingly to the grandeur of the memorial and then locked eyes with Alexander.

"My perfect little brother," he sneered. "Still under the Elder's complete control."

Heat rose in Alexander's neck, and he regulated his breathing into the measured rhythm that kept his focus from the pain, mentally thanking Peter.

"Perhaps we can discuss this privately in the library." With another steady breath, Alexander approached his brother and gestured to the hallway behind him.

The closer Alexander got, the clearer it became that his brother was past reasoning. Benjamin was seventeen years older, and the second youngest of the six Koch brothers. Only Alexander remained in the Clan, and Benjamin resented him for it.

Benjamin stood nearly as tall as he was, but instead of the

broad shoulders and heavy build Alexander had inherited from their father, his brother was wiry like their mother. Both had their father's red hair and light complexion, but Benjamin's eyes were a pale gray like their mother's. In those eyes, Alexander saw a lifetime of devastation and bitterness lying just under the sheen of alcohol.

"You, their little prince," Benjamin spat. Alexander huffed in amusement. Benjamin's hands balled into fists as he glared around the room. "How many of these pretty people know the truth about you, Alex? About the deal..."

"What would you know about anything?" The Elder, Res Detrich, swept between them, her champagne-colored gown swishing loudly in the deafening silence.

When Benjamin turned his gaze on her, Alexander tensed at the dangerous look on his brother's face, but she didn't pause.

"Your parents followed the rules and released you at twenty-five." She pointed out the broad window to their left where a rare snowfall dusted the ground. "You married a human and left this life. Don't think you can come in here—"

"My *wife* and the rest of the women you despise are people just like you!" He spit the words at her and leveled a finger at Alexander. "What you are allowing him to do by waltzing into their lives, flashing our family wealth, and taking whatever he wants is a disgrace!"

A collective gasp rose from the room, and Alexander's carefully guarded control slipped. He reached out to take his brother by the arm, but before he could react, Benjamin swung a fist. In his drunkenness, he missed, striking Res in the shoulder and sending her toppling to the ground.

Alexander's fist instinctively shot upward, connecting solidly with the bottom of his brother's jaw. The impact lifted him off his feet, sending him flat backward onto the floor. Alexander snatched his brother's body up from the floor. As he drew his arm back for another punch, a familiar strong hand caught his wrist.

"Alexander, stop!" Peter twisted his hand painfully. The room spun, and Alexander dropped his brother in disgust.

"Get him out of here!" He turned to see the wide eyes of everyone in the room staring at his loss of contorl.

Curling his lip, he shook Peter off and helped Samuel steady Res as she slowly rose to her feet. Rage and embarrassment surged through him as his pain levels rocketed off the charts. From the corner of his eye, he saw the pair of girls running out of the mansion as if a demon were after them.

Disgusted with himself, Alexander ordered everyone out. "The service is over. Get out of my house. All of you!"

Not waiting to see who dared stay, Alexander spun on his heels and stalked up the stairs to his room. Slamming the door, he ripped the tie from around his neck and reached for his phone.

The comforting voice of his father's former secretary, now his secretary, promised a quick relief from the pain. She'd been willing enough to lie in his bed for the past few months. Playing the grief card should gain him even more attention.

"Rebekka, leave your door unlocked. I'll be there as soon as I can get my pilot to the airfield." Her murmured assent was all he needed to hear before placing the call to his pilot. He was getting out of this house and didn't care if he ever came back. The pain was too much.

His penthouse in Seattle was already fully furnished in anticipation of his graduation, so there was no need to pack anything. Out of habit he straightened the room and pulled the door shut behind him. By the time he descended the stairs, the only people left were the servants tidying up.

The Clan wasn't getting anything from him anytime soon. Until they forced him to honor the farce of a bonding his father had arranged, he would run his father's company and enjoy the freedom his insane wealth provided.

Expecting his father's driver to be waiting for him, Alexander exited the house and crossed the driveway, pausing at Peter's massive form leaning against the limousine.

"Where are you going?" Peter's level gaze should have made him stop to think, but he was too angry to care.

"To Seattle." He snapped and opened the rear door. "I have a company to run now that my father is dead."

Peter rested a hand on the door and pressed it closed. "That's not why you're leaving."

He knew better than to challenge Peter, but he wasn't staying. "Doesn't matter why. I'm leaving." He tipped his chin toward the empty driver's seat. "Are you driving, or am I?"

Peter stepped away from the car. "This is all you, my friend. One day I hope you realize you can't do it alone."

"Watch me." Alexander pushed him aside and slid into the driver's seat, gunning the car down the drive. In the rear-view mirror, he saw Peter's shoulders fall before he turned and re-entered the mansion.

As the landscape rolled past and Alexander approached the tiny private airfield and hanger, he rubbed a hand over his heart as a new kind of pain pierced his chest.

CHAPTER
ONE
ALEXANDER

Alexander shifted weight onto the balls of his feet as the heavy bag drifted in a lazy arc to his left. Rivers of sweat ran down his back and soaked into his white t-shirt and the top of his black shorts. Refusing to acknowledge the burning in his eyes and the ache in his muscles, he kept his gaze trained on the bag. He focused on a ripple in the black leather before his tightly taped left hand flashed out to strike the target. He followed up with his right knee, punishing the leather with a brutal impact and sending the bag spinning away from him once again.

The rest of the gym was empty this early in the morning, echoing with the sound of his grunting exhales and the violent impacts of his fists, knees, and feet on the slick black leather bag. It rotated back toward him, and this time, he dropped a shoulder, bent his knees, and swiveled his hips to land an uppercut that would lay an opponent out backward.

Alexander had trained in a gym like this, *exactly* like this, in

Arizona as a young boy. His father had brought him to the front door of it after Alexander lost his temper and kicked a hole in the wall of his bedroom. The gym's owner, Peter Samuelson, had immediately escorted him into one of the fighting rings and substantially lowered Alexander's lofty opinion of himself. Peter led him back to his father, bleeding from his nose and nursing a sprained wrist, casually advising his father to bring Alexander back the next day.

Panting, Alexander remembered the weeks following that first encounter. Six mornings a week his father dropped him off at five am, and Peter took the angry, undisciplined young man and instilled the necessity for control.

The clock chimed four am, and Alexander rolled his shoulders, squaring his hips as the bag rotated clockwise and he prepared to land another series of kicks and punches. His exhausted body was weakening, and each impact stung. Hours and hours of time spent like this had conditioned his body into the machine it was, since exhausting himself was the only effective way to drown out the constant pain.

Still slightly crouched, Alexander sighed at the memory of the one touch that had soothed the pain. Almost exactly a year earlier, he'd encountered his intended. But all he knew was her name. *Jessi.* Just the thought of her name soothed him because he knew she was out there. However, as quickly as the relief came, frustration ratcheted up the pain again.

Alexander could still see the fear that blazed in her eyes when their gazes collided the first time. Fear so intense she'd fled the Gathering before he could stop her from disappearing without a trace. Months and thousands of dollars later, the only lead he had was a consistent trail of suspicious phone calls between Southern California and Phoenix, Arizona. Circumstantial at best, but it was all he had to go on.

Alexander sometimes regretted using the reality of his pain to guilt Baden into using the Clan's network to track her down, but he was desperate. The dark-haired beauty was the only one who could permanently relieve his pain. But it was so much more than that.

Alexander shook out his arms, bouncing lightly from one foot to the other. Though the wealth he'd inherited from his parents satisfied him for a while, even before his brief encounter with Jessi, something inside him shifted. Eleven months ago, life in the Clan flipped upside down when Koen Lockton, Emerick Tate, and Baden Dietrich challenged the Elder, Res Dietrich. They exposed her years of deception and saved their people from extinction by reuniting them with other Vampir around the world. He hadn't believed them until Leisel Lockton's courage forced him to stop feeling sorry for himself, open his eyes, and take a stand.

However, none of that relieved his pain. Only Jessi could do that. She must have sensed his agony as well as the way her touch alleviated it. What he didn't know, was what he'd done to make her run. Was it his reputation? The sheer intensity of his pain?

Frustration coiled his muscles and launched the uppercut he had perfected years ago. The chains holding the bag sang with the impact, and he winced at the memory of the one time he had used such force against a person outside a boxing ring.

In the ten years he had spent perfecting the discipline he was so proud of, Alexander had only lost control once. The memory of his brother's lifeless body slumped on the mansion floor haunted him. Not long after it happened, he had sworn to both himself and Peter it would never happen again. Late nights spent here releasing the tension and frustration had enabled him to keep his promise.

Sweat dripped into his eyes, and as he hastily wiped it away with the back of his forearm, a voice behind him made him flinch.

"At it again, Alex?"

"Alexander." He corrected automatically and dropped his fists to his sides.

His hands stung painfully, and his shoulders were on fire. He'd been beating the bag in front of him for nearly two hours and could finally feel true exhaustion setting in. Reaching out, he caught the bag and stopped its movement. Glancing over his shoulder at the man behind him, he grimaced. He'd been so lost in his thoughts he hadn't heard Peter approach. The man would make him pay for that mistake in the ring later.

"Still nothing on Jessi?" Peter asked.

With a huff of a laugh, Alexander shifted toward him and barely managed to dodge the roundhouse Peter aimed at his head. He ducked and caught the other man's foot in his hand.

Peter swept his body around, jerking his foot out of Alexander's grip and grinning as he rotated away, landing lightly on the balls of his feet. Peter stood half an inch taller and thirty pounds of solid muscle heavier.

Alexander warily surveyed the man he now called a friend and wondered if he would ever beat him in a match. Even when he wasn't exhausted, those odds were not very high. Alexander was reaching the end of his strength. Not just tonight, but all of it. He'd spent the last year looking for her.

Jessi.

If he closed his eyes, he could still feel the graze of her hand across his lower back, the touch of her hand so light he might never have noticed it if not for the intensely soothing effect she'd had on his skin. He knew instantly she felt it too. He heard it in her voice; had felt it wrap around him like a cold compress.

And he had seen the light of recognition in her beautiful hazel eyes at their connection—just before it dissolved into a fear he didn't understand. Then, she was gone. Running from him as though he were the devil himself.

Peter watched with a calculating look. Alexander both admired and hated that stare. Peter had a knack for not just leveling punches, but knocking down excuses, doubts, and worry in the lives of those he mentored. More than once, he'd pulled Alexander back from a self-destructive ledge, and he would always be thankful for it.

Alexander stepped back from the heavy bag, peeling the grayed and torn tape from his hands and wrists. His breathing had nearly returned to normal, and his heart rate slowed. Shaking his head to dislodge the sweat from his brows, he winced as his long ponytail slapped his cheek with a wet sting.

"You can't stay here all morning, Alexander," Peter smirked then jerked a thumb over his shoulder. "Hit the shower and I'll buy your coffee."

The Broken Bean coffee shop was quiet when Jessi arrived. She parked her truck next to her manager's Honda at the back door and pulled open the heavy steel door to enter the brightly lit hallway. The familiar scent of freshly roasted coffee greeted her, and she leaned into the roasting room to inhale the rich buttery smell of the batch currently spinning in the old machine. The smell alone was enough to wake her completely.

It was crazy early in the morning, but the bill for her horse's emergency vet visit would set her back a week's worth of pay, so coming in early for a few weeks would certainly help.

After hanging her jacket on the peg and slipping an apron around her neck, she crossed the hallway to wash her hands in the tiny bathroom. Humming to herself, she heard men's voices filtering toward her over the hum of the roaster.

Sighing, she rinsed her hands, shut off the water, and reached for a towel. She had intended to put the extra cash back in case she needed to move again. The thought caused her to run a palm over her chest, wondering if the ache of hiding from her mate would ever go away. Just as she grabbed the towel, a booming male laugh from the front sent chills down her spine.

It can't possibly be him. Not here! She tossed the damp paper then pulled the bathroom door open to listen.

A smell she would never forget swept through the cracked door, and she fought the same stinging tears she wrestled with every time she thought of him. She slowly inhaled Alexander Koch's crisp orange and clove scent. The smell that haunted her nightmares and fueled her dreams. Her hands shook as she fought down the desire to rush to him.

"Oh, Alexander," she breathed. Her eyes pinched closed as the ache intensified, stealing her breath for a moment. She opened her eyes and tried to block out his pain.

Hesitating in the bathroom, she picked something different out of his scent. She couldn't explain it and didn't want to get close enough to find out, but it was different from when she unexpectedly touched him a year ago at the Gathering. She cursed herself for weeks after that night, angry she let her friends talk her into going.

Before then, she had been so careful to avoid any place members of the Clan might be. But when she heard there were other Vampir Clans around the world, and they would be at the Compound, curiosity got the better of her. She had never personally been to the huge home they called the Compound, and just being there that night set her nerves on end.

Her parents had been out of the country, and her looks had changed enough she wouldn't be mistaken for who she once was, but she knew there was still a chance someone would recognize her. If it had been Alexander of all people was terrifying.

She never expected him to be there. He should have left the Clan at twenty-five. That was the way it was for Vampir males who were not bonded or at least pledged. There were so many more men born than women, it was a reasonable law.

As Alexander's voice and raw scent continued to roll down the hallway, his deep baritone sent her traitorous stomach into a flurry of excitement. The draw she felt toward him was incredibly powerful and stronger than ever. She'd followed his career, and every time she saw his picture in a newspaper or tabloid, her body ached to be near him. She drew in another lungful, sending a rush of chills across her stomach. She tightened her grip on the door to prevent herself from running to him.

"I have to return to Seattle tomorrow." Alexander sounded tired.

She took a moment to assess his state of mind and realized the scent she had memorized was strong but dull like a worn blade.

"I hoped Thomas and his team could handle the transaction, but they are forcing me to attend the shareholder meeting." Frustration cut through, and his anger spiked with a bitter bite of clove.

See? He's as angry as ever. Despite it, or perhaps because of it, her heart refused to stop pushing her to go to him. She rested her head against the doorframe, hoping he would leave before she lost her resolve.

A different man's voice responded quietly. Another Vampir, she was shocked to realize. Completely focused on Alexander, she'd nearly missed the mix of salty water and pine riding underneath the other smells.

This man was steady, measured, disciplined. "I'll keep my eyes open for her, Alexander. Baden is confident she's in this area somewhere."

Oh, gods.... with a jolt she realized they were talking about her. *How did they get this close?* The scent of his frustration bled away from Alexander as he answered, and his sudden calm left her even more confused.

"Thank you, Peter. I've run out of places to look." The front door chimed, and their voices faded on their way out. "I'll call you when I get to the office."

The door banged shut and her manager yelled, "Jessi! I need to leave. Are you back there?"

Cringing, she stepped from the hallway into the subdued lighting of the store front. Brandon's head was down as he wiped off an empty table. Presumably, the one Alexander and Peter just vacated. He looked up and smiled. "Thanks for coming in so early."

"I don't mind." Jessi glanced nervously out the window. Not seeing any cars, she relaxed. "Armani racked up another vet bill last night, so I can use the money."

Brandon shook his head, straightening and tossing the cloth into a bucket of water that smelled faintly of bleach. "That horse is going to kill someone." He carried the bucket and followed her behind the counter as the door chimed again. "Are you sure he's worth all the trouble?"

She turned to straighten the bottles of flavorings and bags of coffee that lined the mirrored wall behind the espresso machine. "The broken ones are always worth the trouble, Brandon. They just take a special touch and lots of love." The breeze from the door swept over her, and she froze. Salt and pine washed over her as her words faded.

In the mirror's reflection, she met the eyes of the man who matched the scent. The other Vampir, Peter. His eyes narrowed, and dread rose in her stomach even though she knew he would see someone who looked nothing like the twenty-year-old girl who ran away five years ago.

The straight hair that had once been long enough to sit on was cut and fell in rough layers around her shoulders, the tips dyed deep pine green. Gone also were the perfectly tailored suits and dresses. Instead, she wore a thigh-length patchwork skirt of muted greens and blues over gray tights and a pair of gray knee-high boots with bright blue laces. Under the coffee shop apron, her green cotton shirt was dyed unevenly, and the light blue cardigan frayed at the seams. Her once perfectly manicured hands had a ring on every finger, and stacks of bracelets encircled her tiny wrists. Only her height and eye color might yet give her away. Or her voice.

Did I disguise my voice?

She had never met this male, but her father had posted her picture everywhere after she disappeared. If he looked closely enough, he might see the resemblance. Especially if she had just given herself away as a Vampir female.

The male's eyes flicked over her, but she held her gaze steady, unwilling to give him reason to think she identified him. She schooled her stare into a look of cool amusement at his perusal, though she knew from his scent that was not his intent.

Careful to keep the echo out of her voice, she turned to face him. "Is there something I can help you with?"

Her confidence wavered when she realized the man standing across the counter from her was huge. Easily over six and half feet tall and shoulders wide as a truck. He filled the room with his presence, but there was a gentleness about him she couldn't put her finger on. He reminded her of her older horse, Ulysse, the tall, powerful beast of a sport horse who was as gentle as a kitten.

A long sleeve shirt hugged his upper body, and the burgundy sleeves were pushed up just below his elbows, accentuating his massive size. She always thought Alexander was the largest man she had ever seen, but this man was clearly larger. His intelligent blue eyes drifted down to her shoulders, and her cheeks flamed.

"I was just admiring the color in your hair. I like green." She bristled, but before she could respond, he reached for something on one of the chairs. "I forgot my gloves." With a tight smile, he nodded. "Have a nice day." His gaze lowered then met hers again. "Jessi."

He turned to go, and as the door swung shut behind him a second time, she cursed and slapped the counter in front of her making Brandon laugh.

"I've never heard you curse before!" When she turned to him, he was shrugging into his jacket. "Do you know him?"

"No." Jessi shook herself out of her shock and wondered what he would say if he knew the truth. "Never seen him before in my life."

The boardroom door swung closed behind him, and Alexander smoothed the navy suit coat over his flat stomach. The door had let him in at exactly the center of a conference table four feet wide and twelve feet long, made of darkly stained walnut. Across it, he looked out a wall of floor to ceiling windows. From the twenty-fifth floor, he could see most of Seattle's skyline.

Stepping further into the room, he braced his hands on the edge of the table and sighed. In an hour, this room would fill with the board of directors, three partners, his attorney, and multiple staff. None of them were going to like what he was about to tell them. Pushing away from the table, he unbuttoned his suit jacket then tucked his hands in his pockets.

His Tom Ford wingtips were silent on the dark brown carpet as he strode around the far end of the table, where he stopped close enough to the windows to feel the coolness of the thick glass on his face. The cars below looked like toys, and the people were nothing but specks gliding along the sidewalks. He felt as small as they looked.

His CFO would be here first to go over the financials before anyone else arrived, but Alexander already knew what he would see. He had kept close tabs on things despite his absence. Over the last twelve months, Koch Architectural Design had grown, nearly doubling their annual profits, making shareholders extremely happy. All without Alexander's influence, making his board and partners very *un*happy.

He hadn't intended to stay gone so long, but once he got away from boardrooms and high-rise offices with fake smiles and even faker personalities, he found himself less and less inclined to return. Especially when he knew *she* was out there.

Before that moment, he had no hope of anything ever being different and therefore *wanted* nothing different. Money, power, the arms of a woman, and the finest things money could buy sustained him. He even believed they were enough to satisfy him. Now, he realized how fragile and hollow that kind of satisfaction was. He was shallow.

I've been *shallow*, he corrected himself.

Spending the past year away from the dynasty his father built had changed him. Changed him too much to think he could ever come back here and be the charismatic and controlling executive he once was. Moreover, he should have already left the Vampir. But as the youngest Koch, and no new heir possible, he was expected to remain, manage the company, and assume his family's place in the Clan. At twenty-six, he was young, and while the business world loved to praise him for having accomplished so much already, the pressure to maintain a Fortune 500 company wasn't what he wanted from life. At least not anymore.

He focused on his reflection in the glass and frowned. His thoughts drifted back to his last conversation with Koen and Leisel Lockton before they left the Compound to begin their new life in Illinois.

Leisel had risen on her toes to kiss him on the cheek, prickling his nerves. "You'll find her, Alexander."

Koen stood beside her, his arm possessively around her waist. "We'll do all we can to help." He reached out his hand, and when Alexander started to shake it, he realized Koen wasn't offering a handshake but trying to give him something. "My father gave this to me when I thought I had no hope left."

Alexander pulled his hand back. "I can't take that."

"As long as your heart beats, there is always hope, Alexander." Leisel took the anatomical heart necklace from Koen and, careful not to touch him, wrapped it around his wrist. She looked up at him with her shimmering green eyes. "We want you to have it. A reminder to never give up hope."

His fingers slid further into his pocket and wrapped around the heavy steel pendant. He stood in the empty boardroom, ready to do the one thing he knew would disappoint his father the most.

But he isn't here. Alexander reminded himself. *He isn't here, and I am not him.*

The door behind him opened, and Alexander sighed as Rebekka entered. He watched the woman in the reflection of the smooth glass. She placed her briefcase on the chair to the right of his at the head of the table.

Rebekka was everything he once chased, though with her, he never really had to. Her long legs strode toward him on a pair of silver Jimmy Choo pumps, and her shapely hips swayed in the gray linen suit, perfectly tailored to skim every curve. The jacket was unbuttoned to reveal a lightly ruffled placket on the pale peach blouse tucked into her skirt.

Her flat stomach and ample chest gave her an almost perfect hourglass shape. At her throat, the flawlessly tanned skin had a light shimmer, and the closer she got, he could smell the fragrance of the perfume he bought her two years ago. Dark auburn hair was swept into a low chignon at the back of her neck, and he knew exactly which pin to pull out so it would cascade down her back in silky curls. As the familiar tension crept up between them, he clenched his fist.

"It's been a year, Alexander." Her voice was like silk. Cultured and smooth, but with a bite of warning hovering just underneath. "I was beginning to think you were avoiding me."

"And what would you think if I *was* avoiding you?" She sucked in a breath, and he turned to face her. Her eyes were as sharp as ice; the blue having gone glacial in her anger.

"If you were, I would at least like to know *why*." She stopped less than a foot in front of him. Heat rose in his stomach as he searched the face he once thought he could love. Carefully composed and expressionless, but her questioning eyes cut like knives to his gut. She was right to be angry. He had used her, and now, when he knew things would never be the same, he couldn't tell her why.

They stared at each other, and Alexander watched the emotions rage across her face. A face he had often held in his hands. Her full pink lips turned down, and when he focused on them, a flood of memories washed through him.

Their first encounter had been in this very room. He had come in here to hide from his father under the guise of studying a report. Alexander's father demanded he educate himself on the financial status of the company while he was home for the summer. He'd carelessly tossed the document on the table with a curse; unaware Rebekka was in the room.

"What did my report ever do to you, Alexander?"

He looked down to see her sitting at the opposite end of the table, pages and pages of reports and two computers spread in front of her. The blouse she wore was his favorite color. Peach.

She watched him with interest. Her hair had been shorter then, curling softly around the tops of her shoulders, and he remembered the shiver that raked his body when she leaned back in the seat, then pushed away from the table and slowly crossed her legs.

Uncaring what might happen, he tipped his best smirk at her and left the report where he tossed it. Need built inside him like a pressure valve. He had never been turned down and knew he wouldn't be by Rebekka. He'd caught her watching him enough to know she wanted him, and he was more than willing to oblige. Rebekka was his kind of painkiller.

Alexander had never bothered to answer her question. He'd simply held out his hand, his eyes inviting her to take what she wanted. For months they did just that. Here in the boardroom, in her office, his office, her place, a weekend trip. Neither of them committed to anything, but he knew she expected more. A more he knew he would never give her.

Then, months later, his parents died. At the time, Rebekka was his father's secretary, and in the wake of his death, she helped Alexander take over the reins of the company. Due to her intimate knowledge of the company and her shrewd business skills, she quickly promoted to CFO and took an almost permanent place at his side.

As his mind drifted back to the present, he realized she had stepped closer, taking his silence as an invitation. Her hands slid up his chest and under the lapels of his suit coat. Though he did his best to resist it, his body instantly responded to her touch.

"I've missed you." She breathed before rising on her toes and pressing her lips to his. Her fingers curled into the muscles of his shoulders as she pulled herself closer. He was too stunned by her actions to pull away.

Seemingly of their own accord, his arms went around her waist, and he drug her fully against him. He swallowed her soft cry of surprise as he deepened the kiss, slanting his mouth roughly across hers. It had been a long time since he held a woman's body, and the fire that burned through him at the softness of her curves ripped a tortured groan from him. Her hands slipped around his neck, and when they grazed the skin below his hair, he froze. Suddenly realizing what he'd done, he tore his mouth from hers and firmly set her back from him.

"Rebekka. I apologize. That was a mistake." He withdrew his hands from her waist and straightened his tie and jacket, trying to rein in his breathing. He shook his head, frustrated with himself. "Things have changed." He softened.

"You apologize?" The slap was loud, and his cheek stung as her palm whipped his head to the right. If he thought her eyes were icy before, he was mistaken. "You stay away for a year, Alexander! *A year!* With no contact. No phone calls. I even had to get your attorney to force you to come to this meeting! Then you come in here, kiss me like that?"

His eyes closed, and he exhaled before turning his head back toward her. "I am sorry." He stepped back, and with a jerk of his neck, tossed his ponytail over his shoulder. "I also said things have changed." Walking around her, he gestured toward her briefcase. "Let's go over the financials, and I'll explain when everyone else arrives."

Make her hate you. It's the only way.

When he didn't hear her move, he turned. She stood where he'd left her, hands clenched in fists and proud shoulders quaking. Sighing inwardly, he made his tone cold. "You had to know it would end."

"How would I know that?" Her hand went to her neck, and he realized she was wearing not just the perfume he bought her, but a Tiffany diamond and platinum necklace lay gracefully around her neck and the matching bracelet peeked out of the cuff of her blouse. He'd given them to her before leaving for Arizona last year. Just before his entire life was turned upside down.

You gave her every reason to think you loved her. End this.

"Rebekka." He straightened his cuffs with a nervousness he had never felt before. "You've always known I'm not the marrying type. Did you believe we could continue the way we were forever?"

"Yes! No. I don't know." She marched past him to lift and bang her briefcase onto the table. She stood still for a moment, perfectly manicured hands resting on the leather case. "I loved you, you know." Her normally strong voice broke.

His breath left him in a hiss. "I never asked you to."

She shook her head and clicked the latches to lift the lid. Her hands shook as she withdrew two stacks of reports and laid them aside. "You're right. I should have known." Her jaw was tense, her eyes shimmering with unshed tears, cold as glaciers behind the moisture.

"Though the fiscal year-end report shows a net gain of almost fifteen percent, our revenue was down nearly ten last quarter due to flooding and landslides in two of our building sites in Alaska." She turned and lowered herself into the high-back brown leather chair. "We had to abandon both sites, and the contracts were rescinded."

Steeling himself to be professional, he carried the report and took his place next to her at the head of the table. "What about the new contractor we signed with in Haiti? Any progress there?"

She shook her head. "Not yet, but he assures us he will have the proper permits within the month."

They lapsed into silence as he flipped through the pages, not really seeing the numbers. In less than half an hour, none of them would matter to him anymore.

Minutes later the boardroom filled with people and chatter until his attorney's announcement made the boardroom fall deathly silent. As the sole heir to a privately held company, Alexander currently owned sixty-eight percent of the stock. Two months ago, he agreed to sell all his shares to their closest competitor. The final sale would take place in the next ninety days. Once complete, Koch Architectural Design would be wholly absorbed into the new company.

Every eye in the room focused on him, waiting for his explanation. He set his chin and for what he hoped would be the last time, let the cold and ruthless nature of his father settle on him.

"It is time for a change." He stood and squared his shoulders, meeting the eyes of each of the men and women, daring them to argue. "This has been my family's legacy, but it is not meant to be mine." His attorney presented each of them with an envelope. "Inside that envelope, you will find the contract that was signed by myself and Mr. Dawson Jager of Jager Design Studios on your behalf. Each of you will have the option to maintain your current position at no less than your current salary within the new company for at least five years, should you decide to stay. Otherwise, a generous severance package will be yours ninety days after the merger is complete."

At that, most of the men and women around the table relaxed.

"What if we want to negotiate our own contract?" Colin Smith, a senior engineer leaned forward. Alexander fixed his eyes on the man.

"How do we know we even want to work for this new company?" Jacob Howards, also a recently promoted senior engineer and Colin's office mate, crossed his arms and glared down the table.

Alexander tucked his hands in his pockets. "Anyone else?" He slid his gaze down the row of faces. When no one spoke up, he rested a hand on the table and leaned into it. "Colin, who hired you?"

Surprised by the question, the men glanced at one another. "You did," Colin replied.

Raising his chin as if remembering, Alexander pushed back and lifted his palm up. "That's right. I brought you on board as a senior engineer, didn't I?"

"You did." Colin's ears turned red.

"Really?" Alexander scratched his chin. "And how many promotions were there in your department last year?"

Squirming in his seat, Jacob cleared his throat. "Only me."

"I see." Alexander looked to his left, where Dawson Jager sat. "Mr. Jager, did I mention either of these two gentlemen during our negotiations?"

The man's sharp eyes connected with Alexander's, and he nodded. "I believe you said they were two of your finest structural engineers."

Alexander smiled. "They really are. Would you like to renegotiate their contracts?"

Dawson didn't hesitate. "Absolutely."

Nodding, Alexander returned his attention to the two men. "Why do you think he would want to renegotiate?" He watched understanding dawn on their faces. "If you are unhappy with the contract I arranged for you and think you can do better, I will be happy to pay you one full month of salary, and you can leave the building now. You would then be free to negotiate with Mr. Jager on your own time." Alexander lifted an eyebrow. "What do you want to do, gentlemen?"

Faces red, the two exchanged a look. "We'll consider the deal," Colin said.

"Wise choice." Alexander sighed and straightened. "Koch Architectural Design was my father's dream. With your help he achieved it. I have confidence you will do the same for Mr. Jager and his team. I've spoken to Mr. Jager at length, and I can assure you he is looking forward to working with you." He glanced around the table. "I appreciate all the support and hard work you put in after my father died. I know he would be proud of you."

Alexander nodded to his attorney. "Thomas will answer any questions you have. This will be my final board meeting, as I am relocating out of state in a few days. It has been a pleasure to work with all of you." Not wanting to remain in the stifling room anymore, Alexander exited the boardroom and made his way through the hallways to his office.

His desk was already cleared out. All that remained were a few last-minute contracts and plans he had yet to sign off on. Alexander lowered himself into the chair behind his desk and quickly finished up. He set the neat stacks in the outgoing bin for his secretary to deal with tomorrow.

Alexander opened the lap drawer and sighed. Inside he had tucked the formal invitations to the second Gathering only a few weeks away. Underneath them was the outline of the speech he was supposed to deliver. So much had changed. And quickly.

The Vampir were beginning to thrive again as the Council organized meetings, defining and updating customs to accommodate the cultural changes so many centuries of division had caused.

The simplest solutions usually turned out to be the best. Getting back to the basics of their species and letting their natural instincts guide them had resulted in many Vampir of all ages finding their mates. He rubbed his temples, relieved the pressure of the company had been removed, but unable to decide what to do about his commitment to the Vampir Council.

Alexander pulled his speech out of the drawer and left the invitations. He pushed the drawer closed then stood. There was nothing else for him to do here. Not bothering to glance around the office one last time, he stepped into the hall and shut the door. Letting go of the knob, he turned and nearly knocked Rebekka over.

"Excuse me," he said and steadied her with a hand on her shoulder. She shook him off and slammed the door to her office, refusing to make eye contact. He couldn't blame her.

Personally, he had torn her heart out, and professionally, he had just sold her to the highest bidder. She had every right to be furious with him. Because of it, he'd negotiated the largest package he could for her. She deserved to stay, and thankfully Jager's board agreed.

For a moment Alexander considered going in to talk to her but knew there was nothing he could say. The devastation on her face when Thomas made the announcement told him she would not welcome his attempts anyway. Resigned and hoping she would eventually forgive him, Alexander took the elevator and left Koch Architectural Design behind him.

The evening air was crisp as he walked the short distance to his high-rise apartment building, stopping at the coffee shop in the lobby for a fresh cup of coffee and a sandwich.

The luxurious penthouse was dark and quiet. He pulled the tie from his neck and crossed the expansive living area to his bedroom. His apartment building rose five stories higher than the office building, and his penthouse was the entire top floor. At thirty-five hundred square feet, it was small but had always been all he needed. The open floor plan was sparsely furnished with dark woods, Italian leather seating, and rich marble surfaces.

He flicked on the light in the master bedroom, carefully rolled the tie, and slipped it into the tray of his clothing butler. Emptying his pockets, he separated the change, keys, and wallet into their respective compartments. His cell phone rested on the charging station and from the last pocket he pulled out the stainless-steel anatomical heart.

He rolled it between his fingers. His life was comfortable by any standard, but he wanted more from himself. He couldn't change the things he had done, and he knew it would take a very long time before anyone heard his name without associating it with an arrogant, morally unrestrained lifestyle, but he was determined to try, and the charm reminded him there was always hope.

He set the charm in the tray next to the handful of coins and slipped out of his suit coat, hanging it on the butler and removing his cufflinks. With each piece of clothing he shed, he felt lighter, yet more lost. The suits would always be part of him, but the desire to wear them as a sign of wealth and power fled. Now they were simply clothing, something a gentleman would wear.

A gentleman. *Do you even know what that means, Alexander?* He carefully straightened the jacket and folded the shirt so it could be taken to the cleaners.

Though the sky outside threatened rain, he slid the balcony door beside his bed open and sank onto the mattress to listen to the sounds of the city below. All the traffic, the wind, and the bustle of the city blended into a soothing hum that rose and fell around him.

Most of his personal belongings were already packed for the move to Escondido, California, and the modest house he had purchased in the foothills near the safari park. The movers would deliver his things in two days, and this building would be placed up for sale as well.

Southern California. That's where the trail of phone records led him in his search for her. Though Baden had initially been reluctant to use the new network that way, Alexander convinced him to look for anything out of the ordinary. Someone who might still be hiding something. Obviously, whoever she was, she didn't want to be found, but Alexander refused to let it go.

Within just a few months, Baden found a consistent number of calls from an unlisted landline in Scottsdale to several Vampir owned businesses in Escondido. He was convinced it was Jessi.

With Peter already in southern California, Alexander decided the time had come for him to sell out of his father's company and move on.

Tomorrow, he would meet with his attorneys to finish setting up the charitable foundation he and Peter had been talking about for years.

It gave him a purpose for the obscene amount of wealth he inherited. He didn't regret having it but simply being wealthy and successful no longer satisfied him. The things his money could buy weren't enough. He wanted to make a difference. The only thing missing was her.

The familiar ache in his heart reminded him she was his intended. His blood knew it.

His body recognized her as his mate the moment she touched him. The other males he spoke with who had also recently met their intended described the change in their blood as an ache. A pulling in their veins that drove them to claim their intended. The females said they felt similar. A pull neither of them could ignore, though none of them ever mentioned it being painful. But for him, there were days it felt like his blood was boiling with its desire for her.

Only Emerick described the type of pain he felt, and only because he and Ellen, his mate for over three thousand years, were separated for a year when they were working to reunite the Vampir as a race. Emerick believed Alexander's pain was tied to his inability to touch any other female. Somehow the discomfort normal members of their race felt for these things was hugely amplified in him.

He sighed and rose to his feet. But why did she run knowing they were intended for one another? Pushing the heels of his hands against his eyes, he willed the pain to subside.

He looked out the window hoping she wasn't hurting as badly as he was.

CHAPTER

FOUR

JESSI

Armani tossed his head and whinnied as Jessi approached. His dark eyes watched her eagerly, his golden head bouncing up and down as she got closer. In the next stall, Ulysse shifted, banging his large hoof against the stall door.

"Don't you start!" Jessi chided the large gray gelding whose soft eyes watched her. "I can't afford to have both of you tearing this place apart."

Ignoring Armani, she pushed open Ulysse's door and gave him a gentle shove out of the way. His massive body sidestepped obediently, and she patted his shoulder. "Good boy." He turned his head to watch as she dumped a scoop of feed into the box mounted to the wall.

Ulysse's withers were two inches taller than her. He measured seventeen hands when they both qualified for the junior event trials six years ago.

She got her love of horses and equestrian competition from her father. He'd competed with the German National team before escaping the country during the war. He and her mother were two hundred years old when they came to the States with Samuel. All of them settled in Arizona.

Her mother was the daughter of a baron and inherited a massive estate, giving them the wealth to help establish the Clan in Arizona along with the Kochs and the Gottschalks. All Jessi's siblings, three older brothers and one sister, left behind in Germany, had died during the war. Her parents were so devastated that when Jessi was born, they poured all their attention on her.

When she was young, having a father who spent all his time with her was wonderful. He taught her how to ride, how to handle unruly horses, and how to manage a stable full of world class prospects.

Jessi sighed as Ulysse stamped a foot. Smiling, she scratched him under the cheek as he stretched out his neck toward the food, politely asking permission to eat. "Go ahead, you big baby." With a swipe of her hand down his neck, she left him to chew in peace. The sweet smell of molasses and the contented grinding of his teeth followed her out.

By now Armani was pushing against the door with his chest, and his slender neck stretched in her direction. Jessi squared her shoulders and took a step toward him.

"Get back." Jessi unlatched the door and waited until the horse pulled his head back. She slid the door aside, and just like she had with Ulysse, placed her hand on his side and gently pushed. Armani took one step then resisted.

"Move, Armani." She felt the animal's weight shift but waited until he actually took the step before releasing the pressure of her hand against his side. "Good boy." Though she praised him, she kept her hand on him, watching his head. She knew he was watching her too, waiting for her to drop her guard.

He was especially unpredictable at feeding time and would use her distraction to trap her against the wall. The first time he did it, she was so surprised she struck him. Though it was a light smack on the shoulder, more noise than pain, it sent him into a panic. She managed to calm him, but he cowered in the corner with his ears pinned back. For the next two days, he hadn't wanted her anywhere near him. She had to put his food in a pan and slide it under the door until she could earn his trust again.

She had no idea what the horse had endured before she brought him here, but he could be sweet and docile one second, terrified and unpredictable the next. She had yet to figure out everything that would set him off, but food and aggressive handling were two of them.

She never turned her back on him, and even now when he stood calmly beside her, she remained alert. With one hand on his neck, she slid her palm under his silky mane and scratched. His skin twitched with nervous excitement at being so close to the feed, but she refused to give it to him until he settled.

She held the bucket of feed at her side and waited until his tail relaxed and his muscles stopped twitching. When his nose dropped a fraction and the tension left his neck, she dumped the feed into the newly replaced bin and waited. He twitched again but didn't move. After a moment, she released him. "Okay."

He took a step forward and swung his nose in a circle through the grain, spinning it as he ate. Tomorrow she was going to try putting large rocks in his feed bin in an attempt to slow him down and prevent him from flinging the grain around so much. He'd never had a problem eating as fast as he did, but she didn't want to take a chance.

She ran her palm down his shoulder, checking the stitches. They were swollen and angry looking, but clean and free of debris. She slid her hand down his back as she exited the stall, always making sure he knew she was still there.

At fifteen hands, he seemed like a pony next to Ulysse. She had not yet ridden him, though the people she'd gotten him from assured her he had been under saddle. They purchased him for their daughter, but he proved too much trouble, and they were ready to sell him at a stock farm where he would have ended up in a rodeo, or worse.

The first time she saw him, he was cowering in a dirty stall, his mane matted and his tail thumping against his sides in knots as he swished it nervously. They warned her not to go in his stall, but she slid the door open anyway, offering a handful of raw oats. His ears and eyes told her he wasn't mean or aggressive, just scared. She stood still, turned slightly sideways, trying to be as non-threatening as possible. She kept her eyes on the ground near his feet so she could see his movements but not make eye contact.

She'd stood that way for almost half an hour before he inched across the stall and sniffed at what she held in her hand. His upper lip grazed her open palm, gently sweeping back and forth to pick up the offered oats. His unshaven muzzle felt like velvet against her, and when she finally looked up to meet his eyes, they were intelligent and wary behind the twisted mess of his forelock.

The gleam of their black depths reminded her of two shiny suit buttons, and she immediately named him Armani. Whispering his new name and allowing him to get used to her smell, she carefully stepped closer, reaching out to rub the side of his head.

"Easy, boy. No one is ever going to hurt you again." Her heart melted when Armani responded by pushing against her as she scratched the mud and caked manure from his coat.

Within two hours, she coaxed him into a halter, led him into the aisle, and bribed him into her trailer where he promptly kicked a huge dent in the side. The owners laughed, telling her she was a fool for wasting stall space on him, but they were so glad to have him gone; they even refused the two hundred dollars she brought to pay for him.

Good thing too. She needed the money to repair his new stall the next day after he kicked the door off its hinges in order to get into his paddock. Once outside, he settled down, and she turned Ulysse out with him to see how they would get along. She knew Ulysse was large enough to defend himself and sure enough, within moments Ulysse put the smaller horse in his place with a few well-placed nips and a solid kick to the rump. The two had been pasture buddies ever since.

She slid the stall door shut behind her and checked the latch before turning to watch her charges finish their dinner. Holding the bucket in both hands, she sighed. Everyone had gone home for the evening, and there were no sounds in the barn except for the muffled sound of shifting hooves and the contented chewing of the animals.

Closing her eyes, she drank in the peace, trying to ignore the growing pain in her chest. It came and went, but each time it returned, the ache under her ribs increased. Some nights she could barely breathe. Blowing out a breath as it eased, she filled the horses water buckets and picked up the empty feed scoops.

After securing the feed room and making sure the barn was locked up for the night, she climbed the stairs to her apartment above the tack room. It was tiny, no more than an efficiency with one large room, a small kitchenette, a bathroom, and a huge window that looked out over the pasture to the north. The wooden floors were covered with four large area rugs. A twin bed and dresser tucked into the far corner of the room with a curtain that could be drawn around it for privacy. In the center of the room sat a worn blue and white gingham couch and chair, and beside the door sat her TV stand. Not much, but all she needed. It had been the smell of the horses downstairs and the beautiful view of the mountains in the distance that sold her on the space.

She stood at the window for a long time. The ache in her chest returning. Rubbing a hand over her heart and remembering the bruises that were always on her mother's arms, she whispered, "*Oh, Mom. Which pain is worse?*"

The next morning, Jessi fought off the grogginess and climbed into her car to call Alyssa from the library a few blocks from her house. She crept through the library until she found an unattended phone. Alyssa was the only friend she stayed in contact with after she fled from her father. She was also the one who convinced her to go to the Compound that night.

Allysa kept her up to date on her mom. For months after she left, she told herself she would go back to get her mother, but the thought of facing either her father or Alexander terrified her.

"Hey, Lyn." Alyssa's bright voice calling her by her childhood name made Jessi smile.

"Morning." Jessi leaned around a shelf, and seeing no one, pulled a stool out from behind the counter. "How's work?"

"Good. How are you feeling?" Alyssa asked.

"About the same." Jessi tucked a strand of hair behind her ear. "Have you talked to my mom lately?"

"No." Alyssa sighed. "Last time she was in the shop was last week."

"Did she look all right?" Familiar and well-handled guilt crept over her. "I never should have left her there."

"She looked the same. Tired maybe." Alyssa said. "You know Alexander is still looking for you."

"Please don't start this again." Jessi tensed. "I'm not about to tie myself to him."

"You know you can't avoid it," Alyssa said. "He's your mate, and staying away from him is causing both of you pain. Bonding isn't as scary as you think."

"That's so easy for you to say!" Jessi shot back and glanced out the library window. "You know what my parent's relationship is like. You lucked out. Curt is sweet and doesn't come from our Clan. But for me, this is Alexander *Koch* we're talking about!"

Alyssa was amused. "Oh, yes. The handsome—no—the drop dead gorgeous, powerful, extremely wealthy, Alexander Koch. I see where you could struggle with being his intended." Jessi heard an indignant snort from Curt, who must have been sitting next to her. "Relax, babe. Not my style."

"I can't do it, Al." Jessi glanced around the shelves, watching for the clerk to return. "You know I won't live like Mother does."

Alyssa sighed. "I know, honey. I don't envy you, but maybe he's changed. People around here seem to think so anyway."

She dropped her head back against the wall. "I have to go. I'll call you tomorrow?"

"Sure. At least think about giving him a chance, Lyn." Her voice sobered. "The pain will only get worse for you."

Hearing someone approaching, Jessi leaned over the counter. "I gotta go. I'll call you." She replaced the phone and pretended to be searching for a pen. Jessi snagged one from the basket beside the phone, jotted a note on her hand, and put the pen back.

"Thank you!" she called and hurried away.

Arriving at work, Jessi let the back door swing closed and paused in the shop's hallway, listening to the voices murmuring from the front of the coffee shop. Ever since the day Alexander was here, she hesitated before crossing into the main room. Each time, she found herself hoping he was there and dreading the thought he might be.

"Well, you look like a ray of sunshine this morning, Jess." Dawn, the other barista, poked her in the shoulder as she pulled her apron on. Dawn's waist length blond hair was braided down her back, and under her apron, she wore a gray Broken Bean hoodie and well-worn jeans. "You look like you haven't slept in days. Are you all right?" Dawn's hazel eyes watched her sharply as she loosened the apron from around her waist.

"I'm fine." Jessi nodded and smiled at the next customer in line as the door chimed. "What can I get started for you?" She scribbled the woman's order on a cup and handed it to Dawn.

"Maybe you should see a doctor. You've had a headache every day for weeks now." Her expression narrowed. "Should we be worried?"

Jessi picked up the filter holder and banged out the grounds before flipping on the grinder and refilling it with fresh ones. "There's nothing wrong. I've just had a lot on my mind." She glanced up at her co-worker. "I promise I'll see a doctor if it gets any worse, okay?"

Dawn's lips thinned, but she turned to go. "You know you can call me if you need to talk."

Jessi locked the filter in place and started the steam. "I know. Thank you. I appreciate it." She heard Dawn's boots cross the floor and finished the customer's drink. Maybe she should talk to someone, at least about the situation with her mom. Maybe there was a solution she hadn't thought of.

The hiss of the machine drowned out the sound of everything else, and when she looked up with a smile to hand the cup to the waiting woman, she nearly dropped it when she saw the man standing at the register.

Regaining her composure, she thanked the woman and wiped her hands on her apron. Over the rich smell of the freshly brewed coffee, she finally noticed the salty pine smell of Peter. He stood patiently with a hip against the counter watching her. She was obviously out of practice scenting the approach of a male, and this time, she knew she hadn't suppressed her echo.

His blue eyes bored into hers and seemed to read more than she wanted anyone to know. Dark blond hair, cropped closely to his head and day-old stubble lent a dangerous shadow to his face. His hands were pushed into the front pockets of his jeans, and a pale blue t-shirt was visible underneath the black zip up hoodie. On the upper right side in blue was an embroidered image of a man kicking almost straight up with his fists tucked into his sides.

Jessi pasted on a smile and removed the echo from her voice, hoping he wouldn't notice. "What can I get for you this morning?"

He met her smile, but his eyes never changed their intensity. "I'll have a double-shot Americano." She dropped her head and wrote the order on his cup, then froze when he continued. "Jessi."

Her hand shook as she keyed the order into the register. "That will be $4.50." Trying to keep the fear out of her eyes, she looked up as he reached into his back pocket.

"It's on your name tag." He nodded toward her. "Does it make you uncomfortable that I called you by name?" He held out the bills, and she took them, cursing the fact that her hand still shook.

"No. Why would it?" Dredging up anger, she met his stare as evenly as she could as she returned his change.

He tipped a knowing smile at her. "Because now I know who you are."

She was sure all the color drained out of her face, and she quickly snatched his cup from the counter and repeated the process of making the espresso, adding hot water instead of milk and flavoring. Feeling like a cornered rabbit, she drew a deep breath and held out the drink. "Double-shot Americano."

"Jessi." His voice softened, and she was surprised to see his expression had too. "He doesn't know."

Her heart pounded in her ears. "Who doesn't know what?"

Peter looked around, and she followed his eyes. "Can we talk?"

It was only ten am and the afternoon rush wouldn't start for at least another hour. Though she dreaded the conversation, there was something about this man she instantly trusted. His eyes matched his calming scent, and since the place was nearly empty, she nodded. He gestured to a quiet corner near the register where she could keep an eye on the door.

She sat in the chair he held out for her then warily watched him lower his huge frame into the seat opposite her. Still studying her, he took a sip of his coffee before speaking. She didn't know what she expected him to say, but his first question wasn't it.

"How bad's the pain, Jessi?"

Tears sprang to her eyes, and her throat closed up. "Not bad." Defiance shone from her eyes. She thought about the bruises on her mother's arms and the brutality of Alexander's attack on his brother at the funeral. She tipped her head. "At least, not as bad as the pain he could cause."

Peter was momentarily surprised but recovered quickly. "So, you would rather live in pain than give him a chance?"

"Yes!" she hissed. "You have no idea what I've been through, and I won't go through it again."

His expression went from surprise to confusion. "No one is

asking you to go through anything." Peter rested his elbows on the table. "And you've no idea what he's been through either."

She angrily wiped tears away. "Maybe he brought it on himself." Even as the words left her lips, she regretted them. She squeezed her eyes closed against the anger rising in Peter.

"What he's still going through." His scent was defensive, not threatening, and she lowered her chin.

"I'm sorry. That wasn't fair." She drew a shaking breath. "You're right, I don't know what he's been through. All I know is what I've seen and heard."

Peter weighed her explanation and took another sip of his coffee. When he glanced out the window, she tensed. "Alexander won't be here today." His name sent pangs of longing through her. Peter smiled sadly at her reaction. "He responds the same way when he hears your name, you know." He leaned back. "And his pain isn't bad, Jessi. It's brutal."

She exhaled a shuddering breath. "I know. I felt it when he was here the other day. What am I supposed to do? I don't trust him."

Peter nodded. "I know you don't. Though I don't understand why. Personally, I'd trust him with my life." His expression hardened. "What I don't think you understand is the control it's taken for him to endure the amount of pain he lives with. You'd be angry too—after a while." He lifted an eyebrow when she slumped. "I'm not going to use his pain to make you feel guilty. You need to trust him, not feel sorry for him." Peter crossed his arms. He thought for a moment, and his eyes searched hers. "I have a proposal, and if you agree to it, I'll personally guarantee your safety."

She scoffed until she refocused on just how large Peter was. Her eyes skated over him, and his scent dared her to doubt his ability. Arms crossed, she mirrored his posture. "All right. What do you want me to do?"

Peter leaned back in his chair, and a smile played at the corners of his mouth. "I've known Alexander a long time, and if there's anything he enjoys, it's a challenge." He tilted his head. "You, I think, will be a real challenge for him. He's used to getting what he wants when he wants it."

Jessi cringed. "I'm sure, but how does that help me trust him?"

Peter tipped his chair back. "It doesn't. You are going to make him prove you can."

"How exactly am I going to do that?"

"By pushing his buttons." Peter ran a hand through his hair. "I'm going to let you in on a little secret about Alexander." He lowered the chair back to four legs. "He looks tough, acts tough, and in many ways he is tough. He's one of the strongest males I know." Jessi held her breath. "But he also has a heart that's bigger than even he realizes." He rested a hand on hers. "I guarantee he won't hurt you. It's nearly impossible for a male to hurt his mate. I've seen enough to know better than to claim it never happens, but I wouldn't believe Alexander capable of it. Ever." His eyes were serious. "But it doesn't matter what I believe. Make him prove it to you. I already told you I'll personally guarantee your safety if I'm wrong."

Jessi pressed her thumbs into her temples, the headache pulsing against her fingers. Something had to change, and soon, or she wouldn't be able to function. If Alexander's pain was worse...Jessi met Peter's eyes. "All right. I'll do it."

"Great." He rubbed his palms together. "The first thing Alexander hates is to be called *Alex*." He grinned. "In fact, he hates nicknames period."

"Seriously?" Jessi said. "He doesn't like nicknames?" She gave everyone she knew a nickname at some point. Did he really take himself so seriously he would let that set him off?

"He'll correct you every time." Peter nodded. "And he spends money like water. I'd give him a hard time about it."

She gritted her teeth. That wouldn't be difficult. She resented the way her father liked to wave his money around too. So far there was very little to convince her Alexander could be trusted, especially if something as simple as a nickname could make him angry. "Anything else?"

Peter hesitated. "Judging by the look on your face that might be enough." He folded his hands. "All I ask of you is that you give him a fair chance. You've got to be willing to let go of what you think you know about him."

The door chimed as a customer entered. "Fine." Jessi stood and pushed her chair in. "Tell him I'll meet with him here. *Only* here." If she was going to come face to face with Alexander Koch, she wanted to do it on her turf.

Peter sipped the rest of his coffee. "Fair enough. He's out of town for the next few days, but when he gets back, we'll stop in."

Jessi let her eyes travel over Peter again, reminding herself he had promised to protect her. "Can't wait," she mumbled. But deep in her heart, excitement took hold. Jessi couldn't deny that Alexander was incredibly attractive, or, as Alyssa so easily admitted, drop dead gorgeous. The media loved to proclaim him the sexiest bachelor alive, and from what she read, he played the part.

Peter might keep him from physically hurting her, but what could he possibly do if Alexander ripped her heart out?

CHAPTER

FIVE

JESSI

Three mornings later, Jessi stood behind the counter at the Broken Bean, wiping the gleaming expresso machine down, though it was already spotless. Every time the door chimed, she jumped. She was reaching for a mug when the sound made her knock over the bin holding the used grounds. The wet mess thumped from the counter and sprayed grounds over her shoes and across the tile floor. Swearing under her breath, she reached for the broom to sweep it up as hard soled shoes clicked across the hardwood.

"I'll be right with you," she called, but as she lifted the dustpan full of grounds off the floor and turned to dump them in the trash, the smell of citrus and clove stole all the strength from her hands. The whole thing clattered back to the floor as crippling pain rammed into her with a force that doubled her over.

His pain had increased to a level she wouldn't have believed possible. Exhaling slowly, she braced herself and stood.

Unwilling to turn around, she raised her eyes to the mirror behind the counter and locked gazes with the most luminous pair of green eyes she had ever seen. The intensity and hunger flickering behind them pierced her chest, and made her face go numb as an instant connection caught fire.

"Jessi?"

Hearing her name from his lips sent her heart into a strange pattern and dried all the moisture from her mouth. She closed her hands into fists to keep them from shaking and turned to face the man she had been running from for five years. Swallowing thickly, she watched his cat-like eyes roam her face as he took a step closer to the counter.

His physical presence filled the shop, and the air charged with electricity she was afraid to acknowledge. It tingled across her skin and burned low in her stomach. His question still hung in the air, and doubt threaded through him as silence weighed between them. Too overcome with him to speak, she nodded.

His eyes fell closed, and she was relieved to be released from their intensity. Freed from his penetrating gaze, her eyes slid down his body. His broad shoulders and perfectly tapered torso were expertly fitted into a brown suit coat; his long red hair bound at the back of his neck. A dark brown tie with small white dots surrounded his throat and each collar point of the cream shirt bent with crisp dimples pulled there by the tab under it. The coat was unbuttoned and her breath caught as she followed the neatly clipped tie down his flat stomach and stopped at the dark belt around his waist. Her eyes trailed back toward his face.

The cords of tendons in his neck were taunt, and his pulse hammered at his throat. His red beard was trimmed neatly around a strong, square jaw, and a few loose hairs curled softly where they had escaped the knot at his neck. As her eyes slid across his full lips, her heart skittered when they tipped into a smirk. His gleaming eyes taunted her when their gazes met. He almost looked like he was purring. They stood for a long moment before she found her voice, reminding herself to hide the echo.

"Hello, Alex." His smile slipped, and she blinked in anticipation of a sharp correction.

"I prefer Alexander," he said softly, moving forward with a grace she wasn't expecting.

She took a step back, and her hip bumped painfully against the counter behind her. When she flinched, his head tipped in question.

"May I have a pour over of your house blend?" His voice was as deep as she remembered, but softer. "And the honor of your company if you have a moment."

The combination of his cat-like grace, the ache in his scent, and the intensity of his deep voice threw sparks of want throughout her body.

Traitor! Get a grip. He's pretty, but the moment you let your guard down, he'll hurt you. A small voice argued back. *But what if he's like Armani and doesn't mean to?*

Fighting to keep the echo of confusion out of her voice, she replied as coldly as she could. "I'll have your pour over right up, Alex, but I have work to do."

He stiffened, and she flinched harder this time, sure he would raise his voice. His expression grew puzzled.

"If you don't mind please, it's Alexander, and I can wait until you have the time." His tone never changed, but there was doubt in his face. He slid a fifty-dollar bill across the counter, his stance softening when she didn't immediately take the offered money. "Keep the change."

Frustrated by her body's response to him and angry at his ridiculous tip, she gritted her teeth. Swiping the bill off the counter, she slapped it into the register and slid his full change back.

"I can't be bought." She let her echo punctuate her frustration.

Instead of the anger she expected, he was confused. Hurt flickered on his face before she turned away. Doubt clouded her resolve for a moment, but she reminded herself who he was.

He's just not used to anyone telling him no. He'll get over it.

Her eyes involuntarily rose to the mirror as she reached for a mug and pour over vessel. Peter leaned against the far wall. He lifted his chin toward her as a satisfied quirk curled his lip. Unfolding his arms and kicking away from the wall, he took a seat across from Alexander at a table near the counter. Sitting together, they looked like two lions prepared to wait for their next meal. A cold shiver raked her back at the thought.

Her fist tightened on the hot water pot as the other rubbed her aching chest. Alexander's pain and the depth of their combined need was so much stronger than she ever anticipated. As she watched the timer and reined in the instinctual need for her mate, she realized just how easily Peter had set her up to fall.

By the time she cleaned up the twice-spilled grounds and took out the trash, the morning rush was on. Peter and Alexander still sat at the same table almost two hours later. She watched with mixed amusement, and not a little jealousy, as almost every one of her female patrons, and at least one man, caught sight of them and either did a double take or outright stared.

One woman boldly approached the table with a flirty smile. At the brunette's hello, both men looked up, graciously listening and nodding. Smiling politely, Peter shook his head, lifting his left hand to display the wedding ring he wore. Not all bonded couples wore them, but some chose to adopt the human custom.

The woman shrugged an elegant shoulder before lifting an eyebrow at Alexander. He leaned back in his chair and shook his head, eyes flicking toward Jessi. The woman followed his gaze and looked Jessi over in disbelief. Jessi knew why the woman reacted as she did.

Even on the best of days, she made sure her clothing choices would never be considered business attire. The bottom edge of her white tunic hung loosely past the hips of her worn jeans, with cutout lace around the elbow length sleeves and hem. A green cotton vest layered over it, and a bright red belt circled her waist. Eclectic layers of necklaces, bracelets, and rings wrapped around and hid most of the exposed skin at her neck and wrists. Her hair was artfully disheveled, and a folded turquoise bandanna wove through her hair.

The woman broke eye contact with a wrinkle of her nose and a confident smile. She turned back to Alexander and opened her purse to hand him a business card. To Jessi's bitter surprise, he took it with a matching smile. His dazzling charm continued as he shook her hand and inclined his head to her as she left.

The woman winked at Jessi as she passed, making her hand tighten on the handle of the filter holder so hard it cut into her palm. When the woman was out the door, Jessi let go and rubbed her palm as she glanced toward Alexander.

His green eyes danced as he deliberately lifted the offending card between two fingers. With his other hand, he popped the lid off the coffee cup next to him. Then, he raised a ginger eyebrow, dropped the card into the cup, and replaced the lid. His shrewd grin and sexy wink nearly made her knees give out before he turned his attention back to Peter.

Peter chuckled at the exchange, and Alexander sighed. Just being in the same room with Jessi roused a playfulness he didn't know he had, but her reactions to his earlier advances confused him. She was terrified of him, yet their physical attraction was off the charts.

It's like she expects me to hit her over the head and drag her out of here. He chuckled. *Not a bad idea...*

"Have you contacted Greg at the Ice Box?" Peter's voice drew his attention back to the business at hand. "He's interested in partnering with us to set up a hockey scholarship."

"No. I haven't." Swiping his finger across the trackpad of the laptop, Alexander shook his head and did his best not to think about tossing Jessi over his shoulder and toting her out the back door. "I just got the email from him yesterday. I'll call him tomorrow."

His eyes refused to stay focused on the emails in front of him. Instead, they followed Jessi back and forth behind the counter as she took care of her customers. Her raven hair was pulled away from her face by a sea green bandanna that disappeared into the tangle of black and green locks that twisted at the back of her head and tumbled down her neck. All he wanted to do was bury his hands in the glossy mess and kiss her senseless.

She's incredible.

From the corner of his eye, he knew a couple women had paused hoping to get his attention, but he never gave them a glance. The only reason he noticed their approach was because each time they did, Jessi tensed. Though the tales of his promiscuity were wildly exaggerated, he knew his public reputation gave her every reason to doubt his ability to be faithful.

"Alexander." Peter laughed quietly. "Have you heard anything I said?"

"Not a word," Alexander admitted. He pushed the laptop closed and sat back. "Not with her in the room." He glanced at Peter thoughtfully. "She doesn't trust me."

"No," Peter agreed. "She doesn't."

It was becoming obvious she was creating busy work to avoid talking to him, but her not so covert glances their way told him she was torn.

"She doesn't just distrust me. She's scared of me." He shook his head and slid back from the table crossing an ankle over his knee.

Peter glanced over his shoulder. "Well, you probably seem like a giant to her. She's all of what, five foot two?"

"It's more than that. We've seen these signs before." He twisted the cup in his hand. "I think she's been abused somehow and expects me to treat her the same way."

Jessi paused and turned his way. There were no more customers in line, and she fidgeted nervously with the strings of her apron. When their eyes met, he smiled slightly and inclined his head. Her expression eased, and he relaxed.

"Maybe." Peter tipped his chair back on two legs. "Valid concern if she's heard about some of your less than shining moments."

Alexander met his friend's gaze. "I can't change the past, and if that's what she's reacting to..." His eyes fell to the table, and he flicked a crumb from the surface. "How do I convince her to trust me?"

"You earn it." A slender hand with rings on each finger set a fresh mug of coffee in front of him. He looked up in surprise to see Jessi beside the table, a second mug in her other hand. Her jaw was set, the fragile hold on her courage revealed by her trembling hand.

Alexander rose and Peter followed, the front legs of his chair meeting the floor with a snap. Alexander was acutely aware then of how tall he was in comparison to her. Despite her petite size, there was a strength to her that was undeniable. And irresistible. Wanting to put her at ease, Alexander backed up to keep the chair between them though he ached to hold her instead

Peter quietly picked up his phone and the empty cups from the table. With a nod, he left the two of them to talk.

"Thank you for joining me." Alexander watched a tangle of emotions play out on her face. It was the same reaction he'd seen in her earlier, the thoughts parading across her features as varied as the colors in the rich gold green of her eyes.

A blush crept over her cheeks as they assessed each other. "May I sit?"

Jolted to action, Alexander realized she was waiting on him to offer. "Of course." He held the chair Peter had vacated, lifting a brow when she sat in his chair instead.

"It seems you have me at a disadvantage. You apparently know much more about me than I do you. I don't even know your full name." He sat and reached across the small table for the coffee now on her side, frowning when she drew back as though he intended to grab her. "Have I done something to offend you? If I have, I'd appreciate the opportunity to apologize so we can find our way to a better start."

"There's nothing you need to apologize for." Her eyes searched his face, and he stilled. "It's difficult for me to trust people." She dropped her focus to the table. She clutched the brown mug close to her chest as though it could protect her. He ached to know what she felt she needed protection from.

Alexander lowered his chin until his eyes were nearly level with hers and cleared his throat. Wariness stiffened her shoulders, and he sat a little straighter.

Softly, Alexander.

"I'll do whatever it takes to earn your trust, but I need to understand why you're scared. I would never hurt you." He tilted his head in curiosity. "You are my mate." Her breathing quickened, and he let the gate open just a crack on his need, knowing she would recognize the change immediately. Her beautiful eyes widened, but she stayed seated.

"I know what we are to each other," she said quietly, her gaze burning with challenge. Jaw hardening, she leaned forward and spoke low. "We may be intended for one another because of what we are, but that doesn't mean I will blindly submit to you. I will not be controlled by genetics. Or you. I don't care how wealthy or powerful you are. I've worked hard for my independence and I'm not about to give it up. Not for anyone, including you."

"Why would you think I would want to control you? I freely admit I have not been the man I should have been. I make no excuses for it, but you should realize not everything you may have heard is truth." His hand tightened on his mug as spikes of pain across his shoulders. The pain roiled his stomach, and he closed his eyes. He'd hoped the reality of their combined need would at least convince her to allow him close, but his intensity was only making it worse.

"Control it, Alexander. Breathe through it." Peter's voice coaching him through the worst pain he'd ever experienced after she'd fled the Gathering last year drew his attention inward. Focusing on his breathing, he tried to bring the inferno under his skin back to a manageable level, when suddenly it was gone.

His eyes flew open as cool fingers slid across the back of hand. Like a flood of ice water, relief washed over his skin and numbed the burning consuming his body. There was still wariness in her eyes but growing understanding.

"It's Vogel. Jessi Vogel. I'm sorry you're in so much pain, Alexander. All I ask is that you don't dismiss mine before you know what it is."

He didn't bother trying to hide his delight as he laid his other hand on the table, palm up, hoping she would take it. She stared at it for a long moment, and the look of indecision returned before she carefully set her mug aside and placed her tiny hand in his.

SEVEN

JESSI

Alexander's hands wrapped her fingers in a grip that was as careful as it was strong. The spike of pain their standoff caused him was so much more than she ever imagined. When his startling eyes closed against it, she reached for him before she could stop, and the moment their fingers touched, the pain vanished. Though the ferocity of his stare made her stomach drop and forced her blood to race through her veins, she didn't look away.

Peter approached the table, his expression cautiously optimistic at the sight of their joined hands. Not wanting him to read more into it than there currently was, Jessi pulled back, leaving her hands suddenly cold.

"Alexander." Peter's voice was apologetic. "Our meeting is in half an hour."

Jessi picked up her mug and settled her elbows on the table, gripping the warm ceramic with both hands. She watched as Alexander slid his laptop into a dark brown leather case and then into the matching attaché. He paused for a moment before meeting her eyes again.

"I have to go." His tone was reluctant as he stood. Nervousness crept into his scent, and she sat back in her chair. "May I use this table tomorrow?"

"It's a public coffee house. I can't stop you." She pushed to her feet.

He would expect her to want him around she supposed, but she wasn't at all ready to admit she did. Besides, tomorrow was her day off.

"Then I'll be here." He picked up his case and extended his free hand to her. "Thank you."

She took it, intending to end the contact quickly, but Alexander fixed his glittering eyes on hers, and firmly held her fingers in the space between his thumb and forefinger.

Unable to tear her eyes from his, she watched them darken to jade as he brushed a whisper of a kiss across the back of her knuckles before releasing her. Her legs trembled, and she shivered when a rumble came from his chest. His eyes flashed with triumph.

"Until tomorrow, Miss Vogel." With a slight nod and another knowing smirk, he turned to go. As his long strides carried him across the room, she pressed a hand over her pounding heart and watched until he and Peter were out the door.

"Oh, my goodness, Jess!" Dawn's stunned voice came from the hallway just behind her. "Did *Alexander Koch* just kiss your hand?"

Jessi knew her expression was as stunned as Dawn sounded, and it took her a moment to catch her breath to answer.

"Yes, I think he did." She closed her eyes and folded her still tingling hand into a fist. Jessi untied her apron and turned to face her co-worker's grin. "He'll probably be back tomorrow. Tell him I said hello."

The muted roar of a crowd poured from the TV, but Alexander barely heard it. He stared sightlessly at the hockey game on the screen. The Canucks were losing, and he stopped paying much attention after the second period. Thoughts of his day at the coffee shop distracted him. Part of him was amused, the other frustrated at having been so easily played. Knowing Jessi had intentionally not told him today was her day off made him smile. He was so taken with her he hadn't bothered to confirm she would be there. And her shrewdness only intrigued him more. If there was anything he enjoyed, it was a challenge, and he hadn't been challenged in a long time.

He'd gone to the coffee shop that morning, set up his workstation at the same table as yesterday, and waited for Jessi to come into work. The employees spent the time keeping his cup full and dodging his questions about her. Finally, the blond, Dawn he thought her name was, told him she wasn't coming in. But only after he had been there an entire eight-hour shift. And he still wasn't sure when she was working next.

He called Peter on his way home to let him in on the joke and listened as his friend laughed.

"So, what are you going to do now?" Peter asked. "Are you going back tomorrow?"

"I am." Alexander chuckled. "I don't seem to have much choice. She's holding all the cards at the moment."

"You'll figure something out." The amusement in his friend's voice faded. "Just don't overdo it, Alexander. Be a *little* patient."

At least it was a productive business day. He'd gotten most of his speech written, and the attorneys called to let him know the charitable foundation status had been approved, while three more athletic trainers joined the list of approved sponsorship choices.

Alexander also finalized his travel plans for the Gathering in New York at the Ritz-Carlton Battery Park. The week would be full of meetings, including choosing the location for the following year and discussing candidates for the next Council. Alexander planned to step down to focus his efforts on the foundation, especially now that he had found Jessi.

Ignoring the fire just her name lit under his skin, he stood to pour himself a glass of wine from the newly installed wet bar. He poured a swallow into the glass and absently swirled the contents.

Recently completed, the entertainment room was decorated in browns and light blues. The couches were a comfortable dark grey leather, and he had the walls painted a muted cream. In front of the sofa hung a massive TV still blaring the game. It flickered above a stone hearth fireplace of rough fieldstone that reminded him of his parents' house in Arizona. Moving out from behind the bar, he clicked off the TV and let his eyes travel across the room that was still sparsely decorated. There were no pictures on the walls, and he had yet to choose the fabrics for the curtains or pillows. So far, the only textile in the room was the large area rug that defined the seating area in front of the TV. Over the pale Berber carpet, it was a creamy brown several shades darker than the walls. An abstract pattern of blues swirled gracefully across it, suggesting rain sliding down a darkened window.

The home sat at the foot of a group of tall hills in a small, gated community. With three bedrooms, a master suite, a full media room, game room, and office space that opened onto a large patio with a fully equipped outdoor kitchen and pool, the house was much larger than he needed. A full-time housekeeper and grounds crew for the acre and a half of property enabled him to renovate and landscape to his preferences without worrying about the upkeep afterward. It felt good to test his interior design skills for the first time in a renovation project rather than a new build. He'd bought the home in foreclosure, and had he not found Jessi, he could easily have sold it for a tidy profit.

He carried his glass into the kitchen still decorated in a classic wine country theme. He hadn't had time to redo the kitchen before moving in. He rarely cooked, so he left it as the last project on the list. The stone tile counters and pale cabinets would soon be replaced with dark cherry woods and gleaming black granite. The brushed steel appliances would stay.

The kitchen demolition was scheduled to start next month while he was in New York, and he was looking forward to having the project completed. The single door leading outside from the dining room narrowly framed the view of the hills outside. Taking a sip of the wine, he hoped the view was one Jessi liked as much as he did.

Thinking about her brought a wistful smile to his face even through the pain, and he longed for the day they would call the house he had poured so much of himself into home. For now, he had work to do. Gaining her trust would take time. Meanwhile, he would play along with her game of cat and mouse. Peter's advice to be patient echoed in his mind. He could be very patient. But that didn't mean he would do nothing.

He set the glass on a counter and picked up his phone. She may be holding all the cards, but he knew how to call a bluff. The way she reached out to him yesterday told him she felt more for him than she was willing to admit. His fingers moved swiftly across the screen.

"Hello again, Peter." He braced his hip against the counter. "May I speak to your lovely mate? I have a question for her and a favor to ask."

The next day Alexander pushed open the door to the Broken Bean. The bell twanged softly above his head, and the sweet smell of fresh flowers greeted him. Jessi stood behind the counter arguing with a deliveryman who held a large bouquet of tiger lilies.

"There *has* to be some mistake!" Her voice rose on the last, exasperation filling her echo and pricking his skin. The deliveryman lifted a clipboard from the counter.

"No mistake, miss." He pushed the papers toward her and set the vase beside him. "All the orders are right here. Prepaid and to be delivered once an hour." He shrugged and held out a pen. "Sign here?"

She crossed her slender arms and refused to take the offered pen. Defiance glared in her eyes. "Tell me how many more, and I'll sign it."

The man lifted his ball hat to scratch his head. "I told you the last time I was here I'm not sure." He replaced the cap and shifted from one foot to the other. "Please, miss. I have four more deliveries before getting back to the shop. I'll do my best to find out for you when I do."

Alexander widened his stance and waited. Jessi was so focused on the situation in front of her she hadn't noticed him, and he was enjoying the show. His stomach tightened as Jessi gritted her teeth, and a rush of excitement flooded him when he heard a frustrated growl.

Feisty little thing, he thought, then held back a laugh as she snatched the pen from the man's hand and signed his form. Relief was evident in his shoulders as he picked up the clipboard and pushed the vase of orange flowers toward her.

Alexander nodded at the young man as he rushed past then

turned his attention back to Jessi. She glared at the flowers as though her stare could make them disappear. He slid one hand into his pant pocket and gripped the pendant.

Her cheeks were stained darkly in frustration, and her ring-clad hands pressed flat on the counter in front of the vase. Her hair was loose today, and the green was gone. From root to tip it was jet black and lay in gracefully curled layers around her shoulders.

Her head dropped, and Alexander glanced around the room. A riot of color and shape brightened the space in a chaos of flowers and greenery. Nearly every table had a large vase or basket of flowers in the center of it.

Pleased with the result, he cleared his throat. "Is there a problem?" She drew a deep breath before her head slowly rose and her eyes found him. He did his best to keep the smug grin from taking over his face, but he couldn't. She looked so bewildered he couldn't help it.

"You?" Her head fell again, and she pushed back from the counter. "You did this, didn't you?" She picked up the vase and moved it to the short counter above the register before looking his way again. For just a moment her emotions were unguarded, and he was taken aback by the sliver of joy that flashed across her expression.

Her eyes skated across his face, and he swore it was a physical touch. Blood raced south, and he tensed, doing his best to rein in his physical response before she picked it out of his scent. But he was helpless against the hot rush of pleasure that spiked down his torso. His gaze fell to her lips, and he wondered if they were as soft as they looked.

Gripped with the sudden desire to march behind the counter and claim her regardless of the consequences, his hand clenched in his pocket as he imagined her fangs snapping into place and piercing his tongue. She was his and he wanted to make her so— permanently.

He'd been told several times that the desire to complete the

Blood Exchange would be nearly impossible to resist, but he foolishly believed his years of training gave him an advantage. It didn't.

Turning away, he broke their stare and viciously drove those thoughts out of his mind. What he'd intended to be a playful moment had turned in a heartbeat. He pulled out a chair and carefully placed his case on it. Staring at the basket of variegated green ivy and wildflowers, he gripped the back of the chair to keep from doing something he knew he would regret.

Her fiery nature ignited a desire he knew how to control, but the vulnerability he had just seen in her eyes unwound him. Unless he found a way to resist her, he would burn any chance of gaining her trust to the ground in seconds.

NINE

Jessi wrapped her arms around her middle and drew a deep breath as Alexander turned away from her. His coppery hair was free and contrasted sharply against the white of his perfectly tailored shirt. His muscled back rippled underneath the expensive fabric, and she longed for a glimpse of him without it.

Her friend Alyssa was right when she called him gorgeous. Ruggedly handsome and naturally confident, he shattered any attempt she made at denying her attraction to him. His intoxicating scent filled the room just as thickly as the sweetness of the lilies sitting in front of her. As his hand clenched the chair, his bicep bulged, and she wondered how it would feel to have arms like that hold her.

No sooner had that thought crossed her mind than she smelled the shift in his emotions. A spike of clove hit her, and his need rifled through her. The pain morphed into a shiver of desire, making her sinuses ache. With a quiet grasp, she realized it was her fangs. The pressure in the roof of her mouth continued to build until she closed her eyes and willed her body to relax.

Fear tightened her chest, and she searched for a way to stop the runaway train of their desire. The shop was completely empty other than the two of them, and she didn't expect Brandon to arrive for more than an hour.

Alexander smoothed his hands along the back of the chair, and she shivered at the thought of what those hands would feel like on her back.

This can't be happening. He can't come in here with flowers and make me forget who he really is. Taking a deep breath, she raised her arms from her twisting stomach and crossed them over her chest. She grabbed for her anger with both hands.

"Care to tell me why this was necessary?"

His head swung fractionally toward her, and she lifted her chin. A faint smile arched the muscle of the cheek that was visible in profile, and his strong jaw flexed. She knew he wasn't fooled.

His voice was smug as he shrugged. "I didn't know which was your favorite, so I ordered one of each."

Pompous jerk. "You could have just asked." She threw her hands in the air. "I would have told you it was stargazers, *Alex.*"

The muscle in his jaw jumped. "And when exactly would I have asked you?" He moved toward the counter. "Yesterday when you weren't at work?"

She trembled at his silent grace and once again felt very much like a small animal being stalked. His voice caressed the air like velvet, and she took an involuntary step back. "There are quite a few things I would like to ask you, Jessi."

Her throat clenched, and she savagely resisted the urge to launch herself into his arms. Thinking quickly as he continued to advance on her, she caught herself and held her ground as he reached the counter.

"I only have one question for you."

He paused. "And what would that be?"

Picking up a paper cup and sharpie, she smiled smartly up at him. "What can I get started for you?"

He froze, and the glint of humor returned to his eyes. As they stared, Jessi tilted her ear toward him and lifted the cup and pen in question. His laugh started with a slight shaking of his broad shoulders before the deep sound rolled from his throat. Rough and sexy, it made her toes curl.

"House blend pour over with room." He reached for his wallet and slid another fifty across the counter, keeping two fingers on the bill. "Will you please keep the change this time? I hate carrying small bills."

Is he serious? What an arrogant... Truly angry, she opened her mouth to protest when the bell over the front door chimed. They looked up to see another flower deliveryman. Jessi turned venomous eyes on Alexander's self-satisfied face.

"How many, Alex?"

A low growl escaped him, and she thought she was going to pass out. Or fling herself across the counter at him. His eyes flashed knowingly when she blushed.

He bit out his next words. "Keep the change, *stop* calling me Alex, and I'll tell you." They glared at one another, but her knees were not going to last much longer under the heat of his look. His voice dropped seductively. "I might even be persuaded to call them off if you'll agree to let me take you to dinner."

Blowing a strand of hair out of her face, Jessi reached for the money to cover the need to brace herself against the counter. "Fine, *Alexander*."

He caught her hand before she could draw it back, and once again the searing pain in her heart vanished. They both paused. He shook his head in wonder and whispered, "I'll never get used to that." He gentled. "Are you free tonight?"

"No." The word fell from her reluctantly. The vet would be at the stable to remove Armani's stitches in a few hours, and she knew it would take time. "I have something I have to do tonight."

A throat cleared beside them, and their heads whipped toward the forgotten delivery guy. He was half-hidden behind a huge basket of daisies, coneflowers, and sprigs of greenery. "Flowers for a Miss Vogel?"

Disengaging herself from Alexander's hand, Jessi growled. "That's me." Then she pointed at Alexander. "And this one will tell you what to do with the rest!"

Alexander's laugh rumbled again as he drew out his phone. "I'll call them off, but we have a deal, correct?"

"I suppose." She shook her head to clear it. Taking the basket of flowers from the man, she carried them out from behind the counter to place them on the last empty shelf in the room, thankful her trembling legs supported her.

Alexander backed up to lean on the counter, bracing his hands on either side of his hips, the phone in his long fingers. The door chimed as the deliveryman left, and the back door opened.

Crossing his ankles, Alexander regarded her. "Do you like seafood?"

Before she could answer, Brandon exclaimed in surprise, "What in the name of..." He caught sight of Jessi and Alexander. "Where did all this come from?"

Wordlessly, Jessi pointed to Alexander. His amused exhale brought Brandon's gaze to his, and Jessi's heart hitched as Alexander pushed away from the counter. He was power and grace in huge quantities, and she wasn't sure if she should be frightened or excited.

Excitement won.

Alexander's quiet rumble as he stepped past her told her he knew it. He extended a hand to her boss. "Alexander Koch. Pleasure to meet you."

"Brandon Hills." Brandon's eyes widened a fraction as he grasped Alexander's hand. "Alexander *Koch*? Of Koch Architectural Design?"

For a split-second Jessi scented an intense spike in Alexander's pain before he answered. "Not anymore. Or at least, not for long. The press release was scheduled for today, so I suppose it's no harm to admit I've sold the company."

"You *what?*" Jessi gasped, surprising even herself. "Why?"

Alexander crossed an arm over his chest to grip his opposite elbow; green eyes locked pointedly with hers. "It was time." He turned back to Brandon. "Since I don't have an office yet, I hope you won't mind if I occupy one of your tables from time to time." He nodded to the seat where his untouched case sat. "I've found I enjoy the scenery here." Jessi flushed red but said nothing.

Brandon shifted his gaze between them. "I don't mind, as long as there aren't any complaints from the employees." Jessi's heart swelled at his protective words, then nearly burst in frustration at Alexander's reply.

"Oh, she'll complain." His fierce cat-like eyes turned to her. "But that's because I tend to overdo it when I want something."

Jessi walked away as she untied her apron and remembered Alexander hated nicknames. "Call off the flowers, Mufasa. It takes more than a few pretty blooms to impress me." She exited out the back door, not even caring she was leaving before her shift was officially over.

"Mufasa? I have a name!"

Brandon's bark of laughter followed Alexander's frustrated reply. "Uh oh. She's found you a nickname. I think she likes you."

Armani was in rare form, but thankfully the barn owner, Dennis, was able to help manage the frightened animal while Dr. Richards removed the stitches. Both were patient with him. Jessi held the twitch, carefully keeping the right amount of pressure on his tender muzzle. Dennis held the hoof on the side opposite Dr. Richards lifted and clenched between his knees. She could see the fear in Armani's eyes, but he stood still. His jet-black tail swished in agitation until they were done.

"The wound looks good, Jessi." Dr. Richards peeled off his rubber gloves. "It shouldn't leave much of a scar." He turned his attention from the horse's shoulder to her. "How this animal has survived with so few I've no idea."

Dennis released the hoof and stepped around to where Jessi and the vet stood. He wiped his hands on his jeans. "He's a piece of work for sure."

Setting the twitch on the shelf next to her, Jessi patted Armani's sweaty neck. "I just wish I knew what happened to make him so scared."

Dr. Richards watched her. "Hard to tell." He shrugged. "Doesn't make much of a difference at this point. He is more scared than mean, but the end result is the same. He might not be very big, but he's unpredictable. That makes him dangerous."

She'd heard all this before but refused to give up on him. There was something about the golden animal's eyes that broke her heart. There was hope for him. She just needed to find the key to getting past his fears.

"I don't have any delusions about him." Jessi scratched his chin and was rewarded when he lowered his head into her hand. "He's never tried to hurt me. He just resists any attempt to correct him." She smiled when he pushed at her hip pocket looking for sugar cubes. "He'll probably always be a pet." She slipped one out, and he quickly swiped it from her open palm.

"A big, destructive, expensive one. Are you sure you won't let me find a home for him?" Dennis moved to stand at her shoulder, and she was surprised when he reached out a hand to stroke Armani's neck. "I have a lot of clients who have the time and space."

"I'll think about it, Mr. Bean." She smiled. "I better get him put up and fed."

Dr. Richards packed away his things and was thoughtfully watching her unfasten Armani from the crossties. "Have you ever had a trainer work with him? Someone who could take the edge off and get him started for you?"

She shrugged. "Can't afford that at the moment, and even if I did, I wouldn't know who to ask. He's not a dressage prospect, that's for sure."

"I might know someone who would at least come take a look at him." Dr. Richards picked up his satchel. "He's worked with a couple problem horses for my clients, and they've all been happy with him. He'd come out and evaluate for free if I asked."

Knowing he was loosened from the ties, Armani danced in place. His hooves clacked against the concrete and Jessi placed a hand on his shoulder. "Be still." As requested, Armani stilled, and she smiled. Jessi looked at the vet and nodded. "Sure. I can arrange to be here this weekend if he's free."

Dr. Richards shook his head. "You've got a special touch with that one. I'll call Toby and see when he can come. I'll let you know as soon as I hear." He turned with a knowing smile. "Until next time."

She waved and led Armani back to his stall. Dennis walked beside her, his hands crammed in his pockets.

He cleared his throat. "I was wondering if you would be willing to groom for me next weekend. I'll be riding three of my horses, and I could use an extra hand if you're available."

"I'll have to see what my work schedule is like. Where's the show?" She knew she would turn him down, but it was sweet of him to ask.

"Not far, just across town in lower Escondido." Dennis tossed the shaggy hair out of his eyes, and his next words chilled her blood. "Rumor has it Marcus Vogt will be judging a few of the Level Three and Four tests. I've wanted to ride for him for years, and I'm hoping to get Saturn on his schedule."

Jessi tensed at the mention of her father's name. Working at a competition dressage barn, she knew eventually someone would mention him. He was a celebrity among judges, but to her he would always be a monster. Armani picked up on her tension and shifted away. Refocusing on him, she quietly unlatched his halter and slid it carefully over his ears. Backing out of the stall, she saw Dennis watching her.

"Is he okay?"

"He's angry at me for twitching him." Her voice shook at the thought of her father being so close. He had only been in southern California one other time, and she made it a point to be out of town. "When do you need me to let you know? I can check my schedule tomorrow."

Dennis fell in step beside her as they headed back to the grooming area to tidy up and grab the horses feed. "I leave with Pacemaker tomorrow afternoon, but I should be back by Monday." His earnest blue eyes focused on her, and she did her best to hide the fear in hers. "I'd really like it if you'd groom for me. You're one of the best. You could even catch ride if you wanted to."

She handed him his twitch and smiled. "I appreciate it. I'll let you know tomorrow, okay?"

He took it from her and lowered his hand. "Are you riding tonight?"

It was only seven, but she was exhausted. "Not tonight. I've picked up extra hours at the store to make up for this vet bill, and I could really stand to catch up on my sleep." She grabbed the broom to sweep up the small amount of dirt and hair Armani left behind. "I'm going to feed the horses then head upstairs."

Disappointment flitted across Dennis's features, and she thought he might ask her something else, but instead his lips pressed into a line. He nodded. "All right then. I guess I'll see you when I get back."

"Have a safe trip, Bean." She pushed the small pile of dirt into a dustpan and dumped it into an empty stall.

Dennis had turned to go when she looked up. "Have a good week, Pixie."

She smiled at his nickname for her, and then her thoughts caught on Brandon's words as she'd left the shop earlier today. *"She's found you a nickname. I think she likes you!"*

She could only imagine Alexander's scowl at that. He was far too proper for nicknames, evidenced by his disdain for being called Alex. But every time she saw him, she couldn't deny he fit the image of a proud lion. Thank goodness he never asked if Jessi was short for anything. He addled her brain so badly she might just tell him. And that would be a disaster.

"He filled the coffee shop with flowers?" Alyssa barely got the words past her laughter.

Jessi shook her head and had to admit it *was* funny.

"Yes. They kept coming all day until he showed up that afternoon and..." She paused. "I have no idea what to think." The gas station wasn't busy, and she sank onto a stool beside the register. The clerk had handed her the phone and disappeared into the back room.

"When are you going out?" Alyssa asked.

"Tonight." Jessi rubbed a hand down her arm. "It's a double date with his friends Peter and Hannah."

"The Samuelsons?"

"I think so. Peter is the one who talked me into giving Alexander a chance. If it goes well tonight, I guess he and I are on our own." She twirled the phone cord around her finger, wondering if she'd made a horrible mistake.

"Oh yeah?" Alyssa was smug. "How are you feeling about that?"

"I just said I don't know!" Jessi snapped.

"Whoa. Sorry." Alyssa sighed. "It's only been a couple days. Go out tonight and have fun."

Jessi glanced at her watch. "I have to get to work. Sorry I snapped at you."

"Don't worry about it. I'll talk to you tomorrow, okay?"

"Thanks, Al." Closing her eyes, Jessi drew a deep breath. "If nothing else, you're right about one thing. He is gorgeous."

Alyssa laughed. "Told you! Enjoy it. The Vampir believe in him. I think you should too."

"I'm going to try," Jessi conceded.

"Have a great date. Call me with all the details tomorrow."

"Sure. Have a good day." Jessi hung up, snagged her purse from the floor, and promised herself she would at least try to relax.

The flowers were still in place on the tables when Jessi arrived. From the hallway, she caught sight of Alexander's coppery hair. Brandon called last night to let her know three more deliveries arrived before Alexander could stop them. He also said Alexander stayed at the shop for hours working. Brandon was concerned, and while she appreciated his protectiveness, she was also sure Alexander's smooth-talking nature would win him over sooner or later.

He was seated at what was quickly becoming his table. Pulling the apron over her head, she sighed. Alexander was here to stay, and she was a fool to fight it. There was no denying they were mates, but she couldn't quite allow that thought to bring her comfort yet. So far her interactions with him were here in the coffee house. This was her territory. What would happen when she stepped back into his?

How will he react when I tell him we're already pledged? She winced and decided to put it off as long as possible.

At that moment, Alexander looked up from his work, his brilliant eyes sparking when he spotted her. Glittering peridot green like a finely cut gemstone, they would always be the most arresting eyes she had ever seen.

His full mouth tipped up, and she shivered. A charcoal grey suit jacket was draped on the back of his chair. Over his white dress shirt, was a camel hair waistcoat and a tie the same grey as his suit. One long leg crossed the other at the knee, leaving grey, tan, and burgundy argyle socks peeking out from his cuff. His black wingtips were polished to a high shine.

"Good morning, Jessi." He stood to greet her, and she felt the eyes of everyone in the room on her. There were several tables of businessmen and women scattered across the space, and she cursed internally when all the chatter died. Alexander Koch commanded attention, and when his attention was on her, so was everyone else's. It both thrilled and annoyed her.

Directly in her line of sight was a table with two housewives and their babies. The women watched wistfully as Alexander lifted her knuckles to his lips. His mustache tickled the back of her hand, and she did her best to stifle the undignified noise that escaped her throat. His resulting chuckle did sound amazingly like a purr.

"Good morning, Mufasa."

His eyes narrowed as he released her hand. Annoyance thinned his lips.

"Does everyone have a nickname?" he growled.

She turned away to take her place behind the counter and smiled at Dawn, who was handing an order to her last customer. "Only the people I don't like."

"Liar," Dawn whispered. She pushed her chin in Alexander's direction. "And how exactly do I get one of those?" He had settled back into his chair, sipping from a Broken Bean mug reserved for their regular customers.

Jessi scowled at the back of his head. "One of what? The pompous jerk or the thousand-dollar suit?"

The customer in front of her barked a laugh, and she looked up in surprise to see Peter. She was again distracted by Alexander's presence and hadn't noticed his seaside scent or the amusement that came with it.

"And how *is* our evil plan working, Jess?" He dropped a couple dollars into the tip jar and raked a hand through his hair. Without the hoodie over his t-shirt, the muscles of his arms bulged and took Dawn's eyes with them.

"Good grief, Jess." They grew even wider as she took in Peter's impressive size. "Two in one day? If you don't want this one, can I have him?"

Peter raised an eyebrow and laughed. Movement to his left drew Jessi's attention to the tall blond standing beside him with an amused but no-nonsense expression.

"Ask me tomorrow, honey, and I might let you have him. But I bet you send him back within a week." Her pale eyes were bright as they flicked over Jessi and Dawn's faces. "He's pretty to look at but a pain in the—"

"Jessi," Peter hastily interrupted as he wrapped his arm around the woman's shoulders and gently squeezed her neck. "I'd like you to meet my wife, Hannah. She's sweet most of the time, but she bites."

Jessi almost choked, and Hannah shrugged. "Only when provoked." She kissed his cheek. "I'll have my usual. I'm going to go keep Alexander company while you chat with your fan club." With a wink at Jessi, she walked over to Alexander.

Hannah was a perfect match for Peter. Her head came to his shoulder, and she was obviously a fighter. Her lithe body moved with the same confidence and grace as the two men, though with a decidedly feminine swing to her narrow hips. She wore slim fitted white pants and the snug grey sweater that skimmed closely to her upper body hugged her hips. Jessi realized with a grin that most of her startling height came from the tall stiletto platform boots. They had to be at least a five-inch heel, but she walked in them with such confidence Jessi was sure she could fight in them too.

Wildly layered blond hair fell just past her shoulder blades and the stack of silver bracelets around her wrist tinkled against each other as she quickly hugged Alexander then stepped back. Jessi felt his needle of pain at the contact and drew a breath.

"All yours, Jess," Dawn whispered in her ear as she lifted her apron over her head and watched Alexander hold a chair for Hannah. "That woman scares me."

Peter chuckled again. "We'll both have a double shot Americano. But make Hannah's a decaf. Caffeine makes her mean."

ELEVEN

Hannah sat quietly across the table from Alexander. She always struck him as sharp edged, but as she watched Jessi and Peter, he wondered what she thought about his mate. Before he could ask, her pale blue eyes swung to his.

"Well, she's a tough little thing." Hannah leaned back in her chair. "She's the one, huh?"

"She is." Alexander pushed the computer back and folded his hands on the table. He ticked his head back toward the counter. "What gives you the impression she's tough? Not that I disagree. I'm just curious."

Hannah's lip tipped up. "Well, she called you a pompous jerk in a thousand-dollar suit." Her laugh was soft as Peter approached. "Takes guts to be as small as she is and be willing to take shots like that at you." One shoulder shrugged. "I'd do it, but I know I can take you in the ring."

Alexander's laugh was genuine. These two had seen him through the darkest times in his life. He was grateful to share the brightest with them now. "I'd like to see you try. Your mate is the only one who's ever been able to best me."

"Don't challenge her, Alexander. She fights dirty." Peter pulled out a chair, flipped it backwards, and straddled it

Taking a sip of coffee, Hannah scowled. "Decaf again?"

"You need to be nice tonight." Peter patted her hand. "We're chaperones for the lovebirds, remember?"

Still scowling, Hannah tilted her head toward Alexander. "Where are we going anyway?"

"There's a seafood place not far from here I've been wanting to try. It looks like a good place to take potential donors. I made reservations for us at five." Alexander shifted in his seat, pushing back to cross his legs. He deliberately seated himself with his back to the counter. Despite telling Brandon he enjoyed the scenery, watching Jessi work was far too distracting. "After that I plan to take us all over to my pier."

"Your pier?" Peter asked. "You moved the yacht down here? I thought you were selling all your toys."

Alexander shrugged. "I sold the helicopter and decided to keep the yacht. The jet went with the sale of the company." He glanced at Hannah as her expression grew concerned. "Something wrong?"

"I don't think your intended was impressed by that." Her eyes were thoughtful. "She was on her way over but stopped when she heard you mention keeping the yacht. She looked almost offended." Her gaze shifted to his. "What do you know about her, Alexander?"

"Nothing but her name." He straightened his cuffs in a gesture that was more habit than anything else. "She's scared of me for some reason and hasn't been willing to tell me anything. Not that it matters much, but I don't even know which Clan she's from."

Peter braced his arms on the back of the chair in front of him and pointedly looked at Hannah. "That's why you need to be nice tonight." He leaned away when she swatted his arm, and they all laughed. "No. Seriously. I thought it would be a good idea for the four of us to go tonight. I hoped you could talk to her." Peter's rueful grin turned to Alexander. "Besides, I can already tell these two are like matches and gunpowder. Without someone to keep them apart they'll either kill each other or..."

"Yes." Alexander's face grew warm. What Peter suggested was true. There was a need between himself and Jessi that if left unchecked would be devastating in the light of morning. "I'm well aware of the effect we have on each other."

Hannah's eyes shifted from amused back to concerned. "Does she know about your pain?"

For the first time today, Alexander let the pain register in his conscious thought. It rippled through him like fire. "She not only knows, she feels it like I do."

Her brows shot up. "And you haven't...she knows that would relieve it for both of you, right?"

"It's not that simple." Alexander let out a breath. "I can't ask that of her until she trusts me. If I do, I'll betray everything the new Council is trying to put in place." He ran a hand down his beard. "She's so scared, she's been hiding for the last year. She knows, Hannah, but it's got to be her choice."

Peter grinned. "Well, if your statement about keeping your toys offended her, that last bit made her cry."

Alexander stiffened and started to turn, but Hannah stopped him. "Wait until you have time to really talk about it." Alexander pushed down the urge to at least glance over his shoulder. "She heard you, Alexander. Let her process it."

TWELVE

essi had been on her way to refill their cups when she heard Alexander respond to Hannah's sympathetic question. His words blurred her vision.

"I can't ask that of her until she trusts me."

Her feet froze to the floor and for a split second, her eyes locked with Hannah's before the woman looked away. Jessi turned back, refills forgotten.

Alexander could not have known she was close enough to hear his response. Even if he had, the way he released the carefully maintained wall he kept around his pain convinced her he was telling the truth. The pain hadn't spiked like it did with a touch. It coursed through him like fire on dry wood, so intense her vision went white. The room was spun, and Jessi stumbled as her foot caught on the rubber mat. Catching herself against the rear shelf, she drew a deep breath and forced herself upright.

Alexander was nothing like the man she thought he was. Arrogant and self-assured, yes, but that was part of what made him so magnetically attractive. He wore the arrogance like he wore his suits, but she was beginning to see that underneath it all, he was someone far more charming and real than she ever expected. She set the pot on the warmer and blinked up at the ceiling lights to force back the tears.

"Jessi?" Hannah stood at the end of the counter, her expression gentle as though approaching a frightened bird. "May I have a refill?"

Jessi smiled shakily. "Sure. Decaf right?"

Hannah tossed her hair and glanced back at the table where Peter and Alexander sat. "Make it regular. I won't tell him if you won't."

Jessi exhaled in a small puff. She found her smile widening in appreciation for Hannah's sensitivity. "Does it really make you mean?"

"Nah." She watched Jessi pour the fresh liquid. "Well, sometimes. Are you all right?"

The room begin to right itself again as Alexander's pain subsided and her own heart rate slowed. "Yes. Thank you for checking on me," Jessi said sincerely.

"You bet. He can be a lot to deal with." She held the cup between her slender hands and regarded Jessi. The blue eyes watching her were sharp, missing nothing.

Are they all *like predators? S*he poured herself a cup as Hannah rested her arms on the counter. *If that's the case, I don't stand a chance.*

"How long have you known Alexander?"

Hannah took a sip. "Since he was sixteen. His father brought him to the gym in Phoenix hoping Peter could knock some sense into him." She shook her head wryly. "And he did. Alexander left that day with a bloody nose and a broken wrist. They've been best friends ever since. Though Alexander is the same age as our youngest son."

Hannah appeared to be in her late thirties but looks were very deceiving among their people. Her own mother was two hundred thirty-five but didn't look a day over fifty. "How many children do you and Peter have?"

"Three boys." Her eyes were distant for a moment. "They've all left the Vampir. Our oldest passed away three years ago, and the other two are raising families somewhere out east." She set the mug down and crossed her arms. "Peter talks to them about once a year. Their wives don't know about us, and it's easier for me not to know. I worry about them enough as it is."

Jessi wondered what it would be like to have a brother or a son leave and never speak to them again. She had never known her siblings. They all died before she was born. Would she have to watch *her* children leave? How would Alexander feel about it? Shaking off that thought, Jessi glanced at the clock.

"I need to finish up some things before Brandon gets here." She set her mug in the small sink and nodded to the half-empty one beside Hannah. "A quick refill before Peter finds out?"

"I knew I liked you." Hannah held out her cup, then caught Jessi's hand. The pot stilled between them. "Give him a chance, Jessi. I promise he's not the man he used to be."

Tears swam back into Jessi's eyes, and she nodded, afraid to speak. Hannah released her and headed back to the table where Peter and Alexander were deep in conversation.

Jessi stared at his wide shoulders and fiery red ponytail. *If I give him a chance, I'll never be able to resist him.* As she watched him laugh with his friends, her heart pushed back.

Do you really want *to resist?*

When Jessi crossed the room, Alexander followed her with his eyes until she disappeared into the back room. When she was out of sight, his attention dropped back to the computer screen in front of him, not quite registering what he was reading. The press release announcing his sale of the company hit the media the day before without much fanfare. Mergers and acquisitions happened all the time, and since his company had never been a media draw, he'd expected it to go mostly unnoticed.

That made the news story in front of him even more startling. The article with his picture in brilliant color announced the company was being sold in order to avoid a massive lawsuit. As he finished reading, his attorney's name flashed on the screen of his phone.

"Thomas. What is going on?" Alexander listened for a moment as Peter's head snapped toward him. Alexander pushed the computer around. He leaned back in the chair and caught Hannah's gaze. Gesturing with his chin toward the hallway where Jessi re-emerged, he silently asked her to delay for a few minutes. Without hesitation, Hannah stood and led Jessi outside to wait for them.

"I understand. Is there anything you need from me at the moment?" Alexander said as Peter closed the computer and slid it into its case. "All right. Call me as soon as you know." He stood, lifting his suit coat from the back of the chair. "Thank you, Thomas."

"Did you know about this?" Peter tossed their cups in the trash.

"No." Alexander shrugged into his jacket and tucked the phone into the inside pocket. "This is the first Thomas has heard of it either. He has no idea what prompted the article, but he assures me there is no need to worry. He said he would call as soon as he knows anything."

Peter picked up the briefcase and handed it to him. "In that case, let's go have dinner with our smoking hot women."

Through the front window, Alexander spotted the women waiting on the curb. Jessi's back was stiff, and her hands kept clenching and un-clenching at her sides. Hannah stood beside her with a slightly amused expression hidden behind the fist she held pressed to her lips.

Alexander made his way through the shop with Peter right behind. Jessi was glaring at his brand new, bronze Maserati Ghibli. He placed a hand on her shoulder. "Is something wrong?"

"This is your car?" Her voice was exasperated, but he heard the edge of admiration in it.

"It is." The lights flashed, and the doors unlocked as the proximity sensor registered the fob tucked in his pocket. "I picked it up at the dealership yesterday." He stepped off the curb to place his bag in the trunk and heard her muttering as he got a few strides along the car.

Jessi sighed audibly. "It's a beautiful car, Mufasa."

Alexander lingered behind the deck lid after he put his case inside. He drew a deep breath to quell his frustration before pulling it shut. As it glided closed, his eyes locked with Jessi. Behind her, Peter and Hannah were doing their best to control their laughter.

"All right," Alexander said. "I can see I need to make another deal with you."

"Oh, this should be good," Peter whispered to Hannah. They moved around Jessi and with a grin, Hannah slid into the dark leather seat.

Alexander deliberately slowed his steps as he advanced on her. She was taunting him with the nicknames, and he planned to return the favor. Her delicate throat convulsed as she swallowed hard, clearly fighting the urge to run. He relished the fact he could rattle her as easily as she did him. He smoothed his features and blocked his emotions to hide the thrill chasing her would give him.

Someday.

When she actually wants *to be caught.*

"Here's my offer." He extended his elbow to help her off the curb, wishing her trembling wasn't because of fear. "Every time you call me by something other than my *actual* name, I buy you something." Her brows shot up. "And - each purchase I make will be more expensive than the last." He still waited for her to take his arm. "I am not afraid to spend my money, Jessi, and I would enjoy a good excuse to spend it. Especially on you."

Finally, she lay her hand on his forearm, bringing with it the now familiar rush of relief. "Fine." Her echo betrayed her defiance with a longing so deep he ached to pull her against him. "Does this extend to common courtesies like sir or mister?"

Alexander opened the passenger door and leaned forward to whisper in her ear as she lowered herself into the car.

"Try it." Her shiver was satisfying.

FOURTEEN

JESSI

Alexander's challenge made Jessi grit her teeth, while the seductive whisper against her ear shattered her nerves. She lowered her chin and glared at Alexander as he rounded the front of the car. Smug satisfaction rolled from Peter in the back as he clearly enjoyed the way she and Alexander played the game.

"Your move, Jess." Peter said, followed by a slight grunt when Hannah elbowed him. "Woman," he growled.

Jessi laughed slightly at the antics of the couple as Alexander got in and started the car. He looked sideways at her but didn't comment on her amusement. For a moment she allowed herself to drink in the sweetness of his scent. His happiness soothed her nerves as much as his preening behavior annoyed her. He was obviously pleased with himself, and his growing bravado only increased her laughter.

"You really think you're something don't you?" She crossed her arms, then rested her chin on her fist.

Alexander's brows furrowed at the question, but his lip quirked at her teasing tone. "Of course I do. But what really matters to me is what you think."

I think you're funny, endearingly sweet, hotter than an Arizona summer, and frustratingly over-confident, but no way am I admitting that to you.

Alexander Koch was quickly breaking through her defenses, but there were still too many questions in her mind, too many concerns and things she didn't know to allow herself to be swept away by his charm alone.

"Actually, I try to think about you as little as possible." They both knew she was lying, and she realized too late that all she had done was give him one more excuse to plague her.

"Then it seems I have a new challenge." He lifted a shoulder. "You never did answer me the other day when I asked if you like seafood."

"I don't mind it." Jessi settled back in the soft leather seat and studied his profile. Traffic was heavy, and his eyes never strayed from the road, but the smoothness of his scent told her he knew she was staring. "I prefer to cook, so I haven't had good seafood in a long time."

"Well, I hope we're not disappointed then." Alexander glanced sideways at her, considering something. "Would you tell me why you suppress your echo? There's no need to hide from us."

Jessi's gut twisted. "I already told you. I have a hard time trusting people."

"Fair enough," he said, and effortlessly guided the car through a sharp turn. "Mind if I ask you where you learned to do it?"

"Family secret." She hadn't meant to sound so harsh, but she didn't like where this conversation was going.

"You ran for a reason, Jessi. That much I know." The car came to a stop at a traffic light, and Alexander swung his head toward her. She stared at him, refusing to say anything else. His voice was soft, concerned. His eyes went to Peter's in the mirror then back to the road as the light changed. "Whatever you're afraid of..."

Defensiveness flared, and she snapped at him. "Look. I didn't agree to go out with you so we could have a counseling session, okay, Dr. Phil?" She wasn't ready to let him close and had to shut this down before the questions went any further. "Honestly, you haven't earned the right to ask those questions." Her heart pounded in anger, and she knew her response only served to confirm what he suspected, but maintaining her distance was the only safe way to make sure he couldn't hurt her.

Although, she was quickly coming to realize that keeping any kind of distance from him was going to be impossible. The physical attraction between them, coupled with their natural instinct to bond was already nearly enough to drive her into his bed without a second thought. Forcing him to keep his distance was the only way out, but she wasn't so sure anymore she really wanted out.

His hands had tightened on the wheel until she thought he was going to snap it, and his tension prickled across her skin like thousands of needles. As his hurt continued to increase in the silence, she couldn't take it anymore. She sighed and touched his hand. When she did, the tension her anger created diffused instantly. As their emotions calmed, he relaxed his grip, and she lowered her voice.

"I apologize. I'm just not ready to talk about it, okay?" She withdrew, but Alexander caught her hand and laced his fingers through hers.

"*I* apologize. You are correct. I haven't earned that right." He gave her hand a gentle squeeze she felt all the way to her toes. "I promise, no more questions about your past tonight."

"Matches and gunpowder," Peter murmured, and Alexander grinned.

Jessi glanced into the back seat to find Hannah's eyes. The sorrow she read in the other woman's face embarrassed her, and she turned back to stare at the hand engulfed by Alexander's. When she looked up, he was watching her guardedly. They had pulled into a parking lot, and he reached across with his left hand to shift the car into park, unwilling to let go of her. He rested his wrist on the steering wheel.

"Truce?"

"Truce," she replied and watched as his eye color shifted to a luminescent satisfaction. He shook his head as the sweet tang of playfulness returned to his scent. "What?"

"Dr. Phil?" He grunted. She blushed and turned away from him. "That's your last warning."

She was still blushing when they exited the car, and she placed her hand inside his elbow. He tucked her hand close and used the motion to button his suit coat. Alexander was so tall she was sure she looked like a child next to him. However, the stirring in her stomach at the feel of the bicep under her hand was anything but childish. Unable to stop herself, she ran the palm of her hand up the hard muscle and stumbled when he turned it into a full flex. He caught her with a wicked grin, and Peter puffed a disgusted breath from his nose.

"I don't know whether to give you two boxing gloves or hose you down." Peter said, and

Hannah laughed as Jessi tried to free her arm from Alexander, but he pulled her even closer. Hannah's blue eyes danced when Jessi looked back, begging for help.

Instead, she egged it on. "Water could make it interesting either way. But my money's on Jessi. I'm betting she's a lover and a fighter. Win win for you, Alexander."

Alexander's amusement vibrated against the back the hand he had trapped against his side, and the sweet orange of his contentment was intoxicating. She didn't try very hard to get away from him because she knew why he didn't want to let go. He loosened his grip and covered her hand with his.

He's nearly pain free for the first time in a very long time.

His easy smile faded when he turned toward the restaurant entrance, and she followed his gaze. The outside wasn't fancy, no name or signage, but the parking lot was full, and there was a line of people waiting to be seated. It took her a moment to realize they were holding cameras, microphones, and recorders. Alexander's grip tightened and his anger flooded her as one woman stepped in front of them all.

"Rebekka?" He stared down at the woman as anger and embarrassment rolled off him, but he kept his expression calm as she approached.

She was tall, leggy, and drop dead beautiful. An elegant cream suit skimmed her every curve, and she strode forward confidently on a pair of Louboutin's.

"Alexander." The woman's voice was chillingly hard, and Jessi was surprised to see tears in her eyes when her venomous gaze landed on Jessi's arm threaded through Alexander's. "Is *this* the one you sold the company for?"

"I've no idea what you're talking about." Alexander ran a thumb over Jessi's hand, and she squeezed his forearm in acknowledgment. "Why are you here?" he demanded.

Rebekka whipped her eyes to his and hefted a bound sheaf of papers. "The business office was served these papers yesterday, *Mr. Koch.* Your lawyer was kind enough to tell me where I could find you and deliver them in person, as directed." Her brittle stare bored into him. "Consider yourself served." She stepped forward and slapped the papers into his chest. He caught them, and she lowered her voice. "This *isn't* over, Alexander." Jessi's grip tightened on his arm when the woman raked her over with a sneer. "What a waste."

Rebekka stormed away as the reporters closed in, pushing cameras and microphones toward them. A flash went off, and Jessi twisted her face into Alexander's arm. His large hand engulfed the back of her head as he shouldered through the crowd.

Peter's voice rocketed through the air. "Mr. Koch has no comment! You can contact his business office for his attorney's number."

More questions were shouted, and Alexander's pain crested, nearly bringing her to her knees. Even her touch wasn't enough to calm the fury-driven arc of pain Jessi could smell racing though his body. She clung to him for support while he kept her face tucked away from the cameras. Alexander pushed the reporters aside as Peter repeated again that they needed to contact Alexander's attorney.

Step by step, they made their way into the restaurant, where he released her. Inside, curious patrons watched the chaos outside with mild interest. As the door swung shut behind them, Hannah took charge, quietly apologizing to the staff and asking the manager for private seating away from the windows.

Jessi kept a hand on his arm, and Alexander's breathing evened as his pain receded. After several seconds, he spoke quietly to the hesitant manager. With a gentle squeeze to her shoulders, he stepped away to address the man.

"I apologize for the scene outside. All meals and drinks for your patrons this evening, including compensation for your staff, will be covered by me, and any damage the press causes to your property will also be covered." He smiled charmingly and produced a black credit card from his wallet. "I would appreciate your assistance by allowing us to impose on you for dinner. We do have reservations, and your hospitality will not be forgotten."

The man's eyes widened as he took the card and nodded. Alexander relaxed, and Jessi could breathe again. With his palm warming her lower back, Alexander guided her as they were led to a table behind the bar with a shoulder high wall separating them from the other guests. Once seated, they were safely hidden from the view outside.

Peter reached across the table and took the papers from Alexander as he attempted to read them. "Oh, no my friend. This is why you pay your attorney." He put the stack underneath his butt. "Thomas said he'll call you tomorrow."

Jessi sat frozen, her hands in her lap. She had no idea what to say or do until the waiter handed them menus. She took hers and stared sightlessly at it. Alexander hadn't looked at her since the other woman confronted him. Who *was* she?

His hand covered hers, and he waited for her to look up before speaking. "I owe you an explanation for Rebekka's behavior." Her heart lurched at the emotion in his eyes. "She and I were involved for a time." Peter cleared his throat, and Alexander flinched then amended his statement. "She is, *was,* the CFO for my company, and until last year, we...she expected me to marry her."

Jealousy flared red hot, and Jessi fought to keep it from her voice. "How long?"

His eyes closed. "Almost four years." He drew a deep breath and rested an elbow on the table. "We met the year I graduated college. Just months before my parents died." He kissed her knuckle, the citrus essence of him begging her to understand. "Other than the board meeting last week, I haven't even seen her in over a year. The last time she and I saw each other was before I found you at the Gathering. She...hasn't taken the separation well." His regret calmed her, but she sensed he still cared for her.

"Do you love her?" She was immediately sorry she asked. Jealousy was an evil thing, and she knew the question alone gave away her growing feelings for him.

Recognition lit his smoldering eyes, and she waited to hear the rumble from his chest, but the remorse for his previous actions was stronger. "I may have thought I did, but no. Any feelings I have left come from realizing my behavior toward her was unfair." He signaled the waiter then turned back to her. His thumb stroked the back of her hand, and he lowered his voice. "You have no competition, Jessi."

Peter huffed indignantly. "I thought I had a chance. We do shower together often enough."

The waiter paused, and in exasperation, Hannah took control. "We'll start with a bottle of your best wine and the appetizer sampler." She shot a glare at Peter. "Can you at least let them get through their first date before you let her in on your gym activities?"

Alexander chuckled, and the dam of tension around the table broke for everyone but Jessi. The reality of Alexander's life crashed in on her. He was beyond wealthy, and the chances of him being head-line news was probably high. *If my picture ever makes the news...*She glanced toward the front door where the reporters could be heard milling around each time it opened. She wouldn't be able to keep her secret much longer.

"Are you all right?" Alexander followed her gaze. "The authorities will be here shortly, and the reporters will be gone by the time we leave. They're looking for a story about my business practices, not my relationships."

She nodded and did her best to push the thoughts away, but at least one camera had gotten a clear shot of them together. She only hoped it didn't make the cut.

J essi was more relaxed when they exited the restaurant and saw that the reporters were indeed gone, but she remained subdued even after they arrived at the pier. Alexander parked in his spot and led them all to his berth and onto the yacht. His captain was waiting for them as the stepped onto the aft deck.

"Welcome aboard, Mr. Koch. Though we will remain docked this evening, I'll be on board and available should you need anything. Carmina will see to your refreshment needs."

"Thank you, Captain." Alexander introduced everyone, then gestured toward the starboard stairway where a dark-haired woman escorted them onto an open deck. The sun was setting in a glorious display of color, and he watched Jessi glide across the open space where a small table of appetizers and fruit were artfully arranged.

"Give her time, Alexander. Your lifestyle is a little overwhelming." Peter wrapped his arm around Hannah and led her toward a long, padded bench facing the water. His friend patted his shoulder as they passed.

Alexander paused to watch Jessi. She surveyed the food and ran her hand along the damask tablecloth before turning away to lean against the railing. A light breeze off the bay smoothed the fabric of the plumb chiffon dress against her curves and lifted her raven hair just enough to expose the gentle slope of her neck where it met her shoulder.

The image of his lips pressed to the spot sent his blood racing. He wanted to run his fingers under the thin straps crossing her bare shoulders and smooth his palms down her graceful arms. The dress fluttered against her upper thighs, and his stomach tightened as the wind caught it and threatened to expose even more of her leg. She was absolutely breathtaking, and he found himself reaching into his pocket for the charm. The desire to have her under his hands and lips burned through him.

Before he approached her, he turned the charm in his fingers and let the cool steel remind him what she meant to him. She was the manifestation of his hope, and the one thing in his life he wanted to make sure he never took advantage of.

He hadn't been surprised to see the media tonight, but Rebekka's presence caught him off guard. If she made it a point to deliver the paperwork personally, then there was more to the suit than money. He shook off thoughts of Rebekka and lawyers. There was nothing he could do tonight. Thomas would call with the details. Gaining Jessi's trust was his top priority.

He'd heard the jealousy in her voice at the restaurant even without her echo, and there was real fear in her eyes when the cameras flashed. She was shaken by that more than she was jealous of Rebekka. He suspected she realized her association with him would put her picture in the news, and that terrified her.

It solidified the theory she was hiding from more than just him. But she wasn't going to talk about it until she was ready. Hopefully, the little media skirmish encouraged her in that direction.

Alexander crossed the deck and lifted a pair of long-stemmed glasses already half filled with his favorite after dinner wine. He leaned backwards against the railing next to her and offered one of the glasses. They shivered when her fingers brushed his as she took it from him.

"Penny for your thoughts?" he asked.

She glanced up, and he marveled at the way the glow of the sunset shone in her soft hazel eyes, the orange and yellow on the horizon deepening them to a warm earthy brown. There was sadness in their depths, and he reached for her hand. She looked back and forth between his eyes, and he carefully kept his expression open, willing her to understand he wasn't going to push, but neither was he going to give up on the conversation either. After a long moment, her gaze fell to the water and then to their intertwined fingers.

"I don't know what to think, Alexander." She took a sip of the wine, and he wanted her lipstick smeared on him instead of the crystal. The breeze shifted, and her head snapped up in frustration.

"I'm sorry, Jessi." He chuckled. "I am trying, but you have to know it's impossible for me to resist you." He released her hand and turned to lean his forearms on the rail. He rolled the stem of the glass between both sets of thumb and forefingers. "It's the way we males are made." He looked down at the waves lapping against the hull and drew a breath. "On top of the drive I have to bond with you simply because of what we are, you *are* a beautiful woman." Shifting his feet, he leaned further forward so he wasn't towering over her and watched the emotions play across her face.

The wind pushed her hair forward, and he reached over to sweep it back, letting his hand rest at the nape of her neck. Her skin was soft and cool beneath his touch.

"I asked you not to dismiss my pain until you knew what it was, but you already know, don't you?" She closed her eyes as his thumb slid across her skin.

"I can make some guesses, but I'd rather hear it from you." When her gaze reconnected with his, she looked so frightened he resisted the urge to tuck her against him. He tightened his hand on her just a little, silently asking her not to withdraw. "I'll never hurt you. I hope you believe that." The breeze caught his open jacket, brushing it against her arm. A rush of air left his lungs as she sidled up next to him and pulled it around her.

"I want to believe you." She shivered again, and this time he felt it all along his right side. "It's been a long time since I trusted anyone, and you're...intense."

He exhaled through his nose in gratitude. She was at least trying to trust him. Afraid to move but unwilling to give her the option to get away again, he slid his hand down her arm and pulled her in front of him. Grateful she didn't resist, he was careful to keep space between their bodies, as he wrapped his arms in front of her to grip his wine glass again. He wanted to shelter her from anything that might cause her pain, realizing with a jolt he had to put himself on that list. Until she truly trusted him, he would have to keep as much distance from her as he could force himself, and the few inches separating them at the moment was the best he could do.

He pressed a kiss to the top of her head and contentment flooded him. "Talk to me. Tell me everything. Help me understand."

SIXTEEN

Alexander rested his chin on top of Jessi's head, and she ached to press back against him. His charisma filled any space he occupied and even here, in the openness of the evening sky over the harbor, his intensity overwhelmed her senses. She paused for a moment and drew a deep breath of him. His every move was calculated and controlled, but tonight the bittersweet scent of him was flooded with a fierce protectiveness. The radiant warmth of his arms on either side and his huge frame behind her made her feel invulnerable. Instinctively, she knew that was his intent.

Occasionally taking a sip of his wine, Alexander was patient. Inside her chest, she felt her heart thaw, and words began to flow. Words she had never spoken to anyone. Not intending to tell him more than a general idea what her life had been like; she drew a deep breath and let his strength give her courage.

"My father is a controlling man," she began. "When I was at home, he made sure my mother and I were always perfect in front of others. When we weren't, there were...consequences." Alexander stiffened. "Most of the time I was forced to do extra chores." Hours spent cleaning stalls and grueling training sessions on horse after horse made her muscles twitch in remembrance. "Mother wasn't so lucky."

Her head dropped, and she stared at the way the fading sunset stained the waters up to the glossy white surface of the ship's hull. The rolling waves split the shimmering orange and gold into scattered pieces of reflected color as the water lapped against the yacht's sides. It reminded her of the trail of broken things her father left in his wake, and her voice choked. "Afterward...I would come inside and help her clean up. I never saw him hit her, but there was always some treasure of hers broken or a room ransacked."

Alexander shifted further backwards and braced his wrists against the rail. He pressed his forehead to the back of her neck. She resisted the urge to lean into him for comfort as a bite of rage drifted on the air.

His tone was like steel. "Did he ever hit you, Jessi?"

"Twice." She flinched when his hand clenched, shattering the glass in his hand and sending it tumbling over the side. Her voice fell to a whisper. "The second time, I left."

He didn't move, and she felt the heat of his breath down her back. Blood dripped from where the broken stemware cut his finger. Her vision flashed to an image of her mother's bleeding hand as she picked up the broken shards of a flower pitcher smashed against the floor at her feet. Regret surged through her, and the admission of feelings she had suppressed for years left her lips in a rush.

"I left her, Alexander. I wasn't strong enough to stay, and I left her alone with him." Tears wet her lips. "I abandoned her."

He gripped her shoulder and turned her to face him. He set her glass aside and wrapped her inside the warmth of his coat as she wept into his chest. Guilt poured out, and as it did, Jessi came to the sudden realization that her mother wasn't the only one she abandoned. Her arms slipped carefully around him, the hard contours of his torso rolling under her hands as she clung to him. She understood then what Peter tried to tell her.

The physical strength Alexander had attained was all the result of his attempt to control his pain but inflicting himself with a different kind of pain. She was the only one who could relieve any of it. She couldn't help her mother, but Alexander was here. Fear washed over her at the thought of surrendering her hard-earned freedom, but she pushed it aside, knowing there was no getting around what she had to do.

His arms tightened, and he whispered her name over and over, promising to protect her, promising no one would ever hurt her again. The words only made her cry harder as she let the blame for his pain rest completely on herself. She blamed her father for so long, but he'd been right, she was the one who was too selfish and weak.

Shame and guilt streamed from her in sobs until her legs gave out and Alexander swung her effortlessly into his arms, cradling her gently in his lap. He sat and tucked her tightly against him. She buried her face into the space between his chin and shoulder, her hand gripping the lapel of his jacket like a lifeline in a storm.

When she was finally able to form words again, she sucked in a heaving breath and pushed back from him slightly. His eyes were gentle, and his hand smoothed the hair back from her face. In the keenness of his emerald eyes she saw no condemnation, no blame, only a soft acceptance and a burning need.

Her voice wobbled. "I'm so sorry, Alexander. So sorry."

"You have nothing to be sorry for, Jessi." His thumb swiped a tear from her cheek, and he shifted to pull a handkerchief from his pocket. She accepted it and ducked her head to wipe hastily at her tear-stained face. His voice was husky in her ear. "Thank you for trusting me with your pain."

SEVENTEEN

J essi's body curled against him as he lifted her with an arm around her tiny waist and another under her knees. The grief wracking her body and the shame resounding through her cries broke him. The depth of her emotion shook him to his core, and he was left wresting between his desire to avenge her and his deeper need to comfort her.

From the corner of his eye, he saw Peter and Hannah move closer and nodded to let them know he was aware and in control.

For the moment at least.

Her sobs eventually receded, and he loosened his hold when she relaxed into him. She kept repeating over and over again that she was sorry, and his frustration rose at the one who had made her feel like the abuse was somehow her fault.

"Please listen to me. None of this is your fault." His fingers were wet with the tears he kept brushing from her face, and each one lodged in his heart like a shard of glass. He pressed a kiss to her forehead before tilting her face up to his. Her eyes were luminous and pleading, and the blood that wasn't already boiling in anger erupted with need.

Control, Alexander. She needs you to be in control.

"You didn't abandon your mother. Even if you had stayed, he would have continued to hurt her, and he would have hurt you, too. You can't blame yourself for what he chose to do." He struggled to decipher the thoughts raging across her face, but what she said next chilled him.

"She's not the only one I abandoned." Her hand cupped his cheek, and he fought with a strength he didn't know he possessed to maintain the distance they needed. "I ran from you that night. I left you in your pain. I'm a coward."

"Now is not the time to have this conversation." His mind screamed at him, but his hand curled around her neck and his lips touched her hair again. He needed to move her to the chair beside him, but he couldn't make his arms let go.

Her moist breath warmed the skin of his throat, fanning the flames of his desire, pushing him to his limit. He clenched his teeth and lifted her away.

"Jessi, listen to me." With great effort of will, he set her down in the chair and dropped to his haunches in front of her. Clasping her hands in his, he sat back on his heels. "You need time to deal with this. Have you talked to anyone about it before?"

She shook her head. "No."

"Thank you for telling me." He kissed the back of both her hands and hoped the wind was blowing his scent away from her. Her tear-soaked face and swollen lips forced him to drop his gaze, but the view of her delicate form shaking in front of him didn't help either.

He closed his eyes, startled at her touch on his face. When he opened them, he very nearly lost what little control he had. She was so close, and he could see what she wanted plainly written in the plea of her soft eyes.

"You are in so much pain, Alexander." Her tongue swept across her lower lip as her finger trailed a matching path across his, making them both shudder. "I can't help my mom, but you..." She drew a sharp breath, preparing for the pain of her fangs.

He stood and backed away a step. "You are not ready, Jessi, and I won't take advantage of you." Shock whitened her face and in a desperate attempt to regain control, he let some of his anger go. "It's my responsibility to protect you. Even from myself." The anguish in her eyes softened him. "If I take advantage of you tonight, you'll resent everything I am. I can't, I won't, risk losing you again." She started to protest, but he stopped her. "Look around at who I am." He spread his arms and let his gaze travel across the luxurious yacht before resettling on her stunned face. "This is who I am, and I am not going to change. Can you say right now that this is a life you want?"

The truth of his words clenched her lips closed. He wanted nothing more than to have her under his roof. To have her bonded to him forever, but he knew she wasn't ready. Despite her confession tonight, she didn't fully trust him, and he wasn't going to let a moment of weakness drive her to a decision too soon.

The evening air had cooled considerably, and she shivered. He shrugged out of his jacket and draped it around her shoulders.

"Thank you." She held the jacket closed and lifted a palm to his cheek. He was thankful his jacket covered her but even so, he made sure his eyes stayed fixed on hers. "You are a good male. Much better than I've given you credit for."

Tilting his head, he replied with a wry grin. "Don't give me too much credit. My self-control does have limits. Limits that are not very firm when it comes to you." He held her chin and ran a thumb across her lower lip. She blushed. "Will you let me take you home? Peter and I can bring your car to you later."

EIGHTEEN

JESSI

She stared up at the man in front of her in wonder. He could have claimed her. She was his. They both knew it—yet he held back. She had practically begged him to, but he refused. Another layer of her heart melted, but a small voice clawed at the back of her mind.

Maybe he doesn't want you. He already sent you away once.

Inside the jacket she was wearing, Alexander's phone rang. Time froze when he reached for the lapel and pulled it open. The back of his hand grazed her, locking their gazes together as almost visible electricity danced in the air between them.

"Matches," said Peter.

"Gunpowder," Hannah said at the same time.

Alexander grinned wickedly but pulled both his hands back and dropped his eyes to the phone. His smile vanished, making Jessi's chest tighten.

"It's Thomas." He glanced at her. "I need to take this."

"Of course." Jessi closed the jacket again.

"Thomas?" Alexander answered. His grip on the phone tightened, and the smell of clove bit at her nostrils. "Rebekka? Yes, I saw her tonight, why?" A muscle in his cheek jerked before he sighed. "Is she that upset?"

Jessi's blood went cold.

Alexander's tone softened. "Tell her I'll call her when I'm done here." He pushed a hand into his pocket and walked a few steps away.

Jessi's hands fisted in the fabric around her, not hearing anything else he said.

When he's done here? What did that mean? Could Rebekka be the reason he wasn't willing to claim her?

Jessi couldn't take any more. She met Peter's gaze. "Will you take me back to the coffee house? I'm ready to go home."

"Let Alexander drive you," he replied as Alexander ended the call.

"No." She shook as the events of the evening swirled around her; regretting having told Alexander so much. She was letting him too close.

If he really wanted me, he would have claimed me. Rebekka's possessive glare flashed in front of her. *What if Alexander wanted both of them? How could I have been foolish enough to forget who I'm dealing with?*

"Are you all right?" Alexander laid a hand on her arm, but she shook him off.

"I'm fine." She squared her shoulders. "You're right, Alexander. I'm not ready for this, and I think I need to call it a night."

"I understand. I'll drive you home," Alexander offered.

"No. You apparently have other business to attend to." She lifted her chin defiantly.

Alexander tilted his head. "I apologize for the call. I have obligations that sometimes require my attention at inconvenient times." He stepped closer, and she gripped the jacket tighter. "But trust me when I say you come first."

"I have yet to find a reason to believe you." Jessi backed away, shedding the jacket and handing it to him. "Take me to the coffee house," she said.

"Will you let me take you home? Peter and I can bring your car to you later." Alexander took the coat.

"Take me to the coffee house," she repeated firmly. "I can drive myself home."

"You can." Alexander shook his head and draped the jacket over his arm. He cupped her cheek in his palm. "But it's my honor to take care of you. Things might go smoother if you just got used to the idea."

His tone was genuine, but something inside her unleashed at his statement. Memories of her childhood rose unbidden, and Alexander's words sounded too close to the admonishments she received from her father.

"I'm only protecting you, Lyn. That's my job as your father. Things will go easier for you if you just do as I say." As her father's voice overlaid Alexander's, an irrational disapproval swelled.

"Please try to remember I was a responsible adult living on my own before you came along, Mufasa. I don't need you to protect me. I've done just fine on my own." She crossed her arms and stopped at the top of the stairs. She looked back. "Take me to my car."

She refused to acknowledge the pain her rejection caused Alexander. They had spent almost the entire evening without it, and now it raged back to life.

Alexander's eyes narrowed in concern and over his shoulder, Peter watched her thoughtfully. "It's apparently me who upset you. Would you prefer Peter drive you?"

"I would." She tried to ignore the shot of agony that pierced her stomach and lowered her eyes. "I'm sorry, Alexander. You're right. I'm not ready for this, and I need time to think."

"I'll stay here tonight. You and Hannah take the car and go home." She glanced up at him through her lashes. The set of his mouth hardened, and he tossed something to Peter. His gaze returned to her, and she immediately felt his disappointment. "Will I see you at work tomorrow?" When she nodded, he turned and stepped through a doorway leading below deck. Just before the door fell closed behind him he spoke quietly over his shoulder. "Good night, Jessi."

"Yeah," she whispered. "Good night."

NINETEEN

Peter stepped out and regarded Jessi across the roof of the car at the Broken Bean after twenty minutes of painful silence in the car. She crossed her arms and glanced into the shop where Brandon waited by the door.

"We all know you're hurting, but you can't take it out on him." Peter warned. "Giving him a hard time is one thing, leading him on is another. Whatever is going on with you, do him a favor and be honest."

She walked toward the door and rested her hand on the handle as Peter backed the sleek vehicle out of the space. She tried not to wince when his disappointed eyes met hers before he drove away. Hannah didn't look up as the car rolled into the night.

"You okay, Jess?" Brandon wrapped his arm around her shoulders as she entered the shop.

'I'm fine." She leaned against him for a moment. "I'm just not sure I'm ready for this."

"Ready for what?"

"This!" She waved a hand around the shop. "Alexander's whole life is like this. He's so over the top, and... I promised myself a *simple* life when I came here." She sighed tiredly and admitted she had always been fooling herself. There was nothing simple about being a Vampir, and being the mate of a powerful male like Alexander only made her station in life more complex than most.

Her eyes fell on the vase of stargazer lilies, and she smiled wistfully. Alexander had moved them to his table. As Brandon talked to Dawn and turned over the cash register to her, Jessi walked to the table and let her fingers stroke the delicate blooms. Brilliant pink and edged with white, they always reminded her of the way the setting sun made the red stone of Arizona's desert look pink as the sun rimmed the mountains.

Now, these colorful flowers were forever associated with Alexander. Closing her eyes, she let the memory of his capable arms around her soothe her fears. She had seen the desire, the desperate need in his eyes tonight, had felt it in the way he held her against him, but he had done nothing. Shame blotted color into her cheeks at the way she begged him to claim her. She dropped her hand from the bouquet and followed Brandon out the back door.

"He seems like exactly the kind of man a woman would kill for. It's about time you put yourself out there." Brandon waited until she unlocked her car. "Why not let yourself have some fun and try trusting someone for a change?"

Her head snapped toward him, but he was already in his car, completely unaware of the impact his statement had made. Peter was right, she'd treated Alexander unfairly. She had opened up to him, then took swipes at him when he tried to get to know her. But that didn't explain why he'd refused her.

The apartment was dark, and she didn't bother with the lights as she sank onto the sofa and pulled out her cell. Staring at the screen for a moment, she sent a quick text to Alexander.

> J - I'm home.

His reply was immediate.

> A - Thank you for letting me know. I will see
> you tomorrow.

Jessi sighed. She needed to talk to someone about the disaster she had made of the night, and someone needed to talk her through the confusing emotions Alexander caused. Did she risk calling Alyssa? She'd never called her friend from her personal phone, worried her father would somehow find her. Yet Alexander had anyway, even under her alias. An alias that was delicate at best. Changing her name by only a few letters seemed the easiest, but now she wished she'd chosen something less obvious.

"You're over thinking this," she said. "Just call her!"

Jessi drew a deep breath and dialed.

"Lyn? Are you all right?" Alyssa's voice was alarmed.

"I'm fine. I just needed to talk to you." Jessi leaned her head back on the couch.

"You never call me at home, and you're home early." Alyssa lowered her voice. "Are you sure you're all right? What happened?"

"Tonight was a disaster. I am such a mess!" She threw an arm across her face. "How do you know who you can trust, Al? How do you know for sure someone is trustworthy?"

"You trust them." Alyssa laughed at Jessi's groan. "I know. I suck at giving advice, but that is the truth. Want to tell me what happened?"

Jessi dropped her arm, and while staring at the wooden beams across the ceiling, recounted the evening to her friend. Alyssa listened patiently, offering encouraging words when necessary.

"I want to trust him," Jessi sighed. "But he represents everything I left behind. All the posturing and the pretense. How do I know he's any different than my family?"

"Well," Alyssa drug the word out. "You stop looking at what he has and find out who he is."

"I'm trying!" she whined.

Alyssa snorted. "It seems to me you can trust Alexander because he cares enough about you to accept his pain a little longer and put off the bonding until you're ready. If what I've heard is true, I don't know how he does it."

Jessi froze as the gravity of her assumptions about him hit her. Alexander cared enough that he refused to take what he desperately needed and let a moment of emotion ruin her trust.

"You are not ready for me, Jessi, and I won't take advantage of you." She thought he was talking about what had been between them tonight, but clearly, he understood her emotions regarding him were much more complicated than that.

Alyssa continued. "I don't know much about him, but he's willing to spend thousands of dollars on flowers just to get you to agree to go on a date with him, and then he doesn't even try to claim you?" She huffed. "I say trust him and see what happens."

Jessi swept a hand down her face and pictured Alexander's face just before the door fell closed between them. Confusion had marred his rugged features, and she ached to go to him and apologize. But a better idea occurred to her.

"What are you thinking? You're too quiet," Alyssa said. "That usually means you're about to go from the frying pan into the fire."

"Maybe." Jessi wished she could hug her. "Thank you for giving great advice." She leaned forward, thinking. "I'll call you tomorrow, okay?"

"All right, but be careful, Lyn." Alyssa said. "Don't do anything I wouldn't do!"

Jessi huffed. "You're bonded! That's no help."

Alyssa laughed. "It's all the help you need. Good night, hon, and let me know if you need anything, okay?" She blew a kiss into the phone. "I might be two states away, but I'm still here for you."

"I know." Jessi hung up and stood. Going into the tiny kitchenette, she pulled open her cabinets. After making a quick grocery list, she changed clothes and headed out to the store.

CHAPTER

TWENTY

ALEXANDER

Alexander parked in front of the coffee shop and watched the patrons come and go. He ran a hand through his hair and pushed open the car door. Nervousness was foreign to him, but the way things had been left between himself and Jessi last night, he wasn't sure he would be welcome inside.

Through the front window, he noted the shop was busy. Any other time he would have relished the opportunity to showboat a bit, but today he hoped he could get in and settled before she noticed.

Not likely. You're nervous enough your scent is probably carrying through the glass. He shook his head and reminded himself she agreed she would see him at work.

When the door swung open, he was glad to see Jessi's back was turned and several customers blocked her view of him in the mirror. He heard Dawn call out a greeting at the door chime, but no one looked up. He crossed over to the table he claimed as his temporary office and a slow grin spread across his face. A steaming mug of coffee, today's newspaper, and a fresh scone were waiting for him. Even the stargazer lilies were moved to the far side of the table to make room for his computer. His eyes fell closed when the sweep of a hand crossed his lower back.

"I'm sorry for the way I reacted last night," Jessi said.

He looked down to see her peering up at him. The amber of her hazel eyes was bright, and a touch of gold sparkled around the pupil. His chest tightened at the sincerity of her words.

"So am I." He nodded toward the table. "Peace offering?"

"Maybe." Turning back to her place behind the counter, she glanced over her shoulder. "You're not the only one who pays attention." A contented rumble came from his throat, surprising him, but Jessi laughed. "I knew it! You *do* purr, Mufasa."

Gritting his teeth at the endearment, he pulled out a chair and set about getting to work. Despite her use of the nickname to deliberately irritate him, he detected something different about her today. Sipping the coffee, he startled. He sniffed it and made a face.

Picking up the mug, Alexander walked to the end of the counter and waited to catch Jessi's attention. Her hair was swept up and away from her neck and face in a loose ponytail that draped down her back. The sight of the smooth skin of her throat tugged at his stomach. He saw her tense when her eyes met his in the mirror, and he knew his thoughts were clearly spelled out on his face. Ducking her head, she finished up with her customer, and when she crossed over to him, he set the mug on the counter.

"I think you gave me someone else's mug. This has flavoring in it," he said.

Jessi picked up the mug and took a swift sip. "Hmm. So, it does. I gave you mine by mistake. Sorry about that. Have a seat, and I'll bring you another one." He narrowed his eyes at her nonchalant attitude but did as she suggested. A few minutes later she returned to the table with his mug.

"Here you go." He glanced up at her. There was a glint of mischief in her eyes, and he caught her hand before she turned away.

"Have dinner with me tonight." He kissed the back of her hand, making color creep up her neck. "You choose the place."

She swallowed, and he let his eyes follow the patch of red up her neck until it vanished into the hairline behind her ear. He ached to press his lips to the tender spot and suppressed a shudder.

"Okay." Jessi pulled her hand back and placed it against her throat, nervousness pinching her voice. "My place?"

"I'm not sure that's the best idea." His eyebrows shot up and more thoughts of all the places he wanted to kiss raced through his mind.

"I'm sure." She inched backwards as the tips of her ears turned red. Her smile was sly. "But you probably won't want to wear a suit."

Intrigued, he cocked his head at her. "Okay. What should I wear?"

She was retreating toward the counter where a line was forming. When she met his questioning look, he perked up. The gold in her eyes flashed with a shy heat, and he sucked in a short breath. His heart kicked violently, and he knew the low growl that slipped past his control probably made a few eyes swing their way. Jessi's blush flamed scarlet, and she shook her head at him.

"Jeans and a long sleeve shirt." Roguish playfulness swept through him at her expression. She had something up her sleeve. "Boots might be a good idea also."

"I can do that." Alexander lifted the mug, but just before he placed it against his lips, he noticed the layer of foam and paused, chuckling. In the white and brown froth atop the coffee she had artfully drawn a lion. He took a cautious drink and was glad she left the sugary flavoring out this time. He snapped open the laptop and went to work, making good on his bet.

I believe we are up to five.

Hours later, he was preparing to head home to change when Jessi approached the table. "Meet me back here in an hour? My shift ends at seven."

He stood and moved a stray hair from her cheek, letting his fingers brush her skin. "You're sure you want me at your place?"

"Yes." She pressed a kiss to his fingers as they trailed across her lips, and it was all he could do not to yank her to him. "Trust has to start somewhere, right?"

He exhaled in surprise and watched her walk away. The change from last night was startling and made him even more concerned than her previous fear. She was already refocused on work, and he still had to get home, change, and make it back here before her shift ended. He hurried out of the lot, spinning his tires on the pavement.

Despite his misgivings about her sudden change of heart, adrenaline coursed through him at the thought of spending the evening with her.

TWENTY-ONE

Jessi glanced in the rear-view mirror for the hundredth time, watching Alexander's pricey sedan follow her back to her apartment. His sunglasses glinted as his head shook slightly, and the upward tip of his lip indicated he knew she was checking him out.

She was doubly embarrassed when one eyebrow rose above the edge of the aviators, and he pointed with a lazy hand draped over the wheel when she missed a light change. She snapped her eyes back on the road and accelerated forward with barely a glance to check the intersection for other traffic. Keeping her eyes firmly on the road in front of her, she made the last turn onto the lane leading back to the stables, and her tumbling stomach gave a lurch.

The owner's truck was parked at the side of the stable, the rest of the parking lot scattered with cars. She guided her truck in next to a little grey Honda and stepped out into the fading sunlight. Turning around, she watched Alexander exit his car.

If he was devastatingly handsome in his perfectly tailored suits, he was dangerously sexy in street clothes. Leaving her sunglasses on, she trailed her eyes up his body, admiring the way he could make any outfit look expensive, though she admitted his probably was. Surprisingly modern and loose fitting, the dark wash jeans skimmed his long legs, and black lace up ropers peeked from under the cuffs. Her eyes moved upwards, and she held her breath as they took in the torso that flared out in a wide v from his relatively narrow hips. The snug fitting, long sleeve henley gave just enough definition to his chest, shoulders, and arms to make her eyes widen.

Wearing a knowing smile as he paced toward her, she realized he had deliberately slowed his steps so she could look him over. The breeze flipped his ponytail over his shoulder just as he reached her and looked down.

Holding his hands out to the side, he asked, "Am I dressed appropriately?"

The rough texture of his voice nearly sent her to her knees, but she covered it by turning and laying a hand on the stair rail.

"Y-yes." She cursed internally and tightened her hand on the rail when his rumble of laughter only made things worse. "I need to change, then we'll head over to the barn."

"Should I wait here?" He removed his glasses and glanced toward her door before his keen eyes regarded her soberly.

She was already halfway up the stairs. "No. Come on up. It won't take me long." His steps sounded surprisingly light despite his size. He was so cat-like, it made her shiver knowing he was tracking up behind her. Glancing over her shoulder, she pursed her lips in surprise when she saw his eyes were firmly fixed on the step in front of him.

At the top landing she pushed the door open. "I have sandwiches, fruit, and a bottle of wine in the fridge. There's a basket on the counter if you wouldn't mind getting them out." She turned when he didn't respond. His large frame consumed the doorway, and she crossed to her bed and pulled open a dresser drawer, watching his reaction to her tiny home, but his eyes betrayed nothing as he stepped inside.

She withdrew a pair of jeans and a sweater. "I'll be right out. Make yourself at home."

She stepped into the bathroom and glanced back to see him turning in a circle to take in the small space. As the door closed behind her, she thought she saw a slight frown.

A flicker of resentment crept up her neck until she met her own gaze in the reflection of the mirror above the sink. She loved the cozy space and was proud of her independence. She cranked the water on and pulled the loose blouse over her head before tossing it in the general direction of the hamper. She splashed the cool water on her face and dried it with a towel. The flush that had been on her cheeks since the parking lot cooled, and she hurriedly finished changing clothes. Lastly, she pulled her wild hair back into a high ponytail.

As she reached to open the door, she caught sight of herself in the long mirror on the back of it and frowned. The outfit she had chosen hugged all the curves she normally worked so hard to hide. Cursing herself but knowing what was done was done, she stepped out.

He was seated on the sofa with his back to her, the basket on the coffee table in front of him. He looked completely relaxed with one ankle resting on his knee and a heavily muscled arm stretching along the back of the gingham couch. His broad shoulders bunched under the shirt, and the tautness of the fabric hugged the dips and rises of his hard-earned physique.

Unable to resist the desire to feel the thick veins of his forearms under the pads of her fingers, she ran them over the exposed skin just above his wrist. His only response was a tightening of his fist and a slight tick of his jaw. When she braced her hands on the back of the couch, he tipped his head back toward her. As they held their breath, Jessi fought the desire to lean forward and press her mouth to his.

TWENTY-TWO

ALEXANDER

From the moment Jessi stepped into the bathroom, the pressure built in Alexander's chest. Knowing she was undressing on the other side of a thin wooden door lit his skin on fire. Barricading those thoughts away as best he could, he turned to the large window that overlooked the pastures below. Next to it was a short counter, stove, sink, and refrigerator. A woven basket sat on the counter with a blanket folded underneath it. Thankful for something to do, he opened the refrigerator and loaded the sandwiches, wine, and container of sliced fruit into the waiting basket.

Water ran in the bathroom, and once more the images of her undressing played out in his mind. The irony of it all amused him, and he glanced around one more time at the sparse living area she called home, looking for something to distract him. The apartment was neat, though his heart ached to see that nearly everything inside was worn and second hand. Not that he thought any less of the things she had, but he desired so much more for her. He lowered himself onto the faded sofa and ran a hand down his beard.

He crossed his leg, settled back, and let his thoughts wander around the room. There were no pictures on the walls or on the table beside her bed. He followed the line of a heavy drape that fell from floor to ceiling near the head of the mattress that would apparently circle the sleeping area for privacy. The simplicity of her life struck him as surprisingly appealing. The room was quiet except for the faint sounds of Jessi's feet as she dressed and the whisper of the wind as it swept past the eves of the barn outside the window.

Allowing the peace of the moment to sink in, he was almost startled when her fingers brushed up his arm sending chills through him. He focused on the wall opposite them, but when he felt her weight press against the cushion behind him, he leaned back to look up into her fluid gaze.

Her midnight hair was tightly contained atop her head, and a closely fitted shirt revealed curves he hadn't expected. When her eyes dipped to his mouth, he rolled to his feet and paused to take in the rest of her. The thin sweater and snug jeans that molded to her body made his stomach flare, and he lowered his lids at her in warning.

"Let's go," he said.

He picked up the basket and held the door open, watching her lope down the stairs ahead of him. Without her oversized clothing he realized she was even tinier than he thought. She looked so incredibly fragile. He would nearly be able to wrap his hands entirely around her waist. That thought led to more places he wanted his hands, and he roughly pulled the door shut, trying to refocus his thoughts.

"Should we lock it?"

She turned to look up, shielding her eyes with her hand. "No need. There's always someone here." She tipped her head toward the stone walkway beside her. "Come on. There are others waiting to meet you."

He lagged slightly behind to absorb this new vision of her. Though she was only five foot four, her legs were long and lean in the dark denim that wrapped her from hip to ankle. Her waist was wasp thin above the belt that rode low to give her an almost perfect hour-glass shape. She turned sideways, and her cheeks blushed. She slowed, and he adjusted his stride to walk beside her.

"How long have you lived here?" He gestured toward the expanse of barns and pastures.

She hesitated before replying. "It's been four and a half years." They reached the barn, and she paused as he stepped ahead of her to open the door. "The owner lets me work off the horses' board and feed by cleaning stalls and making sure the place is secure at night." She led the way past a large arena, through a seating area of benches and lawn chairs, and down a long aisle, gesturing as they walked.

"This is the tack room and feed bins." The doors stood slightly ajar and from the feed room came a smell similar to beer or aging wine. She ran her hand down the wall to their left. "On the other side of this wall are the stalls reserved for the competition horses. My stalls are down here to the right."

The hallway widened then turned sharply to the right. Alexander counted five stalls on either side of the aisle that ended in a corrugated steel wall. Jessi paused beside one of the boxes and sighed. A pale horse slid his nose through the bars.

"Hey, Pace. You're getting a new home soon." Alexander smiled as she cooed to the animal and scratched his nose before turning to look at him. "These are Dennis's stalls." She pointed toward the last two in the row. "Those two are mine. You'll meet Ulysse in a minute but come say hello to Trouble first."

"Trouble?" He peered into the stalls as they approached the one she pointed to.

"Otherwise known as Armani." Pushing open the door, she paused at the edge of the concrete. "Armani, meet Alexander."

He set the basket down, and just as he stepped forward to see the animal she was referring to, a golden head pushed into her chest. Jessi braced herself in front of the horse who didn't appear inclined to stop. Instinctively, Alexander moved forward, and the animal immediately retreated back into the stall. Jessi looked from him to the horse and back.

"What's wrong?" Alexander stood beside her. The horse's jaw worked as it rested his nose in the palm of her hand. He placed a hand on her shoulder and watched the horse lower his head and push gently against her hip.

She smiled crookedly. "I'm not sure, but Armani might like you." She pulled a small cube of sugar out of her pocket and pushed the horse away when his upper lip swung out for it. Obediently the animal pulled back she handed Alexander the cube.

"Here. Offer it to him, and let's see what he does." She took his hand and pulled his fingers flat, leaving the sugar in the middle of his palm.

Intrigued, Alexander extended his hand toward Armani and the horse bumped his fingers with the flat of his nose before gently lifting his muzzle and sweeping the cube from his hand with a whisper of touch. Letting go of Jessi's shoulder, Alexander reached out and slid the palm of his hand under the lock of black hair that fell across Armani's forehead. He rubbed gently for a second then withdrew when he heard Jessi huff.

"What did I do?" He stepped back. "Did I do something wrong?"

Her eyes were soft when she looked up at him. "No. You didn't do anything wrong."

Tears pricked Jessi's eyes as she watched Armani stand motionless while Alexander's large hand disappeared under the skittish horse's black forelock. The horse sighed.

Seeing Armani submit completely to someone he had never met, even allowing them to touch his face, was astounding. Alexander's expression was questioning, and she shook her head.

"Armani doesn't take to people well. He's a rescue. Probably abused at some point, and it's taken me months to pet him like you just did." She leaned against the open door and watched Alexander approach the horse. The stall floor was a few inches lower than the concrete walkway, and Alexander stepped down. Armani lowered his head and stood calmly as Alexander ran a hand down his neck. It was like seeing a different horse.

"Is everything okay, Jess?" Dennis's voice broke her spell.

"It's fine." She gestured into the stall. "It appears Armani has made a friend."

Dennis's long legs hurried to the open door, and his eyes widened. "Imagine that."

Alexander looked up, and the two men appraised one another.

She hid a smile behind her hand as Dennis stepped closer to her. He extended his hand toward Alexander.

"I'm Dennis. You must be Alexander."

"I am. Good to meet you." Alexander dusted his palm against his jeans and stepped out of the stall. "Jessi tells me several of these horses are yours?"

Dennis glanced at her as she pushed the stall door closed. "Yes. Six of them are mine." He gestured to Armani. "Have you worked with horses before? I've never seen him react that way to someone."

Tucking a hand into his pocket, Alexander shook his head. "No. They've never been an interest of mine." He looked at Jessi. "Until now."

"Well, it certainly seems you have a way with them." Jessi turned to lead the way back to the arena. "Come on, let's meet the other man in my life." As they walked, she ducked her head in amusement as Alexander fell in step with her on one side, Dennis on the other. "I've been riding Ulysse since he was first broken to saddle. He's a giant teddy bear."

The three of them rounded the corner, and she pushed open the gate into the arena. Dennis's horse was tethered and tacked up at the far end. Alexander trailed her across the sandy arena to where Ulysse stood waiting. His silvery tail flicked, and he lifted his head to wicker at her as they approached.

They stopped beside the tall grey, and she patted the horse's glossy flank. "I thought you might like to see what I do for fun." She lifted the flap of the saddle and rose on her toes to get the leverage she needed to tighten the girth. Once both stirrups were down, she unclipped the lead from his head and loosened the reins from under the saddle.

"Give me a leg up?" Alexander looked puzzled for a moment until she bent her knee and gripped the front and back of the saddle.

"You want me to lift you?" His brow rose and his lips tipped up in amusement.

She nodded then felt her heart flutter as he placed a palm under her shin. Ulysse took a step sideways at her nervousness, and she cursed herself. Bending her other knee and springing lightly into the air, she swung it over the horse's back as Alexander effortlessly gave her the extra boost she needed. Tucking her feet into the stirrups, she glanced down at the hand he kept on her thigh.

"Thank you." Her voice was breathless, and the twinkle in his eyes let her know he was pleased.

Alexander stepped back. "What should I do?"

She gathered the reins as Dennis warmed up his horse. "You can see the most if you stand in the center of the arena." She relaxed and followed the wide swing of Ulysse's gait with her hips as he moved to the outer edge of the sandy ring. "We'll just go through a couple of exercises to give you an idea, then we'll eat."

Dennis was already making half passes down the far wall, so she urged Ulysse into a light trot. He tugged uncharacteristically at the reins, and she settled back, hoping he would give her his head. He was unusually distracted, and she ended up so focused on working him through his sour attitude that she completely forgot Alexander was even watching.

After a while, Ulysse's back and neck rounded underneath her, and she gave him his head. As he stretched down and forward, Dennis's mount startled at something just outside the door and Ulysse jumped violently to the side. Jessi managed to stay seated for his first jump, but the second jolted her forward, and when the horse bolted to the side, she tumbled off. Instinctively, she ducked her shoulder and took the impact along her upper back and right side, hitting the ground with a grunt.

Instantly, Alexander was beside her, his gentle hands cupping her head as she rolled toward him. Frustration reddened her cheeks. She wasn't hurt, but the embarrassment of losing her seat in front of Alexander was mortifying. His concerned eyes flicked over her and his scent spiked with worry.

"Are you all right?" He held her still when she tried to stand. "You should give it a minute."

"I'm fine!" She huffed and pushed his hands away.

The hurt on his face and a twinge of pain registered, but she looked away searching for Ulysse. Jessi dusted herself off with Alexander's strong hands still on her shoulders.

"Seriously, I'm all right." Her cheeks burned. "I need to catch the stinker."

Ulysse was trotting back and forth in front of the gate leading to the outdoor arena, his ears pricked to what was going on outside. The stirrups swung freely against his sweaty sides and the reins were dangling dangerously near his left foreleg.

Dennis maneuvered his mount between where she'd landed and the gated door where Ulysse paced, making sure the large animal didn't bolt back toward her.

"Are you all right?" His gaze swung from her to her horse.

"Fine." She waved a hand at him. Alexander was still right behind her as she strode purposefully toward her wayward ride. "Whoa. Be still." Obediently, the horse paused, and she caught hold of the reins. Shaking her head, she turned to lead him back to his stall.

"Well, that was fun," she mumbled.

TWENTY-FOUR

ALEXANDER

Alexander's breath froze the moment Jessi swung her leg over the back of the horse. Her lithe body moved in perfect tandem with the animal underneath her, and he forced himself not to allow images of her doing the same atop him take over his thoughts.

She was sure and confident as she maneuvered the animal through a series of dancelike exercises. For a few minutes he watched in fascination as she and the horse seemed to become one. With no visible movement from her, the horse pivoted, paused in mid-stride, and trotted in place with smooth controlled steps before gliding forward to some invisible cue from her.

Seconds later, Alexander's heart stopped when the horse reacted violently to a flash of light outside. When she tumbled to the ground nearly beneath the hooves of the animal, he felt it like a kick to the chest that restarted his heart in a pounding fear. Without a thought he raced to where she landed, relaxing when her startled eyes clearly glittered with embarrassment and not pain. He knew she was likely uninjured when her body coiled instinctively into a roll, but seeing her impact the ground with such force still shook him.

Impressed by her recovery, he followed a little behind as she led the enormous beast back to his stall. His skin prickled with residual concern, driving him to wrap her in his arms and make it go away. Her ponytail hung skewed sideways on her head, loose loops tumbling across her right shoulder where the dirt of the arena was ground into her pale grey sweater. Sand caked down her right side and the pockets of her jeans were dusty. He longed to reach out and brush the dirt away but jerked his eyes upward to focus on the back of her neck.

She carried herself stiffly and while frustration laced her body language, her hands were gentle on the horse as she slipped his bridle off and clipped long ties to either side of his halter. Once he was secure, she paused and wiped her shaking hands on her jeans before turning toward him with apologetic eyes.

"I'm sorry you had to see that."

"You do this for *fun*?" He plucked a stray piece of straw from her hair, letting his hand linger against the side of her head. The contact soothed the tingling of his skin.

"Yeah." A laugh escaped her as she also relaxed. "Believe it or not."

"Aren't you supposed to get back on after a fall?" He stepped closer to rest his hands on her shoulders, and she tipped her head up. His thumbs brushed the skin above the collar of her shirt, and he did his best not to react to the quiver that went through her.

"Yes." She turned to look at Ulysse. "He's never like that. I was just too embarrassed to think about it." She stepped back and reached for the still dangling stirrup. "Let me get him settled then we'll have dinner." From the other side he heard her mumble, "Hopefully I won't choke on a strawberry."

He covered his mouth to hold in the huff of amusement and tipped his head toward the ceiling; thankful she was all right. She was quiet as she striped the saddle from the horse's back, wiped him down, and settled him back in his stall with a large sheaf of hay.

Alexander leaned against the wall and watched her work. His

respect grew as she hefted a five-gallon bucket from a rack, refilled it with fresh water, and replaced it with little effort. Admiration rose in him, and so did his desire.

She paused with her back to him after latching the stall. She tugged the hair tie from her head and swiftly put it back. When she turned, her eyes were wary but clear.

"Are you hungry?"

"I can eat." He pushed away from the wall and reached for her hand. "Where are you taking me?"

"A little place just around the corner." She slid her hand into his, and he wondered again at the change in her. "It is likely to be much less entertaining than the earlier demonstration."

He tugged her in front of him and did what he was aching to do. As his hands swept across her shoulders and down her side, Dennis called out from behind them. "The small arena is cleared out for you." When they turned, his disapproving eyes were on Alexander. "Yell if you need anything, Pixie."

She waved. "Thanks, Bean."

"Pixie?" Alexander growled. The other man seemed surprisingly unconcerned about Jessi's fall and his familiar tone made the hair at the back of his neck bristle.

"Yes, Pixie. We've known each other for four years." Jessi ticked her head back toward the way they had come in. "Come on. Grab the basket and let's eat. The sunsets are gorgeous from here."

Alexander followed her through a small door and into an outdoor ring behind the barn and swept his gaze along the horizon. Looking down a slight depression as the last of the sunlight spread across the low hills in warm shades of orange and red. Jessi spread a large blanket near the fence. He set the basket down, and she laid out the food.

"This is my favorite place to eat. I come out here every chance I get." She lowered herself onto the blanket and waited for him to join her. She was still covered in dirt, but he had never seen her look more beautiful. She pulled a bottle of wine from a bucket, turning the label toward him. "Not exactly what you would serve, but it'll do, right?"

"It's perfect." He took the bottle, expertly removed the cork, and poured the dark liquid into the glasses she held.

They satisfied their hunger as she talked about what happened to cause her fall. He leaned on his side, propped on an elbow. As he listened to her talk, he relaxed, unable to remember ever having been on a picnic before, and as he laughed at her stories, he vowed to make sure this wasn't their last. Her whole demeanor was different. And in this atmosphere, he was different. He stilled when her voice faded. She sat beside him, knees drawn to her chest and her arms wrapped around them. The faint smile on her lips pricked his heart. It was obvious she was comfortable here.

He reached out to caress her cheek, grateful when she leaned into his touch and sighed. He pulled her toward him until she was propped against his upraised leg.

Her silken hair spilled across his arm as she rested her head back, and the sensation sent his thoughts to the wind. Resisting the urge to trail his fingers under her chin and satisfy the hunger in his veins by tasting the wine still glistening on her lips, he slid his palm down her shoulder and averted his eyes.

The sun disappeared below the horizon, and one by one, millions of stars glowed above their heads. Minutes stretched, and he felt her body soften as the wine took effect.

Alexander's hand drifted up and down her arm, and she pressed closer to him. He shifted so he could place his shoulder blades against a fence rail before drawing her against his side. He wrapped his arms around her, and her cheek fell comfortably against his chest. Puling the tie out of her hair, he ran his hands through the black strands, soft as silk even after her tumble. His skin tingled as it slid between his fingers over and over. She inched closer, and he cupped her head to lower his lips to her hair. His other hand curled around her back, the tips of his fingers toying with the edge of her shirt.

Stillness settled, and her breathing slowed and deepened until she drifted fully to sleep, and her arm landed across his hips. Alexander let his cheek rest atop her head. Closing his eyes with a contented sigh, he imagined the two of them curled together like this night after night. As a chorus of howls rose and echoed around them, a chill crept up his neck, and he tightened his hold on the woman in his arms. In that moment nothing else mattered. Nothing but Jessi and her safety.

"I believe I am in love with you, Jessi Vogel," he whispered, and wished she were awake to hear him. As though she heard, she snuggled closer. "One day soon, when you are ready to accept it, I'll tell you again." When she mumbled, his pulse raced and fear crept through him. *What if that day never comes?*

Refusing to let those thoughts ruin the moment, he closed his eyes and pretended for just a few minutes that today had been that day.

TWENTY-FIVE

JESSI

J essi rolled over and sat up with a start, wincing as pain lanced her shoulder. The familiar grey fabric around her bed blocked the rest of the room.

"Oh, my gosh!" She fell back on her pillow, taking quick inventory of herself. Her right arm and hip twinged when she moved, and her temples throbbed faintly, but everything else felt fine.

Glancing at the clock, the events of the night before washed over her, and she groaned. Bolting up again, she tossed the sheet aside. Horror and shame crept up her cheeks as she realized she was wearing a thin nightgown over the bra and underwear she wore yesterday. Neatly folded at the foot of her bed were her sweater and jeans.

"Oh, my gosh." She repeated louder and was mortified when a deep chuckle from the other side of the curtain confirmed her fears. She leapt out of bed, stumbling against the wall with a thump.

"Good morning, Jessi." Alexander's voice was low, sleepy, and achingly sexy.

"Wh-what happened last night?" She snatched a fresh change of clothes from her dresser, pulled the sheet and coverlet back in place, then peeked around the curtain. Alexander's huge frame stretched the length of her couch, his legs propped up and hanging off the end of the coffee table.

"Before or after you fell asleep?" he rasped.

She stepped toward the bathroom but clung to the curtain as an anchor when he dropped one bare foot to the floor. Her gaze ran the length of him and instantly snagged on the bulging muscles of his arm where he had a hand tucked behind his head. When she jerked her gaze to his, his green eyes searched her face.

"I don't think you have a concussion, but the fall combined with the wine..." His voice trailed off when his eyes slid from hers down her body. His rich scent filled the room, making her acutely aware of how little she was wearing. He moved his focus to the ceiling, visibly shaken. "I didn't think it would be wise to leave you here alone."

She should be angry, but the desire he held at bay made it impossible not to respect his control. Despite passing out and remembering very little, she knew nothing happened. He met her gaze again. The concern she read in his eyes made Jessi pull the curtain closer as warmth spread from her belly to engulf her chest, shattering the armor around her heart. How could she continue not to trust him?

. "Who changed my clothes?" Her voice shook, but she was able to suppress the echo of her own raging need.

Alexander smoothly rolled to his feet. "Dennis's wife. He saw me carrying you up here and offered to call her. I think he wanted her to stay instead of me." He yawned and raked the hair out of his face.

When his stretch revealed a sliver of skin above the waistband of his jeans, she sucked in a breath.

"Wh-why didn't you let her?" This time her echo wouldn't be suppressed, and he chuckled in response.

"I probably should have. But I couldn't make myself leave you." Crossing the room, he stopped and looked down at her. "I woke you a couple times. Do you remember?" His intense eyes grazed her face.

"Not really," she whispered.

His finger brushed her cheek, sending a cascade of sparks down her already tingling body. He backed up, and she wished he wouldn't.

"A hot shower will help." He turned away. "Do you have coffee?"

"Top shelf above the stove." Jessi said, trying to wrap her mind around the sight of Alexander Koch making coffee in her kitchen. Barefoot. Somehow, that made it even more surreal. "I'll be out in a minute."

She shoved the bathroom door shut and threw the lock. Flipping on the water, she lowered herself to the closed toilet seat, her head in her hands. The last thing she remembered was Alexander holding her while they watched the stars light the sky.

Steam filled the room, and she stood painfully to lift the cotton shift over her head and drop it to the floor with the rest of her clothes. Her shoulder ached. There would be a colorful bruise there and on her hip. Glancing into the nearly fogged up mirror, she saw the edges of the purplish-green bruise she would be sporting. *Perfect!*

The hot water soothed her aching muscles, and the steam helped clear her pounding head. Apparently, a nasty fall did not combine well with wine. Groaning, she rested her head against the cool tile of the shower and wondered what Alexander must have thought of her after she passed out on him. Literally *on* him. She lightly struck her head against the wall with a muffled thunk.

Please tell me I didn't drool.

Shutting the water off, she heard Alexander's voice outside the door and hurried to finish. Instead of drying her hair, she wound it and pinned it in a loose bun atop her head. Pulling on a clean pair of jeans and oversized sweater, she gave herself one last glance in the haze of the mirror and opened the door.

He stood staring out her picture window and caught her gaze in the reflection. "Feel better?"

"Yes." While she was showering, he had changed into a pair of black dress pants and tucked in a button-down shirt left open at the throat. The gap revealed a dusting of red chest hair on the exposed skin, and a pair of sunglasses hung from the breast pocket. "You changed."

"I keep a spare set of clothes in the car." He turned, took a sip of coffee, and shrugged. "Late nights at the office got me in the habit." Alexander's sharp eyes studied her face as he crossed the room.

"I suppose I owe you an apology for last night." She slid a palm over her forehead trying to regain her composure. His close proximity jangled her nerves in the best possible ways. "The wine was probably a bad idea after the fall."

"Apparently." His chest rumbled in amusement, and the sound sent goosebumps up her arms. His eyes twinkled, and she wished she could lose herself in them. The deepening of the green in his gaze told her he felt it too. "Are you sure you're all right?"

"I'm fine. You didn't have to stay. I've had worse falls than that," she said.

His scent sharpened, and the tang of orange wrapped around her as he stepped closer. The dull ache of his pain throbbed against her chest until he gently gripped her chin and tipped her face further toward his. Her skin tingled where he touched her, and his thumb grazed her chin.

His voice was rough. "I'm sure you have. But not since you became my responsibility."

"Your *what?*" Jessi twisted away, wanting to snatch the mug from his hand and dump the contents down his designer shirt.

That didn't last long.

He was unfazed. "You are my mate. Therefore, my responsibility." His scent sharpened painfully, and she hesitated. "No matter what you have been led to believe, I have no desire to control you. I only intend to take care of what I'm entrusted with." His tone softened, and he brushed his fingers down her cheek. "I couldn't *not* stay, Jessi. Why does that upset you so much? It's my honor to take care of you. That's the way we're made."

Her breath escaped in a rush, and she pinched her eyes closed against Alexander's intensity. Everything in her *wanted* to believe him. *Try, Jessi. You know he's right.*

"All right." She opened her eyes but refused to back down completely. "That may be truth, but can you please find a less Neanderthal way to express it?"

His expression widened, and he leaned back with a hearty laugh. "I suppose I deserved that." He took another sip of the coffee. "I guess I should be glad you didn't call *me* a Neanderthal. I don't have time to add another purchase to the list today."

Despite the teasing, she saw the calculated way he looked at her, still checking for signs she might truly have a concussion. A flash of smugness crossed his face as he pulled her toward him and pressed a quick kiss to her forehead. As his warm lips met her skin, she wondered when they had become so comfortable with gestures like that.

Probably right after you lost consciousness in his lap.

Alexander's broad shoulders filled her vision, and she resisted the urge to lean into him. Instead, she disengaged herself and took a step back to give herself space. The air suddenly felt close as his flirtatiousness filled the room with a heady amount orange and citrus now that he was assured she was all right.

"What purchases?" She turned and tried to distract herself with a cup of coffee.

He bent and picked something off the chair. "Have you forgotten our deal?"

She tried to focus on his words, but the plain brown of the box in his hands made her chest tighten and her hands ball into fists at her sides. The scene was so familiar it took all her resolve not to flea down the stairs.

"What's wrong?" Alexander set it on the counter and wrapped his hands around hers on the mug.

When she saw the box didn't have the white Louboutin script she dreaded so much, she took a deep breath.

He's not your father!

"I'm fine." She offered a weak smile.

"Good." He squeezed her hand, then picked up the box and took a seat. His wide frame consumed the chair as he settled in, completely at ease. "Come sit and open the box."

She raised a hand in question. "What are you doing? I have to go to work."

"No, you don't." He leaned forward slightly, resting his hands between his knees.

Her first thought was how odd it was to look down to him, then she resisted the desire to run her hands though his hair and clasped them behind her.

"Come open it." He nodded toward the box on the table.

She frowned. She was so used to his formal, almost archaic mannerisms that seeing him this casual threw her opinion of him even further off balance.

"What is it?" Cautiously, she sat in the center of the couch and reached for it.

"Have you truly forgotten our agreement?" The roughness of his low voice sent her heart racing, and her hands tightened on the box.

He sat back as the lid finally came loose. When she spotted what was tucked into the layers of crisp white tissue paper, she slapped a palm over her mouth as unintelligible sounds leaked past her fingers.

Jessi read the words *Backstage Pass, VIP Seating*, and *Koen Lockton* before her eyes flew up to meet his. He was stroking his beard as a smile played at the corners of his mouth. She stared at him in disbelief.

"Part one." He ticked his head toward the box. "The concert is tonight. I contacted Brandon to let him know you wouldn't be in today or tomorrow."

"Koen Lockton? His shows are sold out for months in advance." Stunned, Jessi set the box back on the table.

Alexander lifted a shoulder. "I called in a favor."

TWENTY-SIX

"We have a few errands to run this morning. Are you hungry?" He stood, took their mugs, rinsed them, and then set them in the sink.

"Where are we going?" she asked suspiciously.

"You don't trust me?"

"Alexander," she growled.

He laughed. "Breakfast, shopping, then a stop at my place before dinner and the concert."

Purse halfway over her arm, she stopped. "I'm not dressed for a night out. We'll have to come back here so I can get ready."

He opened the door and stood on the small landing outside. "You'll have plenty of time to get ready."

Obviously puzzled, but saying nothing, she followed him down the stairs. At the bottom, he paused long enough for her to reach his side then placed his hand at the center of her back. He slid his thumb across her spine as the contact drained the tension from both of them. At the car, he reluctantly removed his hand to open her door.

Before settling in the seat, she turned her face up. Her eyes were bright pools of moss and soft edges that stole the breath from him.

He parted his lips to tell her how beautiful she was, but before he could form the words, she rose to her toes and pressed a soft kiss to his jaw.

"Thank you for taking care of me last night," she whispered and rested a hand on his forearm. Like an idiot, he stood frozen as she lowered herself into the car. When he didn't move, she looked up at him teasingly. "Has no one ever thanked you before?"

A rumble grew in his chest. Alexander reached into the car and pulled her seatbelt forward. Leaning dangerously toward her, he fastened the seatbelt across her lap and met her wide eyes from inches away.

"Don't thank me yet, Miss Vogel." Her moist breath fanned his cheek as she exhaled a slow, trembling breath. Triumphant, he trailed his fingers across her stomach as he withdrew and watched her pupils dilate with desire. "The day is still young."

Forcing himself away from her, he gently closed the door and rounded the car. Through the windshield he saw her cheeks flush red as she stared at the hands she twisted in her lap. A wry grin touched his lips as he slid into his seat and started the car. Her nervousness was palpable, and while he enjoyed keeping her off center, he wondered if he had gone too far. His concern was validated when he reached to shift the car into reverse and her hand covered his. When he tried to pull the lever back, she resisted.

"Where are we going?" There was genuine fear in her eyes. "We're alone and..." Her gaze dropped. "You know that might not be smart."

The fierce protectiveness he'd felt earlier deepened at the yearning barely disguised by fear in her voice. He turned his hand over and laced his fingers through hers. Hers was so small and fragile against his large palm.

"Jessi, look at me." Her eyes slid up his arm until they met his, and he smiled. "This," he said, squeezing her hand gently, "is all that will happen today." Her eyes searched his, looking from one to the other, and he made sure she could see the truth of his words. "I want to spend the day with you. And I want to introduce you to my world a little at a time. Nothing more." He lifted her knuckle to his lips then tilted his head. "Trust me?"

Her eyes bounced between his one more time. "I'm trying. But what agreement do you keep talking about?"

He let go of her and shifted the car. Glancing at his mirrors, he tugged the sunglasses from his pocket and put them on. "How many times do you think you forgot my name?" When she inhaled quickly, a full grin parted his lips, and a laugh escaped. "Oh, yes, my dear. You are about to help me spend some money."

TWENTY-SEVEN

"What do you mean?" Jessi's chest tightened. His wrist draped over the steering wheel, and from under the side of his sunglasses, she watched his eyes follow traffic.

"I think it will be more fun if I let you see for yourself." Alexander's lips tugged upwards. "Let's get some breakfast."

The California landscape rolled by as they crossed town, and she searched for something to talk about.

"Why did you sell your company?" She asked absently.

"It was time for me to do something else. Architecture was never what I wanted." He slowed and turned into a small restaurant lot. "But interior design wasn't what my parents wanted." He shrugged. "Unfortunately, the sale has been delayed, so the company will remain under my control a bit longer than I anticipated."

She reached for the door, but his piercing look stopped her. Sheepishly pulling her hand back, she waited until he rounded the car and held it open for her. "That isn't necessary. I can open my own doors."

He removed his glasses. "I don't do it because I think you can't. I do it because I value and respect you. Is that so hard to accept?"

"No," she whispered, as another brick crumbled from the wall she tried so hard to keep between them. "I suppose it's not." His green eyes swirled in triumph, and she huffed. "But you can be so insufferable!"

Sliding the glasses back on his face, he tucked her arm into his. "I'm glad you're willing to endure it."

A neatly dressed young man opened the restaurant door. "Good morning, Mr. Koch. Your usual table?"

"Good morning, Reese. That would be fine, thank you." Alexander gestured for her to precede him.

The man led them to an outdoor patio covered by wisteria vines whose blooms were beginning to show their purple. Alexander held her chair, and she grimaced at her causal dress in such an elegant setting.

The waiter approached and poured their coffee. "Good morning, Mr. Koch. Your usual?"

"Please. And the same for Miss Vogel."

Jessi opened her mouth to protest, but the waiter was already gone. "How do you know what I want for breakfast?"

He turned his teasing gaze on her. "How do you know what I order?"

"Ugh. This could go on all day." She shook her head.

His smirk was annoying. "Probably will."

Letting it go, she took a sip of the coffee the waiter brought and returned to their earlier conversation. "What did you mean when you said the firm would remain yours?"

Stirring a bit of cream into his cup and setting the spoon aside, he shrugged. "Apparently someone is suing me for trying to sell. My attorney should have it cleared up soon." He nodded to the plate of fruit, yogurt, and fresh bread placed before them. "Eat. Our first appointment is at ten-thirty."

"Appointment?" She spooned some fruit onto her plate and frowned. "Where?"

"All part of the day." He gestured to himself. "I'm not used to casual clothes like this. Is this what you would prefer?"

Brow furrowing, she ran her gaze over him. "It's not hard to look at." She took a bite of cantaloupe, and his eyes followed the fork to and from her mouth.

His deep chuckle curled her toes. "Good to know. I was hoping you would help me update my wardrobe." His expression tightened. "Suits and ties, I know. Jeans, not so much."

"Why the change?"

He rested his elbows on the table. "You once called me a pompous jerk in a thousand-dollar suit." She flinched at the memory. "I'd like to change that appraisal."

They shared a dish of yogurt, and Jessi studied him. Tilting her head, she pressed. "Why the change?"

"Truthfully?" She held herself still as his eyes delved hers. "I've never felt more content than I did last night at your barn. I'd like to spend more time there if you'll allow me. But suits and ties don't belong. I am as unfamiliar with your world as you are with mine."

She dropped her eyes as her cheeks darkened. *Tell him the truth.* Fear of returning to face her father held her tongue, and she forked more of the delicate fruit into her mouth. Her closet once held designer labels, custom tailored clothing, and thousand-dollar suits that would make them a perfect match. She had no desire to go back, yet here he sat, believing what she wore now was all she knew.

He reached across the table and lifted her chin. His thumb slid across her lower lip, and it took all her will power not to kiss it. He tore through every one of her defenses effortlessly.

"What do you think?" His eyes followed the path of his thumb, and he inhaled raggedly. "Will you let me into your world?"

A puff of breath escaped her as his finger moved to her chin, and whispered words slipped from her before she could stop them. "I don't think I can keep you out."

For a moment he froze, his hand stalled under her chin. Clenching his fingers, he withdrew, the struggle to remain seated evidenced by the flare of his nostrils. The spike of his desire was obvious, but beneath the sharp clove rode a hint of something she'd never picked up from him before. Silence stretched between them, and she inhaled, letting this new scent permeate her.

He cleared his throat and laid his napkin aside. "Shall we go?"

She nodded, unsure what had just happened. He waved to the waiter standing patiently at the edge of the patio.

The young man lifted the half-empty plates. "Should we be expecting you tomorrow, sir?"

"No, sir." His eyes back on Jessi, Alexander shook his head. He stood and pulled her chair out. "I have other plans. I will call when I plan to be back."

She allowed him to guide her to the car. Once inside, she leaned into the seat and tried to make sense of her scrambled thoughts. His touch and his new scent unsettled her, and when he settled into the driver's seat, it filled the cabin with a rich warmth that was oddly exciting. She had no explanation for it. "Where are we going?"

"Some place I have never been." With a palm on the wheel, he directed the car out onto the busy road toward Interstate 15. "A friend told me I should start at the shopping center on Via Rancho."

"A mall?" Jessi stared at his profile. "You mean you don't want to have your jeans custom made?" She didn't try to keep the sneer out of her voice.

Unruffled, he shook his head. "No. I don't. For once in my life, I want to feel normal."

TWENTY-EIGHT

Alexander let her out at the entrance to the shopping center and pulled away to park the car. The mall was upscale and beautifully landscaped. She watched people come and go around her when suddenly a woman's voice shrieked to her left.

She spun around in time to see Alexander catch a toddler up in his arms while narrowly avoiding a car. The car's brakes skidded, and the driver's eyes and mouth were wide in shock.

"Oh, my! Thank you! Brenna, oh, my Brenna!" The woman plucked the child from his arms and crushed her against her chest. With panicked eyes she focused on Alexander. "I'm so sorry! I only turned my back for a second. I didn't know she could even walk that far on her own!"

Alexander rested a huge hand on the back of the little girl's head. "I'm glad I could help." He waved to the driver of the car to let him know they were both all right, then turned and strode to Jessi.

Her heart melted instantly at the sight of him with a child in his arms. What would their children look like? Would they have his red hair? Her hazel eyes? His long strides carried him toward her, and when the wind shifted, she knew what the new scent was. His blood had changed. Alexander's steps slowed.

"Are you all right?" she asked, trying to recover from the visions of Alexander with a baby in his arms.

"Perfectly fine." One eyebrow rose above his glasses. "Are you?"

No. No, I'm not. I'm thinking about babies. Making babies. I want to make babies with you. Holy cow.

She schooled her expression and hoped her voice wouldn't betray her thoughts. "That was pretty heroic. Jumping in front of a car like that."

"The landscaping here is atrocious." If he noticed her struggle, he didn't mention it. Instead, he gestured in frustration toward where the woman was strapping the child into a stroller. "See those bushes over there?"

She followed his gaze. "What about them?"

"The cars can't see anything until they are already in traffic." He cupped her elbow and held the door open. "I'll call the maintenance department and have them removed."

She slipped her hand away and rested it on his forearm. "What makes you think they will remove it just because you call?"

His eyes swept left and right until he spotted the store he was looking for. "Because I own the place." She stumbled, and he chuckled as he righted her. He shrugged. "Thomas thought some real estate would be a good investment, and his wife loves to shop here."

He tucked her arm into his and led them into a dimly lit store. Immediately a young salesgirl appeared at his other side. "Good morning! What can I help you find today?"

Still stunned by his admission and reeling from her own desire, Jessi almost growled when the girl placed her hand on his back. Alexander pulled her closer and angled his body so the little flirt could see he *wasn't* alone.

"My fiancée can tell you what we need. A few pair of jeans and shirts should be enough, don't you think?" Clearly amused, his rumble of laughter prickled her nerves.

"Sure." Jessi pulled her shoulders back and smiled when her glare made the girl take a step back. "What size do you wear?"

Before he could answer, the girl leaned back in appraisal and hummed.

"A tall athletic guy like you, probably a thirty-four thirty-six?" The sweet voice made Jessi grind her teeth, and Alexander quietly laughed as the girl turned to pull the denim off a shelf behind them.

He leaned down and his scent was deliciously thick in her nose. "Are you sure you're all right?"

Realizing she had firmly placed herself between him and the other woman, Jessi cursed herself. What had he done to her? "I am. I just don't like touchy salespeople."

He held back another laugh, and a shiver raked her. He tucked a hand under her hair and his thumb caressed her neck. "Jealous?"

She glared up at him as the salesgirl handed him the stack of jeans and pointed toward the back of the store. "The changing rooms are behind that wall. I'll check on you in a minute but come find me if you need a different size." She ignored Jessi and grinned at Alexander. "My name is Kelly if you need anything."

Gently pushing her in the direction indicated, Alexander slid his hand to rest between her shoulder blades. Once around the corner he paused and looked down at her.

"Don't ever mistake my manners for flirting." His green eyes pierced hers as he pulled open one of the dressing room doors. "You know there's no going back now. I belong to *you*."

She reached for the wall to steady herself when the door fell shut between them. She stood listening to the soft rustling as he removed his clothes and abruptly turned to look for the shirts he'd mentioned. Thinking of him partially dressed brought back her desire to make babies, and she was nowhere near ready for that conversation.

She dug though several stacks of henley and collared shirts while glaring at the girl who appeared to be overly friendly with everyone who came into the store. It should have calmed her to know Kelly wasn't actually flirting, but just the thought of another woman anywhere near Alexander had her on edge. She fought back tears of frustration and draped a rich purple shirt over her arm. His soft footfalls approached, and she was thankful the dim lighting hid the heat in her face.

"I have the jeans, though I think the tailor will need to make a few adjustments. Did you find shirts you like?" He rested a hand on her shoulder, and she couldn't help it, a sigh escaped her. He turned her to face him, and his expression was concerned. "Jessi?"

She handed him the shirt and forced a smile. "I did. I think the purple will look good on you."

Narrowing his eyes, he took the shirt and ticked his head toward the exit. "Let me pay, and we'll go."

Behind the counter was a man, and Kelly was nowhere in sight. Jessi relaxed and cursed herself again. Alexander politely checked out and let her precede him out the door, insisting she wait while he got the car. She shoved her hands into her pockets and blew a strand of hair out of her face.

He seemed completely unaffected by the change between them. If anything, he was *more* confident and assured, nearly completely relaxed now. Jessi didn't know whether to feel relieved or worried. She would have expected him to toss her over his shoulder and carry her off the moment his blood changed. The thought tightened her stomach, and she rubbed a hand down her face.

His orange clove scent had deepened, and now that her brain had a chance to register it, the new layer was similar to bergamot tea. Rich and masculine. The quiet growl of his car pulled up in front of her.

He exited the car and offered his arm. Mixed with the unique flavors of his body's scent was the heavy scent of warm leather from the car's interior as she sat inside. Her mind swam in desire, and she looked up at him helplessly.

Satisfaction gleamed in his eyes, but it was tempered by compassion as he slid into the driver's seat and guided the car away from the curb. He took her hand. "Please don't look at me like that. I promise I'm not going to press you for anything tonight, or any other night."

"Thank you. I guess I should have been more prepared for this, but I'm not. Sometimes our instincts feel unfair." He tensed, and she glanced away. "It seems like we don't have much choice, do we?"

"There is always a choice. Some are simply more obvious than others."

They were quiet until he pulled into the driveway of an expansive house. "Welcome home."

She'd gone rigid beside him, and Alexander winced. He hadn't meant to say that, but the change in his blood put her mentally under his roof already. For her sake, he quietly amended with, "For the moment, my home."

She loosed the death grip she'd taken on the seat belt as he stepped out of the car, but before he could get to her, she was on the sidewalk staring at the BMW parked in front of the garage. He skirted around her and opened the side door, gesturing for her to enter the kitchen. The remodel hadn't started yet, but the walls and counters were bare in preparation.

"I take it you don't use the kitchen much?" She ran a hand over the worn tile countertop, making his skin tingle in jealousy.

"Not yet." He ticked his head down a short hallway and dropped his keys into a dish next to the door. "This way. I have a surprise for you." As she passed him, he leaned forward to speak in her ear. "Try to remember this is punishment."

She whipped her head to look up at him and their lips nearly connected. Jessi ducked her chin, causing her hair to fall between them. Alexander stepped back, but not before he felt the tremor of her spine under the tips of his fingers.

Her trembling increased as glimpses of what waited for her became visible through the wide doorway. Lace skirts, print dresses, shawls, and tops lined the walls of the sitting room. Sandals and a table full of jewelry sat pressed against the far wall, and in the center of the room three mannequins wearing formal to semi-formal dresses in lace and beads shimmered as sunlight poured through the wide-open drapes.

With each step Jessi's breathing increased and her shoulders tensed. "What is this?"

"Something I enjoy almost as much as interior design." He leaned against the door frame and watched her turn in a slow circle to take in the impromptu boutique. "Clothing a beautiful woman in beautiful clothes." When her eyes swung back to his, there was fire in her glare. *This* he could deal with. "I warned you that I enjoy spending money." He gripped his hands at his waist to prevent them from burying themselves in her hair and ravishing her mouth until she surrendered to him.

"And how many *beautiful women* have you clothed, Mr. Koch?" she snapped.

Jealousy. Interesting.

"Including you?"

She tossed her hair back and arched a brow.

"Three."

"Liar."

He scowled and stepped toward her. "I never said I was celibate, and I told you I am not proud of who I was. Far from it. But that does not mean I am still that man." He towered over her and allowed his hand to thread through her silken hair to soften his words. "I can't change the past, Jessi. All I can do is promise the future will be very, very different."

"This is too much. It's a silly waste of money." Though she was still angry, her shoulders lost their rigidity.

Alexander let the jet-black tresses fall from his fingertips. "It's mine to waste." He leaned into the hall. "Georgia?"

"Yes, Mr. Koch?" Neatly dressed and in her mid-forties, the woman stepped into the room and appraised Jessi. "Are you ready, Miss Vogel?"

He smiled at Jessi's confused look and rested a hand on Georgia's shoulder. "Georgia will help you make your selections while I attend to some business. Chose as many pieces as you like or keep them all. She will tailor anything that doesn't fit just right." Jessi's mouth was open, but no sound came out. He lifted her chin with his knuckle. "I'll be in my office upstairs if you need me." He turned and pulled the pocket doors closed as Jessi stared after him.

Over his muffled steps on the long carpet runner up the hardwood stairs, he heard Georgia's voice. "Would you like to start with the gowns? I believe you and Mr. Koch have an event tonight?"

Satisfied she was in good hands; Alexander turned his focus to business. His phone had been vibrating in his pocket for the last two hours, and as he checked the call list, he cringed to see Thomas's number.

Two and a half hours later, Alexander descended the stairs to retrieve an aspirin. Thomas had the situation well under control, but the company shareholders were not in the least bit understanding. Rightly so, yet their demands for details were bordering on absurd.

At the bottom of the stairs, he heard laughter floating through the house, and despite the tension lingering in his shoulders, the headache virtually disappeared. Jessi's clear voice penetrated the fog of his frustration, and he followed the sound back to the sitting room.

The doors were still closed, and Georgia's sweet laughter from the other side made him smile. "He is a handful isn't he?"

"He's just so impossibly full of himself, Georgia. Then he goes and does things like this." The longing in her voice forced him closer and he struggled to remain on his side of the doors. "He truly never brought anyone to his own houses?"

"Never." Georgia's smile was obvious in her words. "I've been Mr. Koch's tailor for more than ten years now, and the only woman he ever attached himself to was Miss Wellington."

Alexander stiffened, angered that the woman would so freely reveal his personal business. As his hand reached for the handle to push into the room, her next words stopped him.

"But he never showed any real interest in her, and he never brought her home. You've nothing to worry about. Alexan—Mr. Koch is as honest as they come."

His eyes fell closed, and he tightened his hand into a fist, listening for Jessi's response.

"He's honest all right. Honestly aggravating." Her tone had regained its teasing sound. "How did he know my size? And how was he able to pick out so many things that are exactly what I would want?"

Their footsteps approached the doorway, and Georgia snorted. "I would imagine he pays close attention. He's absolutely taken with you." The door slid open before he had time to withdraw, and he met Jessi's startled eyes.

"Were you eavesdropping?"

"Not intentionally." He stepped back to allow Georgia through.

The tailor patted his arm. "You both have great taste in clothing." Her blue eyes twinkled. "Don't let her fool you. She loved it all."

Jessi crossed her arms and attempted to look annoyed, but the dimple in her cheek gave her away.

"Thank you, Georgia," she said sarcastically. "Mufasa here needs all the encouragement he can..." Her eyes snapped to his. "Crap."

Running his thumb and forefinger over his mustache, he covered a smile. "Yes. Thank you, Georgia." He turned. "I'll show you out."

Jessi followed them down the hall to the front door. "Whatever you decide not to keep, let Mr. Koch know, and I'll send someone to get it." She looked up and appraised him. "The name suits. You do look a little like a lion."

Before he could respond, the door closed behind her. Shaking his head, he turned to see Jessi covering her mouth with a hand. "Are you hungry?"

"I could eat."

"I believe the chef left us some pasta." He paused when Jessi didn't follow him to the kitchen. "Is something wrong?"

Something like frustration crossed her face, but she shook her head and stepped forward. "Nothing."

The chef had indeed left two plates of fettuccine and chicken in the refrigerator. Slipping the plates into the microwave, he turned to see her staring out the side door at the surrounding hillsides.

"Penny for your thoughts?" he asked and opened each of them a bottle of water.

"Just a penny? I would have expected you to spend a Benjamin." Her voice was tight.

"If that's what it will take." He set the bottles aside. "What's bothering you?"

Dark hair swayed against her back as she shook her head. "I don't want this life, Alexander. Personal chefs, tailors who make house calls, luxury cars." Her shoulder rested on the doorframe, and her voice dropped to a near whisper. "This is what I came to California to get away from."

"Where *are* you from?" It seemed like an easy question, but she flinched. If she came from money, it explained her actions. She was comfortable with his staff, yet she resented the fact he hired them. Hip resting on the counter, he waited.

"It's a very long story." Sorrow dripped from her voice, and he ached to fold her in his arms.

"We have all day."

She lifted her eyes to his. Despite the distance they had come, fear shadowed the corners of her gaze. The microwave chimed, but he ignored it as she gave him a rare glimpse of herself.

"Money, power, and appearances controlled my parents' lives." Fear morphed to anger. "I refuse to let that happen to me. So, until I am sure it won't, there are things I'm not ready to tell."

Relaxing the grip he didn't realize he'd taken on the counter; Alexander reached for her. "Fair enough, but understand I am not, and I refuse to be, ashamed of my wealth." She stiffened, but he wrapped her firmly in his arms. "I am, however, ashamed of the way I have wielded it in the past." He brushed a strand of hair from her forehead. He kept her close and watched the anger melt at his touch. "I have several things going on at the moment that I hope will make it clear I've changed. Would you like to hear about them?"

"I would," she husked.

He released her and pulled the steaming plates from the microwave. He gestured to the stools tucked under the island. After they were seated, he took a quick bite, deciding where best to start.

"The most important thing is the work I'm doing with the new Council." Jessi's fork clattered to the counter.

"Sorry." She picked it up and wiped it on a napkin. The echo was gone from her voice. "How is that going?"

"Quite well." Alexander glanced sideways. "I haven't thought to ask if you were planning to attend this year's Gathering. Somehow, I've been chosen to deliver the keynote speech." He lifted another bite of his lunch. "I have meetings for several days before, but I hoped you would go with me."

"I would prefer not to." Jessi's voice was cold without the echo of emotion.

"Why?"

Her knuckles were white around the fork. She looked up, and the terror in her eyes prickled his skin. "I'm not ready to talk about it."

"Why?" Alexander's body tensed.

"Can we please talk about something else?"

"No one, and I mean no one, will ever hurt you again." He touched her hair. "You don't have to be afraid anymore, Jessi."

She leaned into his touch. "I know." She gripped his wrist. "I..." He watched her wrestle the fear back. Her voice strengthened, and the echo returned. "I'll go."

Alexander kissed her forehead. "Thank you. I want you by my

side from now on." He could tell from the sound of her voice she would shut him down if he said more, so he changed the subject.

"The other project is one Peter and I have been working on for years." She relaxed and he made a mental note to bring up the subject of the Gathering again later. "When I went to Southern California University for their architectural program, Peter opened a gym in LA, funded by my father. While in college, I recommended Peter's gym to a couple of my classmates. One of them was my roommate, but he was unable to afford Peter's fees. I paid for him. Months later, the training literally saved him and his girlfriend when they were attacked on their way out of a nightclub." Alexander pushed his plate back. "That weekend Peter and I decided to set up a scholarship fund for those who most needed his training but would never be able to afford it on their own."

"I started it with my own money until others who were trained by Peter heard about it and wanted to contribute. Once we established the funding for fight and self-defense training, word got around. Other places began to approach us requesting we set up a similar program for them. It didn't take us long to realize there were a lot of kids who had passion for what they loved to do but lacked the money to get high quality training. We decided to widen our focus, and soon our scholarships were being used for not just Peter's gym, but a hockey training facility, a football camp, and a whole host of personal trainers in everything from bicycling to archery."

"That sounds noble," she said, and pushed her own plate back. "So, you decided to make it an official business?"

His smile widened. "Last year, Peter expanded into San Diego, and when I received good information you were here, I decided the time had come to sell my father's company and move on."

He took a bite of his pasta, and Jessi shifted. "You were that sure?"

"I was." Alexander smiled. "Our head of IT rarely shares information unless he's confident it is accurate. When he said you were here, I believed him." Alexander stood and carried their plates to the sink.

"The fund has gotten large enough we felt it was time to make it more than a scholarship fund."

She came up beside him and leaned against the counter. "Sounds like you have it all planned out."

"Not all of it." He dried his hands and set the towel aside. "I'd like your input as well." Alexander slid his fingers into her hair and cupped the back of her neck. "I'd like it if we worked together to put all this money I have to good use. Would you like that?" He pulled her close, and a tremor raked him when her arms circled his waist.

"I think I would." Jessi's multicolored eyes skimmed his face, making every inch of him intensely aware of the woman in his arms.

The soft waves of her hair lay across his forearms, and she pressed so closely to him he felt the tightening of her stomach. The effect she had on him was electrifying, heightening his response to her until he had no resistance left. Her upturned face and wide eyes drew his head toward her.

When her lips parted and a gush of her sweet breath fanned his cheek, his body responded instantly. Knowing she wouldn't stop him, he stared at the mouth he wanted to claim as his own, wishing for the fangs that would in turn claim him.

"I am doing everything in my power to wait, but..." He cupped the back of her head and tilted it to the side. "I have to do this at least once."

THIRTY

Alexander's warm breath moistened the side of her neck, and her knees failed to support her as his lips touched the sensitive skin below her ear. All her previous protests and fears forgotten, she was about to turn her head and let his mouth claim what was rightfully his, when the door behind her burst open.

"It is hotter than the devil's backside out there!" Peter pushed the door closed and turned. Jessi stumbled into the refrigerator as Alexander stared in astonishment at his friend. Peter's sparkling eyes moved between them. "Looks like it was getting a little warm in here, too."

Alexander recovered before she did, but the frustration in his tone sent a shiver through her.

"Good afternoon, Peter. Is it that late already?"

Peter tossed a set of keys onto the counter and hopped up to sit on the island. "Nope. But it looks like later would have been too late." Jessi nearly choked, and his grin turned on her. "You're flushed, Jess. Are you all right?"

"Fine," she squeaked, and his smile spread wider.

"Thank you for being so considerate, Peter. Would you like some lunch?"

"No thanks. Hannah and I just ate."

Jessi willed the flush on her cheeks to subside. Refusing to make eye contact with Alexander, she crossed to stand next to Peter. Why had she allowed him to get that close? Now that she had a sample of what his nearness did to her, it would be immensely difficult to keep distance between them. Her only hope was that he would continue to be strong enough to keep his promise.

"Did you bring what we discussed?" Alexander leaned around the corner toward the front door.

"I did." Peter slid off the counter and tossed the set of keys to him. "It's in the drive."

Alexander caught and pocketed them. "Thank you." The doorbell rang. "Give me a moment?"

Brow furrowing, Jessi started across the kitchen, but Peter caught her. "Let's wait here." Alexander's steps retreated down the hall, and Jessi exhaled loudly.

"Thank you for your perfect timing."

He brushed invisible dust from his shoulder. "It's my best quality." His eyes turned serious. "Are you okay?"

"I think so." She crossed her arms as a shiver raked her.

Peter's laugh was knowing. "Matches..."

"Gunpowder." Jessi couldn't help but smile.

Alexander's agitated voice carried down the hall as his pain shot through her. It had been nearly absent for the last several days, and the intensity of its return darkened the edges of her vision. Both she and Peter hurried toward the raised voices, but Peter rounded the corner first and stopped short.

She bumped her nose painfully into his spine and stepped back. "What's going on?"

He turned and took her by the shoulders, deliberately keeping his body in front of her. "It would be best if we waited in the kitchen."

"I know what the contract says, Rebekka." Alexander's voice was rough.

Jessi pushed against Peter's brick of an arm, pain climbing her neck and pulsing in her temples. He didn't budge.

"Don't." Peter's eyes were concerned. "Just wait. Let him handle it."

The front door shut firmly as Rebekka yelled back. Frozen where Peter still held her, she strained to listen.

"I asked you not to come here." Alexander's deep voice was muffled. "I told Thomas I would handle the situation."

"We had an agreement, Alexander!"

"We are not discussing this. Go home." The next part of his sentence was softer, and Jessi didn't catch his words. When the door opened a crack his tone was chilling. "It's none of your business who she is. I will uphold my end of the agreement. It is not your concern how." He stepped inside. "Thomas will call you when it's been arranged."

"But..."

"Not now, Rebekka. I'm doing the best I can to resolve the situation, but I have other things to attend to at the moment. Your car is blocking the drive. Please move it before my next appointment arrives."

Jessi glared up at Peter. "Let me go."

"No."

"It's fine, Peter." Alexander re-appeared in the kitchen doorway. "I apologize for that. Things at the office are a bit chaotic and Rebekka is overly concerned about the lawsuit." Peter released her, and both she and Alexander sighed as his pain levels receded. "Anyway. Did you choose an outfit for the concert?"

"Was she asking about me?" Jessi demanded.

Alexander crossed the room and rested his hand on her shoulder. "No. The lawsuit names a young woman my father once knew. It's nothing you need to worry about." He glanced at his watch. "You didn't answer my question."

"There are a couple things I liked." Pushing the conversation with Rebekka out of her mind, she stepped back. "I need to go home to change though."

The doorbell rang again, and Alexander grinned. "Actually, you don't." Exasperated, Jessi followed him down the hall. "I called an old friend who's anxious to meet you."

Jessi's pulse leapt. If it was someone from the Clan, they might recognize her. She was glad she hadn't associated with many of the other members due to her travel schedule, but until she found the courage to tell Alexander the truth, the risk remained someone would out her. She drew a deep breath preparing for the worst.

Alexander opened the door and stepped aside. "Leisel! You look stunning as always." He kissed the woman's cheek, and Jessi stared wide eyed as a gorgeous redhead entered the foyer.

Leisel swatted his arm and set a large black case inside the door. "Thank you. Is she here? I can't wait..." The redhead's eyes swung to Jessi, and her face beamed. Comfortably stylish in black leggings and a pale blue maternity top, she looked to be about seven months pregnant. She reached out a hand. "You must be the famous Jessi."

Shaking the offered hand, Jessi smiled in confusion. "I am. Leisel? As in Leisel Lockton?"

Laughing, she nodded. "Yes." Her mossy green eyes swept over Jessi. "Koen told me you and Alexander would be coming to the concert and after party tonight, so I offered to come help you get ready." Doubt must have shown on her face because Leisel glanced at Alexander. "You didn't tell her I was coming, did you?"

"He's not been very forthcoming with information today." Jessi relaxed and shook her head as Alexander turned back up the stairs. As far as she could remember, she'd never met Leisel or any of Leisel's family. Her secret was safe a little longer.

Alexander smirked. "Paybacks are fun aren't they?" He pulled the tie out of his hair. "We'll need to leave in about two hours. The guest room is up here, next to my office."

Leisel picked up the case and followed him. "Still always over the top, aren't you, Koch?"

He pushed open the door to a lavishly furnished bedroom and gestured inside. "Everything you need is here. I'll be in my office when you're ready to go."

Jessi paused outside the door while Leisel set her case down next to an antique dressing table. "I'll go down and bring the dress upstairs."

Alexander leaned down to whisper in her ear. "Look in the closet first." Before she could reply, he retreated across the hall. "Leisel will take good care of you," he said, then turned and closed himself inside another bedroom.

"Let him have his fun, Jessi." Leisel waved her inside. "You can make him pay for it later."

The room was brightly lit by wide windows, and sunlight splashed across the bed. Darkly stained closet doors stood open to the right of a gleaming blue and silver tiled bathroom. Jessi scratched the back of her head and crossed the room.

"Thank you for coming, Leisel." Jessi stepped inside the huge closet. It was nearly the size of the kitchen in her apartment and completely empty except for one item. Hanging against the side wall was a plain grey garment bag.

Leisel followed her inside the space. "You're welcome, and please, call me Leis. Alexander is the only one who calls people by their full names." She chuckled. "That looks familiar."

Jessi laid the bag on the bed. "How so?"

"It's kind of a long story. Let's just say he and I helped each other through a tough time." She sat on the edge of the bed. "You were at the Compound the night Koen and I bonded, weren't you? That's where you and Alexander first met?"

Jessi nodded and pulled the zipper open on the bag. "It was. Things got complicated after..." Her voice caught, and Leis giggled.

"Well, that's different," Leisel said.

Jessi pulled the dress free of the bag and held it up. A thin black overlay, embroidered neck to hem in a swirling floral pattern of pale greens, rich reds, creamy whites, and sapphire blues, covered a cotton long sleeve dress with sweet white folded cuffs and a high collar. The a-line shape would flatter her perfectly, and the modest cut looked comfortable and light. Blowing the hair off her forehead, Jessi blinked back tears. The dress was beautiful and something she would have chosen for herself.

She glanced at Leisel. "How does he do this, Leis? How does he just pick things out that are..."

"Darn near perfect?" She brushed a hand over her stomach. "I have no idea. He's one of a kind." Leis tried to stand and laughed. "Give me a hand? I think I'm stuck."

Jessi carefully laid the dress back on the bed, and the tears she'd blinked back slipped loose when she saw the label wasn't designer. It was from a chain store she purchased most of her clothing from. Shaking her head, she reached out to help Leisel to her feet. "I'd fall in love with him if I didn't resent his lifestyle so much."

Leisel's brows fell. "He's a little extravagant, sure, but..."

Annoyance and doubt pinched her throat. "He's controlling. And overbearing. And unbelievably frustrating!" The other woman took a step back. Jessi immediately regretted her outburst. Biting her lip, she heaved a breath. "Sorry about that. There's a saying around here." She ran a hand through her hair. "Alexander and I are like matches and gunpowder. You never know if we're going to kill each other or..." She blushed, and Leis clapped her hands in glee.

"Oh, my goodness, he's met his match!" She nodded toward the bathroom. "Why don't you shower and relax for a few minutes. I'll get everything settled out here."

Running a hand down her face, Jessi nodded even though this would be shower number two for the day. "Yeah. That's probably a good idea."

Leis opened her case and began setting out styling tools and makeup. She glanced over her shoulder as Jessi shut the bathroom door. "Take your time."

The door clicked behind her, and Jessi let out a puff of exasperation. The shower door sparkled in the sun shining down from the skylight, and she slid it open. Pulling her hair loose and stepping out of her clothes, she hung them carefully on the hook beside the shower. Warm water soothed her tense muscles, and the smell of the expensive shampoo and soap calmed her nerves.

Behind the door hung a plush white robe. Pulling it around her, she opened the door and wrapped the towel around the ends of her hair.

"No, I haven't heard from them. I'll call Andrew tomorrow. Hey, I gotta go. Jessi is ready for me." Leis sat at the dressing table bench with her cell phone. She smiled and looked up as Jessi crossed the room. "I'll tell him. I love you, too. See you in a couple hours." Tucking the phone into her case, she stood. "Feel better?"

"I do." Jessi took the spot Leis had risen from. "When are you due?"

"Joseph is due in two months." She took the towel and squeezed the ends of Jessi's hair before setting it aside to run a comb through the long strands. "Koen can't wait. His sister is just over a year old. He loves kids." She separated the hair into sections and picked up the blow dryer. "Have you and Alexander talked about kids?"

"No." Leis began to blow out her hair section by section. "We haven't gotten that far yet."

Patiently, she curled and pinned Jessi's tresses into large soft loops that trailed over her shoulders and down her back. Once that was done, she stepped in front of her and tilted her head.

"You don't need much makeup, but your eyes would be stunning with some wide liner. How does that sound?"

"That would be fine." When the other woman turned away, she closed her eyes and asked, "Did you know Alexander before the Gathering?"

"No. Well..." She turned and began applying a light powder to Jessi's forehead and cheeks. Leis scrunched her nose. "We met earlier that week. He was different then."

"How different?" Jessi opened her eyes and the woman's expression softened.

"He was in a lot of pain, and our Clan wasn't in a good place. He, Koen, myself, and another male got caught in the middle of it all." Stepping back, she met Jessi's eyes. The green of Leis' were bright but soft edged, unlike the crystal shards of Alexander's. "He realized he needed to find you, and he made it his life's mission to do so." She picked up a liner pencil. "He's one hundred percent, or he's nothing at all. And when he sets his mind to something, heaven help anyone who tries to stop him." She leaned closer. "Look up for me?"

Jessi did as she was asked, and Leis' careful strokes lined her lower eyelid.

"Was there ever anyone else?" Leisel moved to the other eye, her pinky smudging the liner to soften the edges. "Was he ever involved with anyone?"

Pausing, the other woman peered down at her. "Why do you ask?"

"I know Alexander and I are mates, but..." Rebekka obviously still cared for him. Did he feel the same way for her? How much could she tell this woman? "How can I know he's not still involved with a human?"

Leis rested a hand on her shoulder. "Trust me when I tell you that's not possible. He's your mate. There *can't* be anyone else."

She clenched her teeth, knowing this woman didn't deserve the anger that statement caused. "I wish I could believe that, but my experience says otherwise."

"I'll admit Alexander might be—what did you call him? Controlling, overbearing, and frustrating sometimes, but he's always been honest. If you have questions, ask him. He'll tell you the truth." She tucked an errant curl back. "It's a story for another day but trust me on this one. He's no good at hiding his feelings. We females have been given an incredible gift in our sense of smell. A gift I was without for most of my life. When I finally received it, a very wise friend told me to pay attention to what other people's emotions were telling me." Leis leaned back against the table. "I don't know what he's done to make you think there's someone else, but I'd have a hard time believing it was possible for any male once he's met his mate, and especially for Alexander. Human or otherwise, they aren't able to be with anyone else. It's not possible."

Then you need to meet my father. Jessi reigned in her argument, knowing this wasn't the time or the place to discuss it. "I'm trying to believe you, but I've seen things that convince me otherwise." Untwisting the vice-like grip she'd taken on the edge of her robe, she smiled at Leis. "We'll have to take it one day at a time."

The redhead picked up a shiny silver tube and uncapped it. "No one can ask more of you than that." Her green eyes moistened. "Just don't..." She shook her head. "I know it's none of my business, but I hate seeing him still in pain."

"Me too."

With practiced skill, Leis applied the mascara, and Jessi couldn't help noticing how deeply she blushed as she swiped the dark ink onto her lashes. "What?"

Leisel turned to gather her things. "Every time I apply mascara I think about Koen." Her cheeks were brilliant red. "I did his makeup for a production while I was a makeup artist in college. And, well, that's when we discovered there was some serious chemistry between us." She brushed the dressing table clean of powder. "It's a great memory."

A light knock came from the door. "Jessi? Leisel? Are you almost ready?" Alexander's muffled voice called.

"A few more minutes," Leis replied.

Jessi untied the robe and hurried to the bathroom to retrieve her undergarments. She heard fabric rustling as Leis moved the garment bag back to the closet.

"Uh, Jessi?" Leisel stopped and turned back.

Her stomach tightened, suspecting what was coming next. "What?"

"You might want to check the garment bag. I think there's more in here."

With an exasperated sigh she did. A carefully wrapped package of tissue paper rested in the bottom. Peeling the foil seal back, her body tingled. A small pool of black and silver lace delicately unfurled in her hands. Meeting the other woman's eyes, she held up the Laperla bra and panties, her face glowing in embarrassment.

Leisel covered her grin. "Yeah. Males aren't exactly subtle sometimes." She fingered the lace. "So, will this be the match, or the gunpowder?"

THIRTY-ONE

For the hundredth time, Alexander paced his office, anxious to see Jessi in the dress he'd left for her. He glanced at his watch as a soft knock drew his attention to the doorway.

"I'll see you in a few hours?" Leis leaned against the frame.

He tugged his cuffs. "We'll be backstage by seven."

She straightened as Jessi's footsteps approached. "Have fun. The dress is perfect."

Leis backed into the hallway as Jessi rounded the corner. Their eyes met, and he inhaled deeply at the sight of her. Leisel styled her raven hair into a braided crown around the front of her head, leaving softer waves of black layered against her shoulders. The dress smoothed over her body like it had been custom made, and her gorgeous eyes were perfectly framed by Leisel's talented makeup application.

"Jessi." He breathed. "You look beautiful."

His chest swelled with pride that the stunning woman in front of him was his, though deep in his gut doubt twisted. There were still parts of her she kept closed to him. He didn't understand it. It was clear they were intended for each other, yet there was a hesitation lingering around her like fog that had not yet burned off in the morning sun. He hoped tonight would disperse whatever remaining fears she had. As he continued to stare, her chin ducked and pink-dusted cheeks flushed a deeper shade.

"Thank you. The dress is perfect." Her echo curled around him in gratefulness.

He took her hand and lifted it to his lips, savoring the softness of her skin. "It's my pleasure. Did you and Leisel have a nice talk?"

Her lips thinned, and he tipped her chin up to look at him. Her eyes were guarded. "We did. She thinks very highly of you."

He chuckled. "That certainly wasn't always the case." Tucking her arm in his, he led her toward the hallway.

Alexander descended the stairs then paused in the entryway to maneuver her in front of him, placing her back to the door.

She sighed. "What now?"

Though he tried not to be, nervousness pricked at him. He wasn't sure how she would react to what was outside. He took her tiny hands in his.

"I counted five times that I needed to make good on my promise, and the last is parked in the driveway." Her gorgeous hazel eyes widened, and he brushed his knuckles down her cheek. "I know this isn't the lifestyle you've been used to, but it's fun for me to do these things for you."

"What did you do?" Jessi released his hand and reached for the door latch.

He didn't stop her. Instead, he followed her onto the front stoop and down the sidewalk to the driveway. Jessi's steps faltered when she rounded the tall hedges and got her first glimpse of what was parked in front of his garage.

Peter leaned against a brand new, bronze super duty pickup truck. Hitched to the bed was a five-horse slant load goose-neck horse trailer. His friend stepped away as Jessi approached and laid a hand cautiously against the passenger side door.

"Seriously?" she whispered.

Peter leaned close. "I told him it was too big, but he wouldn't listen."

Jessi glared up at him, and he raised his hands in surrender as she turned back to Alexander. He couldn't tell if she was angry or impressed. "A new rig? How did you even know what to buy?"

Alexander withdrew the keys from his pocket and unlocked the doors. "I discovered our charity provides funds for one of the students at your barn, and Dennis *might* have had some input on the trailer. Let's say I had some excellent advisers on this one."

"This is the end of it?" Her eyes swung down the length of the truck and trailer before landing back on his, her voice devoid of emotion.

"Yes." His inability to hear her emotions frustrated him.

She was deliberately shielding herself, and he wanted to find a way to shatter her resistance. The pain she relieved from his body was being replaced by a mental and emotional ache that hurt worse than the fiery pain of their physical separation.

She studied his eyes. "Truly, this is it?"

"I promise." Unable to stand it any longer, Alexander cupped her face in his hands. "I will never lie to you." He kissed her forehead then rested his hands on her shoulders.

Peter opened the passenger door, and a step lowered. Jessi nodded as slivers of moisture pooled in the bottoms of her eyes.

"Thank you, Alexander." The echo of her voice danced across his skin and unwound the knot in his stomach.

He helped her up into the seat, and the truck's height put her at eye level with him. He let his gaze trail over her face and enjoyed the way the intensity of his scrutiny made heat creep up her neck. The words he longed to tell her lodged in the back of his throat, but he choked them back.

"You're welcome, *Fräulein*." He brushed the back of his knuckles down her cheek and braced himself when she leaned into his touch. "Buckle up."

Peter cleared his throat, and Alexander drew back. "You two need to hit the road. Your car is already at the barn." Inclining his head to Jessi, Peter shut the door and clapped Alexander on the shoulder. "Remember patience, my friend. Just a little longer and your hard work will pay off."

THIRTY-TWO

The smell of leather and new car filled the cab of the enormous truck. Jessi gritted her teeth against the tears threatening to choke her. *The cost!* Her head fell back, and she fisted her hands in her lap. She watched as Alexander rounded the front of the truck and stepped into the driver's seat.

Instantly he tensed. "Talk to me."

"I don't even know what to say." Closing her eyes and taking a deep breath, she reminded herself of what Leis had told her. Scenting his emotions was nothing new, but this time she let his rich scent wash over her, tagging the emotions as they registered. Relief his pain was almost gone, curiosity, concern, and... her eyes flew open.

Love?

When her gaze swung back to him, his expression was completely unguarded, and his words rang with honesty. "Koen and Leisel gave something to me the night you and I first encountered one another. I had planned to give it to you in New York." Alexander's bergamot thickened in the air. He opened his palm to reveal a heavy charm looped through a length of braided black leather. "They gave this to me after you ran."

"I'm sorry," she whispered.

He smiled sadly. "They wanted to remind me there would always be hope. Hope that so long as my heart continued to beat, the opportunity remained for me to find you." His green eyes brightened. "That hope has been fulfilled." His voice rasped, and the emotions embedded in his scent saturated her. "I want you to have it. I don't know what you are hoping for, but my *new* hope is that whatever it is, you will find it in me. With me."

A vice tightened around her ribs, and a lone tear slid down her cheek. Though she was staring at him, his touch startled her when he wiped the moisture from her skin.

Lowering his gaze to the pendant in his hand, he leaned back in the seat. "I want to be the man you deserve, and I'm doing my best to become him." Alexander's hand shook as he tied the leather strap to the rear-view mirror. "Every time you look at this pendant, I want you to remember that as long as our hearts beat, there is hope for us."

He slipped the key into the ignition and backed the rig out onto the street. Jessi's clouded vision focused on the anatomical heart. It hung heavily, and the polished steel sending spears of light reflecting off its surface. Spears that lodged themselves in her heart.

"Alexander?" He stopped at the light before entering the highway, his chin lowered before his raw gaze met hers. Her voice was a choked whisper. "I'm trying. Be patient with me?"

The corners of his eyes crinkled, and he reached for her hand. It wasn't raging desire that coursed up her arm at his touch this time, but a fierce protectiveness that punched through her remaining defenses.

"Patience is my middle name." His thumb caressed the back of her hand. "I'm not going anywhere. When you're ready, you let me know. I would claim you right now, but this will always be your choice." He exhaled and his intensity subsided. "Tonight is dinner, a concert, and an after party that is guaranteed to be a great time.

Enough serious talk." He winked. "Let's go unhitch this trailer and get something to eat."

Jessi sat silently as he pulled into the lot next to the barn. "Are we taking your car to dinner?"

"Not exactly." He stepped out and came round to help her down from the tall truck. He offered his arm and started in the direction of the barn.

She pulled back. "But my apartment is over there."

He tightened his grip. "It is. But dinner is this way."

"Are those lights in the arena?" Confused, she let him lead her though the main barn, pointing when the open door to the outdoor area came into sight. The glow and twinkle of hundreds of tiny bulbs spanned the opening. Alexander didn't answer until they stood on a blue fabric runner that led her eye to a table set for four in the very middle of the fenced arena.

Tall poles supported the strands of lights, and a tent draped over the table with white and blue tulle intertwined with more lights glowed like a scene from a movie. Dennis and his wife, Janice, were already seated with their backs to them. To the side stood two men in white shirts, bow ties, and black dress pants. Behind them was a table of silver topped warmers and covered dishes.

Alexander's grip tightened when she tried to pull away. "You said the truck was the last thing! How much did *this* cost, Alexander?"

"Probably more than it should have, but it was short notice." He bent to whisper in her ear. "And this isn't for *you*. Watch."

Jessi shifted her attention from the exasperating man beside her to the other couple. Janice turned to Dennis, and though his wife wouldn't have been able to see it, Jessi watched him withdraw a small blue box from his pant pocket and push his chair back.

Janice's eyes widened when it dawned on her what he was about to do. Dennis held the box in front of him, his hands shaking so badly he could hardly open it, then lowered to a knee. Janice sat frozen for a long moment. Long enough that Dennis's shoulders drooped before she reached for him. Jessi released the breath she'd been holding as her friend's head bounced up and down.

Dennis gathered her in his arms and stood, taking Janice with him. Dennis pulled the ring from the box and slid it on her hand.

Alexander whispered. "They've been going through a rough time, and she was contemplating leaving. He asked me to help him win her back the way I've won you."

"Is that what they think? That you've won me?" she asked.

He tugged her forward as Dennis and Janice took their seats again, fingers intertwined between them. "Mmmm. Not sure. But the odds are looking better for me, aren't they?"

Supporting herself with a death grip on his arm, Jessi whispered, "I wouldn't bet against you anymore."

The moment she reached the table, Janice leapt from her seat and threw her arms around Jessi's neck. "Thank you! I didn't expect this at all!"

Still reeling from Alexander's statements, Jessi grinned at the other woman. "I guess I owed you after the way you took care of me the other night. Let me see. What did he get you?"

"A new wedding ring. Mine got lost last year." Janice presented the ring, understated with a single round diamond surrounded by smaller glittering stones. She stared at it, and her eyes swam with tears. "It's perfect. He's perfect."

Jessi hugged her. "He is pretty awesome." Her gaze drifted to where Alexander was congratulating Dennis. "I guess they both are."

Throughout dinner, Alexander kept the conversation going, asking questions about their plans for a second honeymoon, how Dennis was going to adjust his travel schedule to be home more, and the possibility of hiring more stable hands. Jessi listened, trying to laugh or comment at the appropriate places, but her mind raced.

Alexander clearly wasn't the angry, vengeful man she believed him to be, and he didn't deserve her mistrust anymore. When the conversation shifted to Alexander, his interests and travel schedule, Jessi realized she was out of time. With the Gathering and Council meeting looming, she couldn't afford to put it off any longer. Within days, they would come face to face with her father who also served on the Council. She had to tell him tonight.

Resolving that she would confess everything on the way to the concert, Jessi let go of her worry and let the hope Alexander offered her blossom.

The meal was delicious, and after the servers had cleared the table and served dessert, Dennis wiped his lips and set the napkin aside.

"I already gave you one gift tonight, but I have another surprise for you." Dennis pulled a plain brown box from under the table and handed it to his wife. "My passion for horses has kept us from doing the things *you* love." Jessi watched the other woman remove the lid. "Alexander was kind enough to—"

Janice vaulted out of her seat and threw her arms around her husband nearly knocking them both to the ground. "You got tickets to the Koen Lockton show tonight?"

Dennis wrapped his arms around her and laughed. "Not just tickets. Backstage passes and..."

Jessi blushed when his words were hushed by his wife's lips. She glanced at Alexander, and her lower body clenched at the heat radiating from his gaze. She covered her sudden inhale with an embarrassed cough.

Alexander's thumb caressed the back of her hand until her breathing settled, and Janice's voice broke the moment. "Are you sure you don't mind us tagging along?"

Alexander never took his eyes off Jessi. "Not at all. It's my pleasure." Unable to withstand his intensity, Jessi tore her eyes from his and smiled at the other couple. Alexander chuckled and pushed back from the table. "Shall we?" he asked.

Alexander drove them all in her new truck and had secured a parking pass allowing them entrance to the rear of the arena. When they arrived, it was surrounded by police and throngs of fans hoping to get a glimpse of Koen. Alexander led them past the barricades and down a long hallway. Dennis beamed as Janice's steps became more like hops the closer they came to the green room. Jessi laughed when Janice's face paled at the sight of Koen's name on the door.

Alexander knocked, and a gruff man opened the door to step into the hallway. "Mr. Lockton isn't taking visitors."

"If you could let him know Alexander—"

"I know who you are, Mr. Koch." He crossed his arms and positioned himself in front of the door. "Mr. Lockton said he would talk to you after the concert." His harsh expression softened. "I wish I could tell you more. I know you are someone he considers a friend, but I'm not at liberty to explain."

Alexander nodded. "Thank you. We respect Koen's privacy, and I appreciate your candor. Please let him know I would be glad to help him or Leisel in any way I can."

Jessi watched the man's face darken at the mention of Leisel's name, and from the way Alexander's body tensed, he hadn't missed it either.

"I'll be sure to let them know." He nodded and rested his hand on the doorknob. "Mr. Lockton will meet you back here after the show, Mr. Koch." The man's eyes scanned the rest of them. "Sincere apologies to the ladies. He was looking forward to meeting you." He turned and slipped back inside.

Alexander glanced down at Jessi. Understanding passed between them, and she squeezed his arm. "I'm sure she's all right."

He turned away from the door. "So am I." He met Dennis's eyes. "Let's find our seats."

Jessi tried her best to engage Alexander in conversation between the opening acts, but his answers were little more than grunts. It was unlike him to be so distant, and Jessi knew the guard had communicated something more to him than the rest of them understood. Deciding he needed the time alone in his thoughts, Jessi wove their fingers together and leaned against his broad shoulder.

The first opening act was a young woman Jessi recognized as having recently won a reality TV show. She was energetic, and her clear voice carried the crowd through her set effortlessly. When the second band took the stage, Jessi flinched. Koen's listening preferences were well known to be on the harder side, and the volume in the stadium erupted with screaming guitars and vocals singing lyrics she couldn't understand. Janice was thoroughly enjoying herself while Dennis laughed and cheered alongside her.

Jessi was relieved when the second act's five songs ended and Koen's band traded places. Though the lights were down, from the front row they watched as stagehands moved equipment and reset the stage.

The buzz of the crowd increased tenfold as the musicians took their places and the soft glow of the light wall along the back of the stage lit their silhouettes. When the announcer's mic keyed on, the stadium erupted with such force Jessi jumped.

"Ladies and Gentlemen! It is our pleasure to welcome to our stage and to the great state of California, the 2015 Entertainer of the Year—*Koen Lockton*!"

The applause and cheers of the crowd were drowned out by the sound of the opening guitar solo of Koen's number one hit. Always in command of his crowd, Koen's rough vocals preceded his arrival on stage, and when the spotlight landed on him, Jessi's breath was stolen from her.

The rich black guitar strap rode his shoulder, and the matching instrument he played looked like a permanent part of him. Even to her untrained eye, this man was clearly a highly skilled musician. But as he drew closer to the front of the stage, she picked up on his distraction. Though his vocals and the notes he brought out of the guitar were flawless, she instantly knew something was off. Jessi had played his concert videos over and over, and the performer on this stage, while clearly the same person, was lacking the fire she'd seen in those recordings.

If Janice noticed, she didn't let it show. Her hands were raised, and she sang along at the top of her lungs. Alexander watched his friend through narrowed eyes, and Jessi wondered what he was thinking. It was obvious the Locktons meant a great deal to him.

When Alexander's eyes met hers, she saw Koen's pain reflected in his. Conversation was impossible, and she realized, unnecessary. They knew nothing other than something was horribly wrong.

The rest of the set was as amazing as the first song, and the crowd stilled when Koen took a seat on a stool provided by a stage-hand who briefly rested a hand on his boss's shoulder before disappearing offstage again.

Koen cleared his throat. "It's no secret that Leis and I are expecting our first child in a few months." He raised his hand and acknowledged the cheers and applause with a smile and a nod. The arena quieted again as his fingers whispered across the strings of a different guitar. The sound was lighter, almost haunting. "I wrote this song for my wife the day we found out she was pregnant." Despite the glare of the lights, Koen's eyes sought out Alexander. "Today is all we have. When you find the one, the one you've been looking for all your life..." His already rough voice caught. "It changes you. No matter what happens, make today count."

Alexander exhaled and wrapped his arm around Jessi's shoulders, pulling her close. As Koen's smoky voice coiled through the enraptured crowd, Alexander pressed a kiss to the crown of her head. She felt his lips move, but the music and words of the song drowned him out. Breathing in his sweet scent, she knew that was his intent. He hadn't wanted her to hear what he said, and she knew why. He was waiting for her to say it first. With Dennis and Janice in the truck, she hadn't been able to talk to him, but now she vowed that as soon as this concert was over, she would tell him who she really was. Jessi pressed her cheek into his shoulder and listened to the last few lines of Koen's song.

I give you all my todays
every moment of everyday

I can't promise tomorrow
and forever isn't mine to give
But today I will love you
with all I am and all I have

If the bright sun rises
and we get another today
I will be by your side
To catch your tears and
share your laughs
hold you while you sleep

Today is yours
My heart is full
of life full of love
full of everything
you've given me
So, I give you
All my todays

THIRTY-THREE

Applause rocked the stadium as Koen rose from the stool and the kick drum set the rhythm for the next song. Alexander shifted to release Jessi and watched his friend carefully as he did what he did best, but there was something missing from his performance. The song ended, and Koen strode to the front of the stage, his smile broad but forced.

"Thank you for coming out tonight, California!" He lifted the guitar off over his head and handed it to one of his bandmates. "You have been a fantastic audience tonight, and we'll be back to see you soon. Have a great night!"

Following his pattern, Koen shook hands with and hugged each of his band members before leaving the stage with a last wave and blown kiss to the crowd. The roar increased as the lights faded, and though normally there would have been a short encore, neither Koen nor his band returned to the stage.

Alexander stood and led Jessi and the other couple toward the side door. The same man who greeted them at the dressing room was guarding the door. He nodded before opening it to let the four of them through.

Over the noise of the crowd leaving, the man leaned close and shouted, "Mr. Lockton is waiting for you in his dressing room. He asked me to send you alone. I'll see to it that the rest of your party is escorted to their vehicle. Mr. Lockton has made arrangements for your transportation after the meeting."

Dread layered over him, but Alexander nodded in understanding. "I will meet him there shortly. Give me a few minutes to explain." The door shut, and the near deafening roar subsided enough they could speak normally.

"Dennis, I need you to make sure the ladies get home safely tonight. Koen has asked to meet with me privately. His security team will see you out to the truck." He pulled Jessi close. "Janice, I am sorry Koen wasn't able to meet with you. As soon as things are settled I'll make arrangements. Perhaps we can all have dinner together?"

"Thank you, Alexander!" Janice's enthusiasm wasn't dampened in the least. "The concert was enough. I just hope everything is all right."

Jessi rested her hands on his forearms, looking up at him in confusion. "What's going on?"

He glanced down the hall. "I don't know." He grasped her shoulders and placed a kiss on her forehead. "I'll call as soon as I know something. Go home with Dennis and Janice. Apparently security has provided for my transportation after the meeting."

Her hands tightened, and he let his lips linger against her skin a moment longer, drinking in the feel and smell of her. Tonight had gone better than he ever could have imagined, and he was anxious to resolve whatever was happening in time to spend tomorrow with her as well.

"Be careful, and you promise you'll call as soon as you can?" She leaned back, and the trust in her eyes shook him.

"I promise." Reminding himself Koen was waiting; he released her and stepped back. "I'll talk to you soon."

Nervousness glinted in her eyes, and she gripped his hand before he turned away. "There's something I need to tell to you, but it can wait. Koen needs you." She lifted his hand and pressed a soft kiss to his palm. "Go on. We'll talk later."

"All right." Torn between wanting to hear what she had to say and knowing his presence was needed elsewhere, Alexander reluctantly let her go. She turned and followed Dennis and Janice down the corridor. When they rounded the corner out of sight, he exhaled and went to find Koen.

The green room was deathly silent when Alexander entered. Koen stood to greet him, then glanced at his band. "Would you guys mind giving us a few minutes?"

"Sure, boss." The five men stepped past Alexander, all giving him a strange look but saying nothing.

Once the door shut behind the last man, Koen rounded on Alexander, his blue eyes flashing in anger. "What is wrong with your Clan? Arranged marriages and challenges aren't insulting enough? You have to put a contract on your females to make sure they obey?"

Alexander stepped back. "First of all, it's not *my* or anyone else's Clan. We are one people now." Koen didn't back down, and Alexander lowered his tone. Suspecting he already knew what was going on, he said, "Why don't you start by telling me what happened."

The musician raked a hand through his damp hair. "To be honest, I don't even know yet." He dropped onto a stool and rested his head in his hands. "Leis wasn't able to get a hold of her parents for over a week. No one could. We thought maybe they went on vacation and didn't tell anyone." He shook his head. "It's not like it's been an easy year for them." Alexander sat in a chair near the door, and when Koen looked up, he knew what was coming. "We found out a couple hours ago that the Dietrichs took everything her parents owned. The house, the bank accounts, everything. Haydn and Stefanie are gone without a trace." Koen's eyes were tortured. "Because of me."

Alexander sat forward. "You know that's not the truth." He met

Koen's stare evenly. "I'm going to make a guess as to what happened. You tell me if I'm right." Koen's brow creased. "The Gottschalks were required to surrender the majority of their property, likely ninety-five percent of it, to the Dietrichs upon Baden's twenty-fifth birthday if he was not bonded to Leisel by that date?"

Koen lowered his hands and sat straighter. "You knew?" he growled.

"Only because I am in a similar situation with the family of the female my parents pledged me to." Alexander pulled his cuffs. "They are currently suing me for ownership of not only my father's company, but everything I own." He wished Jessi were beside him so her touch would soothe the inferno under his skin. Ignoring it the best he could, he explained, "I am only able to prevent it because she has been missing almost since the day the contract was signed. Technically, her family owes me all they own because of it." Alexander made a fist. "I knew nothing about the contracts until a week ago when I was served the paperwork."

Koen pushed to his feet and began to pace. "That's fantastic for you, but Leis and her brothers have lost everything." He spun toward Alexander again. "Res and Samuel Dietrich should never have been released! Who made that decision?"

Alexander held up his hands. "I don't know." He lowered his eyes. "I wasn't exactly concerned with Clan business when those decisions were being made."

Koen fisted his hands in his hair, then dropped them with a loud exhale. "I know you weren't. Even Emerick had no idea these contracts even existed when he took over as Elder. He would have voided them immediately." He swiped a bottle of water and took a long swallow. "He apparently found all the old records at the Compound, and as we speak, he's working with my dad to translate them." Koen rubbed his eyes. "That's all I know at the moment. The Council has called an emergency meeting tomorrow night. I will be there. Baden can't make it, but with his name tied to theirs it's probably for the better."

"Baden is Res's great-great-grandson. I forgot that." Alexander leaned back. "I'm sure he knows nothing about this, right?"

"Baden." Koen covered his face. Then took another drink of water. "He's frantic, trying to locate where the funds went. He's got enough on his hands. This is the last thing he needs to deal with, but he and Dani are hacking every system they can think of trying to find a trail. Hopefully they'll know something by the time the Council meets."

A knock on the door interrupted them. Koen jumped toward the door just as it opened. Leisel came in, immediately collapsed in Koen's arms and burst into sobs. The burly doorman ticked his head outside, and Alexander took his leave.

"I'll drive you home, Mr. Koch," he said.

THIRTY-FOUR

K oen's men drove him home, and he immediately packed an overnight case and climbed into the Range Rover. The Vampir Council had called an emergency meeting the next day, and he was anxious to do some research at the mansion before then.

Once on the road, he called Jessi.

"Hello?" Her sleepy voice made him smile.

"Did I wake you?"

"No." She yawned. "No. I was just napping on the couch."

He laughed lightly. "You're a terrible liar."

He heard a quick inhale then what sounded like the phone being dropped. "Sorry! It slipped." Her voice shook, and the echo was gone again. "How is Koen? Is everything okay?"

"He and Leisel are managing as best they can, but the Council has called an emergency meeting. I'm on my way to Arizona. I'll be back in time for our trip to New York." A strange feeling crept up his neck. "Are you all right? Do you need me to stay?"

"No. I'm fine." The echo was back, and though she was nervous, he believed her.

"Good. Get some sleep and I'll call you as soon as I know more."

"Be safe, Alexander." Her voice softened. "Believe it or not...I will miss you, Mufasa."

He growled playfully. "You better. Talk to you soon." He hung up and tossed the phone on the seat beside him.

Five and a half hours later, he pulled into the empty garage of his family home. He lived here for only a few months after his parents died, until memories and Rebekka's arms drove him to Seattle. He pushed open the door and stepped into the kitchen. The gleaming old-world style of stainless steel, rough-cut wood, and fieldstone surrounded him with memories. He tossed his keys into the dish that was still sitting on the counter and shook his head at how such a simple habit never seemed to leave him no matter how long he'd been gone.

As he passed through the dining room into the main hallway, he could still hear his father's voice echoing through the cold stone. Until his college years he was his father's favorite, the one being groomed to take over the family business. As the youngest son and only heir to the family name, he had little choice but to go along with his parents' plans or risk his family losing everything. But no one ever asked him what he wanted.

Alexander ascended the wide staircase and paused outside his parents' suite. The door was closed, and he had no inclination to look inside. He knew what it would look like; no one had moved anything after their death. Nothing in the house had changed, except him.

The housekeeping staff wouldn't be back until tomorrow, so there was no one at all in the expansive home, and he felt the emptiness like a hole deep in the pit of his stomach. He pushed open the door to his old room and stood just inside. To his right the bed was neatly made and the dresser with a large vase of exotic flowers lent a touch of color to the otherwise dull white and grey stone walls. Glancing up, stars shone against a velvet black back-drop of sky through the skylight above the bed. Perhaps that's why his parents opted for so little color in the house. They had chosen instead to frame the glorious Arizona skies with expansive windows.

With a sigh, he turned back into the hallway and left the door open, heading to the end of the hall where his father's study was tucked into the back of the massive building. The large mahogany desk and brown leather chair seemed hollow without his father's large frame in the room. After five years, he would have expected some of these feelings of unease to pass, but they felt as fresh as the first time he had come in here after hearing of their deaths.

Ignoring the desk for the moment, he turned to the cabinet where his father kept his brandy, whiskey, and the occasional bottle of vodka. He opened the cabinet and was glad to find it empty. With the lawsuit looming, and Jessi hours away, he was more than a little tempted to get rip-roaring drunk once in his life. But it would solve nothing. Alexander never liked liquor, preferring instead the subtle flavors of good wine, and never, ever to excess or drunkenness. His brother provided enough of that foolishness for the family.

Pushing the doors closed, he inhaled and steeled himself for the real reason he had come. He needed to find his father's copy of the contract, along with the information he would have gathered on the Vogts. His father had always been thorough and missed little in his business dealings.

Hours later, he was still digging through files when he got the call from Thomas. In surprise, he looked up to see the morning sun rising toward afternoon.

"I've had my team working on this since it was delivered to us, and unfortunately Mr. Vogt has a pretty solid case against you." His tone was firm but surprisingly apologetic. "It appears it was originally filed under the assumption that you would be proposing to Rebekka Wellington."

Alexander gritted his teeth. "If that's the grounds for the suit, he's got nothing, Thomas. You know that."

"You are correct, but his case is not based on a marriage, rather the transfer of assets." Thomas took a deep breath. "Closer to say it is based on preventing a transfer of ownership from taking place. Even without the suspected marriage, your sale attempt is still a transfer of assets."

His nerves were already stretched thin after the last two days, and though he didn't mean to, he snapped at Thomas. "What exactly does that mean?"

"It means, Mr. Vogt signed a contract with your family requiring all Koch and Vogt family assets remain under the control of both heirs as co-owners." Thomas cleared his throat. "The documents are strange, but legally binding."

"What do I need to do? What's the bottom line here?"

"Bottom line? Either stop the sale of the company or convince Marcus Vogt to drop the suit. You and the Vogt heir are co-owners of everything, or you own nothing."

Alexander's breath left him in a hiss. "So, if I sell my shares of the company, I truly forfeit ninety-five percent of everything I own?"

Thomas sighed. "It appears so. I am still going through the details of the original agreement to see if there is something I've missed. I don't know why your father would have agreed to such a thing, but I haven't given up yet."

Alexander stood and walked to a window overlooking the pool behind the house. "I suppose I am safe to guess that I am named as my parents' heir, so who is the other?"

"Her name is Jessalyn Vogt." Thomas's voice slid higher, and Alexander heard more papers rustling. "I think I may have found our defense. Don't know why I didn't think of it before."

Something wedged in the back of Alexander's mind. "I thought his daughter's name was Lyn? And didn't she disappear years ago? I thought Marcus gave up on finding her." *Jessalyn Vogt? Jessi? Couldn't be.*

The phone switched to speaker, and Thomas's secretary spoke up. "He did. That's why he had to wait for you to either attempt to sell or marry." Her voice was clipped. "There is a clause that states the contract would go into effect immediately upon the death of either set of parents. But by that time, the Vogt heir was already missing."

Thomas spoke again. "I might be able to make the argument that since she is missing, she has already forfeited."

Alexander tapped his fingers on the windowsill in front of him. "But if we win, the Vogts lose everything?"

"Pretty much. Yes."

Alexander rubbed his forehead and glanced around. It was almost noon, and he still hadn't found anything in his father's files. "I have a meeting this evening. Keep working on it, and I'll call you in the morning before I leave here."

Alexander arrived a few minutes early and paused to admire what had come to be known as the Compound. It seemed to perch on the side of the mountain. Three rectangles stacked and slightly offset from each other formed the massive main portion of the home. A large deck at the top overlooked the sprawling grounds, and a patio at the bottom was open and accessible from inside the house. One year ago, the huge home was the residence of the Arizona Clan's leader and self-proclaimed Elder.

He was approaching the lower patio when he heard a familiar voice call his name. He turned to see the Locktons side by side at the patio doors, and his heart clenched. The last time he saw them standing at those doors they were on their way inside to complete their bonding.

So many things changed that year, and all of them were still adjusting. It was the year the Arizona Clan, as they had come to be known, discovered they were not alone. Others of their kind from around the world helped overthrow the control of a few bitter and arrogant leaders who were determined to avenge a centuries-old wrong by destroying them all.

Alexander's smile widened. "Leisel. I didn't expect to see you here."

Koen flicked his eyes toward the others gathered inside. "It's a long story."

He turned to her and finally noticed her red-rimmed eyes. "Leisel? What's wrong?"

Koen pulled her close when her chin trembled. He answered for her. "It's worse than we originally thought. The Council is waiting for us. Come on, and we'll explain."

Alexander followed the two of them inside. Across the wide stone floors, his eyes went to the incredible view of the Saddleback Mountains outside. Floor to ceiling glass made up the far wall, providing a completely unobstructed view of the stunning landscape. The room was wide open, and in front of the windows two long tables had been set. Half the chairs were already filled with the rest of the Council. As his gaze traveled down the line of people, his shoulders tensed when he met the challenging stare of Marcus Vogt. Alexander inclined his head and chose an empty seat beside Emerick and Ellen Tate.

Emerick rose. "Alexander, glad you could make it."

"Emerick." Alexander turned to Ellen, who remained seated. He rested a hand on her shoulder, ignoring the familiar tinge of pain. "Ellen. How are you?"

She patted his hand, and though her face indicated she was tired and worried, the twinkle in her eyes was as bright as ever. She winked at him then sobered. "We're glad you're here."

As though his arrival was what they had been waiting for, the rest of the Council found their seats as Emerick addressed them.

"We apologize for the short notice, but circumstances have been brought to our attention that need to be addressed immediately." He looked worn out, and Alexander hoped this would be the last time he would have to lead such a meeting. Feeling the hairs on the back of his neck prickle, he turned and wasn't surprised to find Marcus glaring at him. Ignoring him, Alexander's eyes followed Koen as he came around the table to join Emerick. The whole room stilled.

"Leis and I came to ask for your help." He cleared his throat, and Alexander leaned forward as anger flashed from the young musician's eyes. "As you all know, the previous leadership tried to force

Leis into a bonding with Baden Dietrich, who is in actuality her first cousin." Koen braced his hands on the table, dropping his head. "We got a call two days ago from Leis's brother Josh that her parents turned over the house and everything they owned to the Dietrichs. To Samuel and Res." He lifted his gaze to Alexander. "Leis and her family are penniless because of a contract the Clan has had in place for centuries. As the final heir to the Gottschalk name, Leis broke the contract by refusing to bond to the final Dietrich heir, Baden. Her first cousin! Because she bonded to me..." His voice faltered, and he paused for a moment to gather himself. "She forfeited everything her family owned."

Alexander knew this much and held himself in check, refusing to look at Marcus. Alexander's shame for the way he'd willingly pursued Leisel last year was overridden by anger. Marcus and Res had allowed the challenge to happen, knowing the Kochs and the Gottschalks would lose everything had Alexander gone along with the Clan and agreed to attempt to bond with her. The contracts weren't about money or preserving family lines. They were about power and control.

Koen went on. "My family, my Clam, has never heard of such a thing. They are trying to help us. Leis and I are okay. My recording contract pays us well, but her family has lost everything. Samuel and Res have taken everything, and no one seems to know where they are." He pushed back from the table. Tears fell from Koen's cheeks, but his expression was stony. "Then, this morning we found out Haydn and Stefanie took their own lives." A sob tore from Leisel, and Alexander's head snapped toward her. He pushed his seat back, but Koen was already on his way. He pulled her out of the chair and held her. His eyes raked angrily down the older members of the Council. "I don't know how many more of these contracts are out there, but you need to make sure they are never enforced." His tone hardened further. "We won't be controlled or manipulated. Your *children* are not for sale!"

Marcus stood and held out his hands in a cautionary gesture.

"Let's not be hasty in making that proclamation, Mr. Lockton." Alexander's skin crawled. He dealt with enough shady business deals to recognize a swindler when he heard one. Marcus continued, "What happened to you and your family, Mrs. Lockton, is very unfortunate." He managed to sound sympathetic, but his eyes taunted when they turned to Alexander. "However, the purpose for these contracts, as you call them, can't be ignored." He nodded toward Emerick. "Mr. Tate has done the research, and I'm sure he will agree with what I am about to say."

"Don't be so sure about that, *Mr. Vogt.*" Emerick narrowed his eyes. "But let's hear your version first."

Koen and Leisel were escorted up to one of the balcony rooms. He watched until they were out of sight and then settled his gaze back on the man who stood at the head of the table. Marcus Vogt was a stern man, more so after his daughter disappeared. He never seemed to recover from it.

Though his father struck a deal with the man, until they began serving on the Council together last year, Alexander had never met him. Knowing what he now knew about the contract Marcus and his parents had signed gave insight into the man's madness. The power, wealth, and influence Marcus thought he gained was stripped when the girl disappeared, leaving the Vogts vulnerable.

Alexander inhaled and allowed the lingering tension to seep out of his muscles, unwilling to give Marcus any clue to his intentions. The Gottschalk's dilemma saved him from having to present the issue, and he was interested to hear how this male was going to spin the situation for his benefit.

Marcus cleared his throat and looked apologetically around the table. "Before I say anything else, I would like to be the first to contribute to helping Mrs. Lockton's family get back on their feet. I am willing to donate the first one hundred thousand dollars toward a trust fund."

Murmurs of agreement circled the table, but neither Alexander nor Emerick acknowledged it. Marcus's face tightened, but he showed no other sign he noticed their lack of agreement.

"What brought on their unfortunate circumstances could easily have been avoided had they understood the necessity of the agreement that provoked it." Marcus straightened his shoulders and looked pointedly at the elder members of the Council. "Those of us who have been alive long enough remember how hard our families worked to acquire the wealth the younger generation now have the privilege to enjoy." Alexander's jaw ticked, but he didn't flinch when Marcus swung his gaze to him. "We worked hard to gain and preserve the wealth you inherited. Therefore, it was with *your* best interest in mind that we laid out contracts between the key families of the Clan. All to ensure that hard-earned wealth stays in the hands of those who should inherit it."

Winston Parchell's thick Irish accent spoke up from the far end of the table. "And just who decided who those families should and should not be?"

Many of the other Council members came from Clans that didn't have the means or the wealth of the Arizona clan. Parchell was one of those.

Marcus didn't hesitate. "A council of elders like this one. When our grandparents realized we would not survive forever, it was determined that the wealth should be consolidated so it would sustain us as long as possible."

"Actual events were recorded a little differently, but please—continue to enlighten us." Emerick cut in, his eyes blazing, and Alexander chuckled under his breath.

Marcus raised his hand flippantly. "You must remember, our Clan did not have the luxury of allowing our children to miss a bonding opportunity. Think of it as ensuring the survival of the very best of us."

"With the Vampir reunited, this matters very little, Mr. Vogt." Mr. Parchell spoke again, his lilt stronger as he grew more irritated.

"What are the specifications of the contract, and how do we void them?"

Marcus looked indignant. "Void them?"

Parchell stood. He was several inches taller than Marcus, and Alexander bit back a laugh when Marcus took a step back. Parchell crossed his arms in defiance.

"My only daughter is about to complete her bonding with a young male who has been notified by a family from *your* Clan that he is forbidden to do so because of one of these contracts. My daughter is heartbroken, and they are growing in pain every day we keep them apart. If we go through with the ceremony this weekend, his family will be the next in line asking for a handout from the Council." He leaned forward and braced his hands on the table. "So—I expect you to tell me how to fix this."

Marcus didn't back down. "If the Vampir had been left divided, this would never have happened."

Emerick held out his hand as Parchell began to advance on Marcus. "Sit down, Marcus, before this nonsense goes any further. If we'd left our people divided, we wouldn't survive. Don't be a fool." Marcus took his seat and glared. Parchell stopped but didn't retake his seat. "There *is* a valid reason these contracts came to be, but it had nothing to do with money. As you know, what is now known as the Arizona Clan lived separated from the rest of us for several centuries. Their ancestors quickly realized they would not survive with such a limited genetic pool. The solution was to match the families with the greatest chances of successfully producing children who would be compatible through genetic prediction in order to keep the gene pool as diversified as possible." Emerick glanced at Alexander. "This is where the idea of arranged marriages first appeared. Until Res's remaining family and their supporters vanished into the Austrian mountains, arranged marriages were unheard of. They are unnecessary."

Alexander heard the guilt in Emerick's tone. It was his decision to bond to Ellen, Res's sister, that caused the split in their species.

Though he and Ellen had successfully reunited the Vampir of the world, he still bore the guilt for the chaos he caused.

Emerick cleared his throat. "When I got the call from Koen yesterday, I took it upon myself to search the records kept here in the Compound. I was able to locate the original document, and with the help of Koen's father, we translated it." He reached beside him and lifted several bound books. "There are enough copies here for each member of the Council. I don't want you to take my word for any of this." He slid the documents down the table each way. Once everyone had a copy, he continued. "As you know, most of our early ancestors were nomads spread throughout Europe and northern Asia. They were not able to communicate or gather together easily and written documents were often lost or destroyed. It is amazingly fortunate this one survived. Without it, untangling the legal mess each generation created would be nearly impossible."

He opened the bound sheaf of papers in front of him carefully. "This is a footnote added after the family lines and arranged marriages were assigned." He cleared his throat and read. "Let it be made known that this agreement can and should be dissolved upon the agreement of three or more witnesses when and if it becomes apparent that it is no longer needed for the preservation of our species. It is not our intent to put burdens upon the backs of our children or hinder them from finding the one uniquely created for them. A parent's greatest desire is to see the light of recognition in the eyes of their child when they meet their mate. Neither this document nor any to follow should in any way prevent or hinder the natural instincts of our species. It is only a guide should such action become necessary." He flipped it shut and shoved it toward the center of the table. "Read the rest of it on your own time."

Emerick met each of their gazes in turn. "With the growing number of couples who are finding one another around the world, I would think we can safely believe that the preservation of our species would be better served by allowing our natural instincts to guide us rather than being forced to adhere to an archaic breeding schedule. I motion that the Council void all existing contracts, and provisions be made to prevent any attempt to enforce them. There are far more than three of us here. Are we in agreement that based on what we've just heard, the contracts in question are voided and no longer enforceable?"

Alexander pinned his eyes on Marcus's bright red face. He was unsurprised to see the calculating glint still in the male's eyes.

Alexander folded his hands and leaned forward. "I have legal counsel on retainer who would be more than willing to help us draft any documents necessary."

Emerick nodded. "I appreciate your willingness to offer his services. If everyone is in agreement, we will make certain a new document is drafted and ratified."

After watching every head at the table nod, Alexander drew a relieved breath but felt the burning stare of Marcus. "Is there something you would like to say to me, Mr. Vogt?"

His smile was unexpected, and Alexander's eyes narrowed, taken completely off guard by the man's next statement. "I just wonder how much effort you would have put into this little endeavor if you'd known the truth before you left California." He stood and slid an envelope sharply toward Alexander. "You'll find the information inside that envelope...interesting."

Alexander caught the packet under his palm then shook his head as he watched Marcus leave.

THIRTY-FIVE

Seated at his father's desk, Alexander spread out the contents of the envelope Marcus flung at him earlier. On top of the pile was a photograph of a younger Jessi seated atop a grey horse he recognized as Ulysse. She wore polished knee-high boots, cream breeches, and a black long tailed jacket and top hat. Her tiny hands were encased in white gloves, and her familiar face was spread wide in a proud smile as she patted the prancing horse's shoulder in front of the saddle. A fluttering blue ribbon hung from the horse's bridle.

His stomach flared, remembering the way her lithe body moved while riding, but the next picture chilled his blood. It was Jessi in the same outfit, still mounted on the large animal. However, a familiar man held the horse's reins in one hand and a huge silver trophy in the other. *Marcus Vogt.*

Dropping the pictures as though they burned him, Alexander clenched his fists on the desk before pulling the clip loose and spreading out the rest of the pictures. Two more glossy photographs of Jessi and Marcus at other competitions and equestrian events were followed by images that shredded his heart.

There in front of him, were pictures from the night reporters had shown up at the seafood restaurant. Jessi's dark head was tucked tightly against his chest, and his own eyes glared back at him from the desktop. Underneath those were shots of the two of them leaning on the railing of his yacht. His stomach churned at the image of her sobbing body curled in his lap. Pictures from the coffee house and even the concert followed. But the last set of pictures ignited a rage that scared him.

His hand tightened on the slick image of Ulysse in the arena with Jessi once again astride, his neck stretching forward. Alexander flicked it aside to the next shiny page to see Ulysse's ears pricked up as he caught sight of what Alexander now knew to be the flash of a reflection from a camera lens...Jessi in the air...Alexander hovered over her in the area...

There were more, but he couldn't bear to look. She'd lied to him. Jessi Vogel was Marcus Vogt's missing daughter. Her words and her irrational fear of him suddenly made sense.

"She's not the only one I abandoned, Alexander...I ran from you that night. I left you in your pain. I'm a coward."

With a growl he shoved away from the desk and punched a hole in the wall behind him. When he turned, he noticed a white envelope on the floor next to his chair. Angrily swiping it up, he ripped it open.

Mr. Koch,

I trust you've found the photographs I've collected for you enlightening. Jessalyn stole the horse from me and nearly cost both of us everything. I plan to bring her and the horse home. Once I have sufficiently punished her, I will return her to you. I will leave it up to you if you still wish to claim her.

Marcus Vogt

"Did he ever hit you, Jessi?"
"Twice."

Alexander's fury evaporated. No matter how she had lied to him, Jessi—Jessalyn—was his mate. Fear of what her father might do sent ice through his veins. Glancing at the clock, he cursed and bolted for the door. Marcus had at least a two-hour head start. He couldn't let Marcus reach the barn first.

Mindful of traffic, Alexander pushed the SUV to its limits knowing he had no time to waste.

The barn was quiet, and Jessi soaked in the familiar sounds of shuffling hooves and the soft rustling of tails against bodies. She hadn't been lying when she told Alexander she would miss him. Their separation had brought the pain back, and she was anxious to tell him the truth. The lies weighed heavy on her, and she was ready to put it all behind them. He would be hurt and angry, but they would work it out. He was her intended, the one she was created for, and her body ached to finally be bonded to him. A thrill of excitement rushed through her at the thought of kissing him. Jessi's whole body warmed, wondering what he would taste like, and what it would feel like to lie in his skilled arms.

She passed the feed room and smiled. Fresh barrels of grain had been delivered earlier this afternoon, and the smell of sweet molasses and oats filled her nostrils. She slowed her steps to savor it.

Humming to herself, she rounded the corner. Dennis's quiet laugh, followed by another man's voice, surprised her. She had hoped to be alone.

"Dennis, you're here early. Is everything okay?" she called. His back was to her while he looked into Ulysse's stall. He turned with a smile.

"It couldn't be better." He pointed toward one of his stalls. "I think I sold Dexter." He frowned apologetically. "I left the trailer at the door again, didn't I? We were planning to load him up."

"It's fine." She stopped in front of him and peered over the wall into her horse's stall. A gentleman in dress pants and a dark blue oxford was examining Ulysse. The sight of him chilled her.

She tried to force nonchalance into her tone and automatically suppressed her echo. "Who's this?"

"The man who's buying Dexter." Dennis cleared his throat, and terror washed over her as she recognized the dangerous edge of her father's scent. "Jessi, I'd like to introduce you to Marcus Vogt."

She instinctively lowered her gaze but not before she glimpsed the barely contained fury in her father's eyes. Dennis shut the tall sliding door, oblivious to the danger.

Picking up on the tension, Armani banged a hoof against his door, and they all jumped. Her father laughed.

"Jessi *Vogel*, is it? Is this your horse?" His eyes bored into her, and she inched backwards.

"Please don't do this." She held out a hand and took another step back. He was in front of her in seconds.

"Clever name change. But it's not your horse is it, *Lyn?* It's mine. You stole him from me." He gripped her arm, but she jerked free. "Your little stunt could have cost us everything. Everything!"

Dennis stepped between them. "You know each other?"

Jessi looked desperately for a way out, but she was at the end of the aisle and both the men blocked her way. Her father grinned.

"Quite well in fact." Turning from her for a moment, he smiled at Dennis. "Thank you for helping me find my long-lost daughter."

Dennis's wide eyes connected with Jessi's. "What?"

"It's a long story." Her gaze swung back to her father, her whole body shaking as she inched away from his advance. "Just take the horse and go. He's what you came for isn't he?"

Ignoring her comment, her father stepped toward her. "Dennis, would you give us a moment?"

The barn owner positioned himself in front of her father. "I don't know what's going on, but I get the impression she doesn't want to be alone with you." Dennis rested a hand on her father's chest. "Not a step closer, Mr. Vogt."

Jessi's heart clawed at her throat, and she tried to drag in a deep breath. She wanted to plead with Dennis to leave, but no sound came out.

"No one comes between me and my daughter." Her father's lethal gaze moved from where Dennis's hand pressed inches below the collar of his shirt to his face. Before she could react, a fist connected with Dennis's jaw, snapping his head back. "I'd advise you not to touch me again."

He resumed his advance, and she flattened herself against the wall.

"Leave her alone!" Dennis wiped the blood from his lip and grabbed a handful of her father's shirt. Spinning him around, he wound up to throw a punch.

Her father blocked his swing and sank a fist into Dennis's stomach. Jessi's hands flew to her mouth when her friend doubled over with a groan. Then her body jerked in horror as her father brought his knee up into Dennis face with a sickening crunch. Jessi screamed his name as he crumpled to the ground and didn't move.

"I warned him." A large hand latched onto her arm, and her father hauled her forward. "We're done here. Let's go, Jessalyn."

Jessi stumbled but couldn't drag her eyes away from Dennis lying face down on the concrete. When she saw the spreading blood under his cheek, something in her snapped.

The palm of her hand cracked across her father's face, and she twisted her other arm, expecting him to let go. Instead, his fingers dug brutally into the back of her arm, making her cry out as the pain forced her to her knees. When he backhanded her, she caught a glimpse of Alexander's murderous green eyes just before the world went black.

Shouts penetrated the fog and Jessi rolled over to see Alexander and her father squared off, fists raised. Her mouth tasted coppery, and her jaw ached. Alexander's lip dripped blood. Deliberately, he wiped it away and glanced down at her before locking his eyes back on her father.

"You drew my blood. And hers. That was a mistake." Alexander's voice was deadly calm, and his scent burned in her nostrils.

Jessi stared. Alexander's crisp white shirt was sprinkled with scarlet dots across his right shoulder. He stood with his feet braced, hands fisted at chest height. He exuded strength and confidence, but what she saw in his eyes stopped her heart. The compassion she'd grown used to seeing in the green depths was gone. Alexander was prepared to kill. This was not the man she had fallen in love with. This was the man she feared.

Sweat trickled down her back as Alexander's pain and rage scorched her from the inside out.

Tearing her eyes from Alexander, she spotted Dennis on the ground a few feet away. She should run to get help, but his still form chilled her. She had to know if he was alive. Inching toward him, her foot brushed a shovel, and it clattered to the ground. When Alexander's attention shifted to her, her father took advantage by plowing a foot into his stomach.

"Alexander!" She scrambled to her feet and grabbed the first thing that came to hand, but before she could swing the broom, Alexander flipped her father onto his back.

"Get out of here, Jessalyn!" he roared.

Hearing her full name from Alexander's lips was like a bucket of cold water to the chest. Time froze as his lethal stare bored into her. Alongside the fury darkening his eyes, she read the betrayal in his face, and her body went numb.

He knows.

There was a scraping sound, and then Alexander landed on his hands and knees with a grunt. Jessi heard a scream before realizing it was her own voice. Her father was on one knee poised to deliver another blow of the shovel to Alexander's back.

"No!" Jolted back to motion, Jessi stumbled and crashed into a stall door.

Alexander rolled out of the way and onto his feet with incredible speed, positioning himself between her and her father.

"I told you to get out of here!" he snarled. Alexander didn't take his eyes off her father as he shoved her roughly toward the exit.

Jessi staggered, then hesitated. "Dennis..."

"Get out!" Alexander bellowed, and then blocked her father's swing, catching his arm and shoving him face first against the wall. She grimaced when Alexander twisted her father's arm behind him, making him cry out. Alexander rested his weight against him.

"Go to the yacht, and call Peter to come get Marcus." He threw her his phone. "Now, Jessalyn!"

There was no softness in his tone or his scent, and Jessi didn't argue. She turned and ran.

THIRTY-SEVEN

"Yes, run, Jessalyn! That's your answer to everything!" Marcus called after her.

Alexander pulled him back and slammed him against the wall. "Shut up!"

Marcus grunted then sneered, "You'll need this anger to control that little brat. She's just like her mother."

Alexander flipped him around and braced a forearm across Marcus's neck. Fury simmered under his skin, and he leaned forward, wanting to cut off Marcus's air. Pressing his face a breath away from Marcus's, he growled through clenched teeth, "I said. Shut. Up."

This man was responsible for the nightmare Jessalyn lived in. Alexander hadn't missed the terror in her face. It was the same look in her eyes, the same fear in her echo as the first day he walked into the coffee shop.

Marcus's face began to purple, and he eased the pressure. "I'm going to check on Dennis, and you are not going to move." Alexander slid his arm lower, and Marcus coughed. Kicking the shovel out of reach, he stepped back, keeping a hand on Marcus's chest. "Sit."

Marcus sank to the ground, and Alexander took a step back to check on Dennis. With one eye on Marcus, Alexander knelt and pressed a finger to the other man's neck. He had a steady pulse and was breathing. He moved him to his back and tilted his head back to allow him a better airway as Marcus rolled to his feet and tried to run.

Alexander roared and launched himself forward. Marcus whirled around just as Alexander tackled him to the ground. The sound of his fists meeting flesh faded and time stopped as his knuckles connected over and over again with Marcus's head. Out of his mind with rage, Alexander fought and kicked when someone yanked him backwards.

"Alexander! Stop!" Peter's hands shoved him until his shoulders crashed against a stall door. The horse inside reared in surprise and slammed its hooves into the wall. "You can't kill him! Stop!" Peter planted a hand on his heaving chest, and he finally trained his eyes on his mentor. Alexander's vision was white with pain, but he fought it back.

"I will kill him," he ground out. Fury prevented him from keeping his focus on the man in front of him. "He hit her right in front of me, Peter!"

Alexander tried to push past his friend but suddenly found himself face down on the concrete with his arm twisted behind him. Added to the pain he was already in, he almost lost consciousness, but he pushed the blackness away.

Peter balanced on a knee in the middle of his back and leaned forward to growl in Alexander's ear. "If you kill him, her mother will die. *Think*, Alexander."

Alexander rested his face on the cool surface beneath him and relaxed fractionally. "Let me up." Peter held his arm as he rolled to the side and twisted to a sitting position. Nearly blinded by pain, he closed his eyes, he fought to stay alert. When he reopened them, Dennis was propped against the wall opposite him, blood drying on his face.

"Where is Jessalyn?" Alexander rasped.

Peter glanced up. "She's on her way to the yacht. I passed her truck on the way in."

Alexander jumped to his feet then staggered. "I have to go after her." His vision blanked out with agony. Peter caught him and lowered him back to the ground.

"You're not going anywhere, my friend." He looked up as Hannah approached. Alexander tried to stand again, but Peter pushed him back with a firm hand on his shoulder. "You won't do anyone any good until you get a handle on yourself." Alexander fell back against the wall with his knees bent and his forearms resting atop them. Every muscle in his body spasmed with agony and his head felt ready to explode.

The adrenaline jacking through his system set his nerve endings on fire while the rage pounding through his veins carried the inferno into every inch of him. The panic he'd seen in Jessalyn's eyes bit hard into his wildly beating heart, making his chest seize with frustration and fear. She'd seen the murder in his eyes. It would be a miracle if she ever trusted him again.

Hannah handed him a bottle of water, but his hands were shaking so badly he could hardly get the cap off. Peter and Hannah waited until he had taken a few swallows and the shaking subsided. They all turned as Dennis stirred against the other wall.

Hannah crouched beside him. "Can you tell us what happened?"

His glazed eyes drifted from her to Peter then to Alexander who was collapsed across from him. When his gaze finally landed on Marcus's still body, Dennis leaned to the side and retched. Hannah waited until he was finished then handed him another bottle of water. He took it and averted his eyes from the prone form lying a few feet away. He swallowed thickly and then cleared his throat while staring at the floor.

"Marcus came by to look at my horses. Said he wanted to buy one of them." His eyes slid to Alexander and blanched at the bleeding hands clenched around the water bottle. "He saw Ulysse and claimed the horse had been stolen from him." His voice faltered as he drew a ragged breath. "Then Jessi showed up. Marcus said she was his daughter..." He wiped the back of his hand across his face. Seeing blood, he turned and emptied his stomach again. When he regained himself, he glanced at Hannah still crouched in front of him. "Is he...dead?"

"No," Peter said. "He'll live."

"Where's Jessi?" Dennis asked.

Alexander slammed his head into the wall behind him, earning another kick from the horse inside and a shock wave of pain that lanced his spine. "She's safe."

Hannah rose and gestured to Marcus. "Let's get him to the house and call...his wife." She grimaced at Dennis. "Will you be all right?"

He rubbed the back of his head. "I think so." He turned green again when he pushed to his knees. "Should I call the police?"

"No!" All of them answered at once.

Alexander glared. "Do not call the police. There's no need to get them involved. This is a family matter. Understand?" Mutely, Dennis nodded.

Peter lifted Marcus and tossed him over his shoulder. "Hannah, you drive Alexander. Get him to the yacht and stay with them until I get there. I'll take Marcus's car and get him...settled at our house."

THIRTY-EIGHT

The waves of a passing boat lapped against the yacht's hull as Jessi's eyes skimmed the horizon. The breeze coming off the water pushed the hair back from her face as she waited for Alexander to arrive. She barely remembered the drive, making several wrong turns before finding the entrance. Alexander's car got her through security, and she was thankful the captain had recognized her and let her aboard. The man's eyes immediately fell to the spreading bruise on her cheek.

"I'm okay, Captain. Alexander will be here soon." She held up a hand when anger flared his nostrils, though the thought of his arrival made her shake inside.

He nodded slightly. "I expect he will, Miss Vogel. May I offer you some ice while we wait for Mr. Koch?"

Tears burned her eyes. "Thank you."

Muttering, he turned away and disappeared below deck. She gazed up at the overcast sky and blinked back tears. Alexander knew the truth, and she could only imagine how hurt he must be. This wasn't how she wanted him to find out, but she should have known he would. The moment he told her he was going to Arizona, she should have insisted on going with him.

Her father was cruel, and she knew he would take the opportunity to make Alexander hate her. Why did she ever think she could hide this? Her father sat on the Council with Alexander! They were bound to put two and two together. Gingerly, she touched her bruised chin and resigned herself to whatever happened next.

At the sound of familiar footsteps, her breath caught, and her gaze snapped back to the door the captain had gone through. It was not the kind mariner, but Alexander himself who stood holding a towel wrapped around a small bag of ice.

Warily, she watched him approach. He had changed to a clean shirt and jeans, but he didn't meet her eyes, staring instead at her swollen cheek. His large hands were gentle as he cupped her jaw and rested the cool pack against the opposite cheek. Though he was careful, fury churned beneath the surface of his stiff facade, and his pain levels were off the charts.

"I'm sorry I didn't get there sooner, Jessalyn." His eyes flashed across hers before returning to the ice pack. "Marcus is in the Clan's custody. He can't hurt you anymore. You're safe now."

The chasm between the frustration in his voice and the tenderness of his touch shook her. He was seething and the violence she scented from him earlier had not diminished. She reached up to hold onto his forearm, and he jerked back, letting the bag land between them with a wet slap. She flinched and bit her lip, watching emotions she couldn't begin to fathom chase themselves across his features.

He exhaled and met her gaze, but his green eyes were flat and angry. "Are you all right?"

"I'm okay. Alexander, I..."

"Let's go below deck." He stepped to the side, retrieving the ice pack before allowing her to precede him down the steps. His body language was stiff, and she shivered at the barely restrained brutality emanating from him. She dropped her gaze to his torn and bleeding hands as they flexed at his sides. A muscle jerked in his neck, and he took a step toward her. She froze until his hand landed on the small of her back, and he gently guided her toward the stairs. "We need to talk, Jessalyn. My wounds can wait."

The way he said the last splintered her heart. It was more than flesh and bone he was referring to. His scent was raw and biting in her nostrils. They descended the stairs to the open deck where they had fought the last time, and she had a sudden desire to sink this boat for good. She walked to the same spot on the railing and leaned her palms against the cool wood, trying to gather her thoughts. Alexander waited silently behind her until she couldn't put it off any longer.

She choked back her fear. "My name isn't Jessi Vogel." He inhaled and shifted his feet but didn't come any closer. Arching pain blossomed between them, stealing her breath and forcing her to pause. Tears slid down her cheeks and dripped from her chin onto the railing. She tried to form words, but needles clenched her throat. All she could manage was a ragged breath before she felt him move.

His hands landed on either side of her, and his breath fanned the back of her head. She wanted to lean into him and relieve their pain, but after the way he jerked away from her attempt to touch him, she resisted. His fingers gripped the rail tighter and tighter as he pushed the pain back until she was able to speak again.

"It's Jessalyn. Jessalyn Vogt. Marcus is my father, Alexander."

Anger, disbelief, betrayal, and doubt played in the wind that blew around them as he processed her words. He never moved, and her eyes stayed fixed on his hands, expecting at any moment he would jerk her around and take what belonged to him.

She wouldn't fight him.

"Tell me why you ran." His voice was steely hard, and she gulped at the fury behind it.

With barely a whisper she said, "I ran because he hit us, Alexander. He hit me and my mother."

Impatience coursed through him, nearly causing her to jump the railing and take her chances with the water. As if he knew that was her plan, his hands slid closer until his ragged voice was against her ear. "You've already told me that. I want to know why you ran from *me*."

"Because from the first time I scented you, I knew we were intended for each other." She licked her lips and tasted the salt of her tears. His confusion deepened as she continued. "But I heard you arguing with your father about the human women you wanted instead of a mate. Instead of me. You sent me away." Her voice fell. He backed away, and she shut her eyes as his pain ratcheted up again. "I didn't know what you would do when you came home. All I knew was you were angry, in pain, and violent, just...just like my father."

His breathing was shallow, and the sharpness of clove completely overrode her senses. Disbelief washed all the anger out of him. "You were there... That was you I sent away?"

"Yes!" She turned to face him. "From the moment I entered your house, I felt your pain. I didn't know why, and no one gave me any explanation." Jessi's fear roared into anger. "But even scared as I was, I couldn't stay away. I tried coming back. I wanted to believe you were different, until I was at your parents' funeral. I saw you punch your brother so hard he left his feet!" Realization dawned on him, and his bright eyes widened at the mention of his brother. "You were so angry and completely against being bonded. I was terrified of you! I ran because I couldn't stand the thought of being bonded to someone just like my father."

Alexander turned away and gripped the back of his neck. "You weren't running from your father at all. You were running from me."

"Yes." She clutched her stomach, feeling as though her insides were being cut out. The current of scorching pain arched between them like lightning, and she gasped. "I know I was selfish. I didn't know your anger was because of the pain you live with. I abandoned you because I was too scared to get close enough to learn the truth about you."

He rolled his shoulders and dropped his hands. "Is that what your confessions have been about? You think you abandoned me, and now you feel responsible to...what? Accept your fate?"

"You have every right to be angry, Alexander." His chin was down, and she couldn't see his eyes. "I've been selfish, and I lied to you. I was willing to let you suffer." She squeezed her eyes shut. "Without - "

"Stop." Suddenly, he was in front of her and she flinched back against the railing. "Stop. Talking."

Alexander straightened, and she anticipated any moment he would seize her and take what he needed. She knew when his lips touched hers her body would surrender. It's the way they were created. He needed her, and though it had taken her five years to realize it, she desperately needed him.

His chest was inches from her, and his Adam's apple bobbed as he swallowed hard. When her gaze crossed his hard-pressed lips and met his stare, she was shocked breathless at the betrayal in his eyes. His control was still dangerously brittle.

His stance softened, and his hand grasped around her waist. She tried to compose herself, anxious to taste him, ready to give herself to him. For a moment his thumb slid back and forth just under her rib cage before both hands were on her waist, lifting her.

In shock, she gripped his forearms, and a tiny shriek escaping her before he set her feet on the stairs. Once she caught her balance, he let go and braced his hands on the railing to either side of her. Jerking her hands back, she realized he had placed her several steps up, so they were at eye level. Her hands tightened into fists and slowly lowered as she watched his face.

He searched her eyes and then dropped his head. His hands flexed on the railings. Indecision rolled through him, and he moved away. Her heart accelerated when his gaze slid back to hers.

"Alexander?"

"The choice has always been yours." He shoved his hands into his pockets. "I've done everything I know how to prove that to you. I've never pressured you, never tried to force you into anything." He huffed and shook his head. "I don't know how to be subtle, and I'm almost always over the top, but I've tried to make it clear the ball is in your court." There wasn't a shred of emotion left on his face. "If you want to be freed from the pledge, consider it loosed."

His words hit her like a punch to the gut. "What?"

"Your father can't hurt you anymore. It's safe for you to go home." A twinge of doubt flickered in his eyes. It came and went so quickly she was sure she'd mistaken it. "I'm setting you free, *Miss Vogt*. Isn't that what you wanted?"

"All I wanted was my own life. To make my own decisions." Her whispered words fell, and a solid wall leapt up between them.

"Then go."

"No. That's not what I meant!" Jessi's heart shattered and it felt like the jagged pieces of it lodged in her echo. She knew he would hear the anguish in her tone, but she needed him to hear the words. "I don't want to be freed from you, Alexander." She took a step down and toward him. He followed her every move through narrowed eyes. "I came here to willingly offer myself to you."

Alexander tried to distance himself from his anger, but her words only reinforced it, and he needed time to cool off.

"That's not how it works. As a Vampir, you should know that." His hands twitched with the desire to hit something. He needed space to think, and time calm down. "You don't respect me, Jessalyn. You feel sorry for me. *That's* why you're here." He dared her to argue. "The last thing I want is pity. I don't accept it from anyone else, and I am certainly not going to accept it from you." He took a step back and reached for the handle to the interior cabin. "The best thing you can do right now is go home. Your mother needs you. You and I..." He wanted to tell her he loved her but now was not the time. His eyes skimmed her tear-stained face, letting his gaze linger on her swollen lip. "We'll work this out, Jessalyn. Just...not tonight."

The heavy wooden door sealed shut between them, and it took every ounce of his strength to peel his fingers from the handle. Though the individual fibers of his muscles burned with pain, he refused to acknowledge it. His back remained to the tinted glass; his eyes locked on the reflection of the window across from him. Jessi— *Jessalyn*—he corrected himself, stared at the door before turning slowly and climbing the stairs that would lead her off his yacht and back to the pier.

Go get her, Alexander. The warning screamed in his mind, but he pushed it away. Once her feet disappeared from sight, he allowed his focus to drift from the mirror to the couple seated on the sectional below it.

"Are you sure that was the right thing, Alexander?" Peter sat forward, hands clasped between his knees.

"Don't." He stalked across the room and poured himself a rare shot of whiskey. He downed the amber liquid and slammed the glass onto the bar. "Marcus can't hurt her anymore. She's safe. That's all that matters. She and I will work it out, but I can't deal with her lies right now."

He rolled his neck and wished the yacht had a heavy bag installed. Though he had more than enough alcohol onboard to get himself past the point of caring, crashing his fists into something until he passed out from exhaustion sounded like a better idea.

"Alexander." Hannah paused when his angry glare snapped to her, but she didn't back down. She measured her words carefully. "What you said was one hundred percent true, but it was also one hundred percent wrong." He crossed his arms and waited.

Hannah matched his stance. "She does feel sorry for you." His eyes shot to the ceiling. "But she also loves you enough that she's willing to live in fear for the rest of her life."

"She doesn't love me. You can't love someone you're afraid of." He retorted. "And I've never given her a reason to be afraid of me!" He took a menacing step toward her, making Peter rise from the couch.

Hannah's gaze never flinched. "We all know you would never hurt her. The problem is that an abused woman doesn't see life that way. You know that. How many women have we seen come through our training? Even being able to defend themselves doesn't always take the fear away." She searched his face. "I don't care how our species is made. You can't expect little more than a week with you to override a lifetime of living in fear! You're too close to her to see clearly, my friend. She's convinced you're going to snap like her father did, and the way you're acting right now, I'm inclined to agree with her." She shook her head. "You two truly are like matches and gunpowder and you'd both rather burn the world down than give in. You need to get a grip on yourself, and then you need to go apologize. If she's still willing to live with your arrogant butt, you better take advantage."

Peter wrapped his arm around her shoulders, smoothly positioning himself between them. "For what it's worth, I personally believe she respects the hell out of you, Alexander. She doesn't know the pledge is no longer in effect. She had no reason to face her fear other than wanting to be honest with you. You don't do that for someone you don't respect. And you can't love someone you don't respect."

Clearly outnumbered and unable to refute their arguments, Alexander growled. "Fine." He pulled the tie from around his neck and unbuttoned the top of his shirt. "I'll talk to her, but I'm going to the gym first. Lock up when you leave."

FORTY

JESSI

J essi drove Alexander's car back to the barn and stumbled to the truck, fumbling her way inside, tears blurring everything in sight. When she closed the door behind her, the smell of the sweet orange and bergamot of Alexander's blood doubled her over, and she pressed her forehead against the steering wheel. His words knifed through her again.

"The best thing you can do right now is go home. Your mother needs you."

He didn't need her, and after her confession, she was sure he didn't want her either. He was a good man, a man who deserved a woman who wouldn't lie to him. He had spent incredible amounts of money and time trying to convince her to trust him, showing her how different he was despite his ridiculous wealth. He proved over and over again he cared more about others than himself. In all that, she'd done nothing but lie.

She started the truck and backed out. A flicker of light from a passing car glanced off the pendant hanging from the rear-view mirror.

"Every time you look at this pendant, I want you to remember that as

long as our hearts beat, there is hope for us." Was there hope for them? She didn't have an answer anymore. *"I don't know what you are hoping for, but my new hope is that whatever it is, you will find it in me. With me."*

What was she hoping for? Could she dare to hope Alexander would ever want her again? Streetlights nearly blinded her as she drove away from the barn. She wasn't ready to go home, didn't even know where home was anymore.

Paying little attention to the road, Jessi drove mindlessly toward the coffee shop. When she entered the main seating area, Brandon hurried over.

"What's the matter, Jess? Everything okay?" He eyed her bruised face. "Did that horse finally get you?"

Covering the bruise with her hand, she lowered her eyes and nodded. "Yeah. He didn't mean it though." Her eyes strayed to the table beside the register where Alexander had taken up residence in her life. "Brandon, when did these get here?"

"Just before you did." He shrugged. "Late for a delivery, but Alexander seems to get whatever he wants."

Her legs trembled as she made her way to the table. The stargazers Alexander brought daily were fresh and as beautiful as ever. Jessi stared at the tall pick in the center of the new arrangement. Alexander's precise handwriting brought tears to her eyes.

MY JESSI,

I AM LOOKING FORWARD TO OUR TRIP TO NEW YORK.

I KNOW YOU WILL LOOK STUNNING IN THE CREAM GOWN.

I LOVE YOU.

ALEXANDER

The tears ran down her face at his confession of love. After tonight, did he still mean it?

"Brandon?" Her voice shook, but she gathered herself and was able to meet his curious eyes with a smile. "I actually stopped by to tell you I need to take some time off." She cleared her throat. "Alexander wants to take me out of town."

"Are you sure? You don't seem like the type for that sort of thing."

She laughed what she hoped was an embarrassed laugh and not a choked cry. "I'm not." She dropped her eyes and shrugged. "We'll be traveling with friends."

"How long will you be gone?"

"Ten days?" She tried to keep her voice from rising. "I think we'll be back by then."

Brandon's face shifted before he broke out into a wide grin. "Well, be sure I'm the first one to see the ring he gives you." He waved her off. "When will your vacation start?"

Breathing a sigh of relief, she replied apologetically. "Tomorrow?"

He hefted a bag of fresh beans to the counter. "Sure. Just be sensible."

Jessi blushed and headed toward the back door. "Thank you."

The rear parking lot butted up to a local fast-food restaurant, and she was thankful it was well lit; otherwise, she would have bolted back inside at the sight of a strange person leaning against her truck. As she neared the truck, she realized it was a woman, and a gasp escaped when she saw it was Rebekka.

"Hello, Jessalyn." The tall woman was in an expensive pantsuit, and her perfectly manicured hands held a sheaf of papers.

"What are you doing here?" Jessi refused to let the shock show on her face.

A tight smile thinned the woman's lips. "And *you* are Jessalyn Vogt, correct?"

Unsure where this was going, Jessi crossed her arms. "What makes you think so?"

Rebekka extended the documents to her. "Because if you are, you might want to know what your continued association with Mr. Koch will cost him."

Jessi recoiled. "How could my relationship with him cost him anything?"

Rebekka tilted her head in mock sympathy. "He didn't tell you about the prenuptials?"

Jessi felt like she'd been punched in the stomach. "Prenuptials? That's not possible."

"Oh, it's very possible." Rebekka extended the papers again, and Jessi took them. "Your little attempt to disguise your identity wouldn't have worked." She glanced at the cover page. All three of their names stood side by side as parties to the agreement. "You see, Ms. Vogt, according to section 5, paragraph 3a your reappearance is too late." Jessi was speechless as Rebekka turned back to the Lexus parked across the street. Every click of her heels on the pavement was like a gunshot to her heart.

All sound faded away as Jessi stood staring at the papers in her hands. Alexander's words slammed through her. "*She expected me to marry her.*" The pages felt like sandpaper as she turned to the section she indicated, all along the way seeing lists of assets, dates, and both Alexander and Rebekka's names on every page. Her hands shook when she found the section. She skimmed to the paragraph that said 3a.

Baring death, Should either party break this agreement for any reason, the offended party will receive no less than ninety-five percent of all assets.

Bile rose in Jessi's throat at the numbers. She coursed back through the pages, unable to grasp the numbers in front of her. The totals were in the billions. She tried to refocus on the original dates. The form was signed, notarized, and filed in the Phoenix courts four years ago. The year before his parents died. The year he sent her away.

Alexander mentioned a lawsuit that was forcing him to halt the sale of the company, but he didn't tell her why or what the suit was about. Her mind flew back to the night at the seafood restaurant. Rebekka had insinuated then that Jessi was the reason he was selling.

He meant what he said earlier. *"I'm setting you free, Miss Vogt. Isn't that what you wanted?"* He was the one who wanted to be free. He didn't want her. He wanted Rebekka and Jessi's lies gave him the perfect reason to reject her.

Clenching the papers in her hand, Jessi climbed in the truck. Alexander wanted her to believe he loved her. But genetics and lust couldn't change facts. If he had cared enough about this woman to sign such a detailed prenuptial agreement, then Jessi needed to get out of the way.

FORTY-ONE

ALEXANDER

Alexander unlocked the gym's back door, the sound of his gym bag hitting the floor echoing through the space. Slapping his palm onto the light switch, he inhaled the familiar musty smell of leather and sweat. As the lights warmed up, he snagged a roll of tape from the shelf next to the row of heavy bags and sloppily taped his hands. Using his teeth, he tore the tape and set it back where it belonged. The hollow sound of his footsteps was quickly absorbed by the mats under his shoes as he crossed to the line of waiting heavy bags. Not bothering to warm up or stretch, he coiled his arm and lashed out at the black mass.

Time and surroundings disappeared as Alexander loosed all his frustration and pain into his workout. Hours went by as sweat pooled on the floor around him. He yanked his shirt off and tossed it aside, letting the air cool his burning skin. Normally his only goal was to physically exhaust himself, but tonight his punches and kicks vented the rage Marcus Vogt stirred inside him. Every time his fist slammed into the bag, he saw Jessalyn's father getting what he deserved. Even knowing the man was in custody and unable to hurt anyone ever again didn't make him feel better.

He also couldn't believe the Clan wasn't able to stop Res and Samuel from stripping Leisel's family of every possession they owned. He offered to buy back her family home, but Leisel insisted they didn't need anything. She was hurt much more by the emotional trauma of losing her parents than the loss of stuff. How many other families had lost everything before the practice was stopped? His anger raged again, and he pounded that frustration away.

Jessalyn's face flashed in front of him, and he paused, gasping for breath. He was wrong to push her away, but the events of the last few days were more than he knew what to do with. Wiping the rivulets of salty sweat from his face, he rang out the hair dripping down his back in a towel then dropped it to the floor beside his shirt.

He stepped back to swipe the sweat from his face and realized he needed to retape his hands. Flexing his poorly taped fingers, he picked the towel back off the floor and mopped his face.

As he peeled the tape from his hands, his already torn knuckles began to bleed. They had taken the brunt of his anger and frustration. *Just like Jessalyn's heart took the brunt of your stupidity.* He swallowed the regret threatening to overwhelm him and stalked toward his bag. He was nearly finished when he heard Peter's footsteps.

"Give me another hour, Peter, and I'll go talk to her." His voice was rough. "If I go now I'll..."

"Do what you should have done earlier and admit you love her?" Alexander turned to see his mentor leaning against a pole. His eyes raked up and down Alexander's nearly exhausted body disapprovingly. "You can't keep coming here to hide. She's crushed, and she needs to know what you're going to do. She needs to know how you feel."

A hot breath of air escaped his nose, and he took a step toward the other man. "You *know* me, Peter. How gentle do you really think I would be with her feelings right now?" Peter's eyes were as hard and unyielding as his own. "Jessalyn *lied* to me. Marcus could have killed her. *And* I just found out a dear friend of mine lost everything." He turned and tossed the roll of tape aside. "As if that isn't enough, I am expected to be in New York tomorrow evening for a week of meetings, and I have a speech to deliver for this year's Gathering. Now is not a good time for me to have a conversation about feelings with anyone."

He felt Peter move, and his body reacted. Though Peter intended to land a kick to Alexander's ribs, the larger man found himself on his back with a very angry Alexander atop him.

"I *said* I'm not ready to talk." Fisting Peter's shirt in his hand, Alexander hauled him to his feet and pushed his nose nearly against his. "You're not helping." He shoved his mentor backwards and dared him to try again.

Glaring, Peter turned on his heel and left. Alexander's eyes dropped to the floor, his chest heaving in frustration. He hadn't been this angry in a very long time, and if he didn't get a hold of himself, Jessalyn would be the one who suffered the consequences.

J essi left the papers Rebekka gave her on the bed and gathered the few things she planned to take home with her. She pulled the suitcase from underneath the bed, quickly packed, and zipped it closed.

The sun was setting, and she could see the colorful glow at the edge of the window. It would have been a perfect night to sit behind the barn and enjoy the view. Remembering the night she'd fallen asleep in Alexander's arms, tears filled her eyes, but she shook them off, knowing what she had to do.

She had read the legal papers over and over. The thought of Alexander marrying Rebekka tore through her. Squeezing her eyes shut against the images playing out in her mind, she reminded herself that's what he wanted, and she couldn't stop him.

As she moved her bags to the living room and tucked a few final items away, her phone chimed with Hannah's reply to her earlier text.

> J - Alexander won't answer my calls. I need
> to talk to him.

H - He's at the gym.

J - Thank you.

Tucking her cell into her pocket, Jessi pulled the suitcase to the door and took one last look around. The room seemed to be begging her to stay, and for a moment, she considered calling Hannah back to tell her she knew the whole truth about Rebekka. Instead, she glanced at the document laying on the bed and knew they would figure it out.

Resolutely, she pulled the door closed and hefted the suitcase into the bed of the truck. Jessi ran her hand along the bed rail and her knees buckled at the memory of the new rig parked in front of Alexander's house. She resented Alexander then, but now the truck might be the only piece of him she would get to keep.

He was only with her because of what they were. Even if he thought it was more, the feelings would fade in time. Her mother hadn't been strong enough to leave her father, and Jessi refused to make the same mistake. Once she was gone, he could finally be with Rebekka. The elegant businesswoman was a perfect fit for him.

The only thing left to solve was the pain and then Jessi could walk away.

Nervous anticipation wracked her body as she punched the address listed on Peter's website into her GPS. The street entrance was well-marked, but she was sure the front door would be locked. Jessi drove around to an alley at the back. The only vehicle in the lot was a silver Range Rover that had to be Alexander's.

She was about to step out of the car when Peter burst through the back door. His hair was disheveled, and his t-shirt lay twisted askew, looking like he just lost the title round of a fight. He didn't look up as he stalked away in the opposite direction. She watched the door swing shut and hoped it was unlocked.

Climbing down from the truck and drawing a deep breath, glanced around to make sure Peter was gone then reached for the door and slipped inside. Her nose wrinkled at the pungent smell of sweat, musty floors, and the sharp bite of Alexander's clove. Following the unmistakable sound of fists against leather, made her way through the dark space. Jessi flinched when a particularly hard impact sent something crashing to the floor. Alexander's deep voice let roar a stream of German curse words that would peel paint.

She crept forward and peered over the corner of a roped boxing ring. A set of three chains dangled above Alexander. His hands were clenched behind his head; his knuckles wrapped in blue tape that stood out vividly against his soaked red hair. His head was thrown back, and the ponytail that hung down the center of his spine dripped sweat. Inching forward, she was confronted with all six and a half feet of him in a pair of black satin shorts and nothing else.

The dim lighting far above cast shadows down his back, and every contour of his ripped body stood out in sharp relief. She watched in fascination as the muscles slipped and slid under his glistening skin. There wasn't an ounce of fat on his perfectly sculpted body, and his broad back was ripple after ripple of chiseled perfection that would make an anatomy chart look like a child's drawing. She had seen photoshopped ads trying to sell supplements and health club memberships, but Alexander, with his incredible physique, was five feet away in living breathing color. He stood a moment longer then lowered his arms, cracked his neck, and rolled his shoulders back. He stepped even closer to square up with the next bag in line, and she involuntarily gasped as the reality of his massive size and strength sank in.

"Gym's closed," he gritted out and stepped toward a bench to swipe a towel from the surface. Alexander glanced over his shoulder, but she knew she was hidden deep in the shadows.

Unable to tear her eyes from the fluid grace of his every movement, she cleared her throat. "Alexander?"

Her whole body tingled when he froze with the towel halfway down his face. She knew the moment he realized it was her, and the smell of sweat was overtaken completely by the intensity of clove and bergamot. Pain was a fleeting thought just before the chills of arousal swept her body. His desire raced off the charts and took hers with it. The intensity of him was intoxicating, and she didn't even try to suppress the echo of her own emotions.

"Alexander?" She breathed. "I need to talk to you."

He squared his shoulders and chuckled roughly. "Now you let me hear what you're truly feeling." He took a step away from her. "Talking is not exactly on my mind, Jessalyn. You would be wise to leave before something happens we'll both regret."

FORTY-THREE

"I needed to see you before I went home." Jessalyn's voice stoked the fire already blazing inside him, and Alexander knew if she didn't leave now there would be no turning back.

"You shouldn't be here." His shoulders twitched.

His control hung by a thread, and the desire in her voice sent every ounce of his blood, and testosterone, screaming for her. Unable to help himself, he rolled his shoulders back and flexed his arms. He was rewarded by her swift inhale and whirled around to face her. Her eyes were wide, and when their gazes crashed, the heat between them caused the hazel depths of hers to melt like chocolate with unabashed desire.

"It is not wise for us to be alone right now. Why don't we *talk* tomorrow?" Jessalyn's chest hitched as he stalked toward her.

Her eyes left his and skimmed his bare torso, throwing a delicious shiver up his spine. The only thought raging through his brain was the one driving him to make every part of her his. He ground his teeth with effort when it hit him that she was deliberately taunting him.

If that's what she wants, why wait? He clenched his jaw and fought to temper his need with the other, more reasonable side of himself. *Not like this. She deserves better. We deserve better.*

"I wanted to tell you I'm sorry," she stated.

"Sorry for what?" Not a shred of fear or doubt swirled in her expression. Concern flickered in the back of his mind, but the hunger in her eyes kept him from letting it register any further. Alexander lowered his voice and measured every word. "What are you sorry for?"

He watched her lower lip tremble and his jaw clenched with the effort it took not to still its shaking by locking it between his teeth. She opened her mouth to take a deep breath, and his lip curled as the image of her viper-like fangs rocketed through him.

More than anything he'd ever desired in his life, he wanted to see them. He wanted to feel them shred the tender skin of his tongue. As that thought scattered what remained of his patience, a warning flashed against the backs of his eyes at something in her demeanor.

Something isn't right. He tried to focus on what her body language was really telling him, but the moment his eyes dropped from the pulse pounding in her throat to the curve of her waist all he could think of was pressing his lips against her pale skin.

"If you're not going to answer me, then I'm asking you one more time to leave." He ripped the rest of the tape from his hands and tossed it aside. She flinched but didn't move away. He tried to soften his tone. "This isn't healthy for either of us right now."

She stepped toward him, and he was in motion before he could complete another thought. Sweeping her up, he set her on the edge of the ring and wedged himself between her knees. Her hands pressed flat against his wet chest, and his fingers gripped her waist. They stared at each other as the heat built in blinding waves. Her eyes were desperate, pleading, begging him to claim her. When her lips parted for a breath, he groaned.

His hands latched onto her face, and with thumbs under her

chin, he gently tilted her lips to his. Brushing the lightest of kisses against her, he growled.

"Stop me now, Jessalyn." She slid her hands to his shoulders, and he moaned her name as a last warning. When her eyes dipped to his lips and her breath fanned across his mouth, he couldn't hold back any longer.

He nipped hard at that trembling bottom lip and relished the way her whole body shook in response. She pressed forward, and the instant her soft body molded to his, he was lost. He slanted his mouth across hers and teasingly ran his tongue along the seam of her lips. They both shuddered, and he groaned into her as she parted to grant him access. Desperate for her to taste him, he swept his tongue across the roof of her mouth and was rewarded by the searing pain of her fangs raking across his flesh as they snapped into place.

He groaned again, this time at the wash of relief that drove the pain from his veins as their blood mingled. He dragged her off the ring and flush against him, relishing the taste and feel of her. Her sleek legs wrapped around his waist and locked at his back. She scraped her fangs across his lower lip then pulled the torn skin into her mouth. He let her suck the blood from his wounds as her hands went around his neck to pull him closer.

When the wounds closed, he slid his mouth from hers and trailed his lips across her jawline to her ear. Their breathing was ragged, and he buried his face against her neck. Her head fell back, and he grazed his teeth across her collarbone, ending with a wet kiss to the hollow of her throat.

The lack of pain fully registered, and the gravity of the situation sank in. Alexander's reason slowly returned. He nuzzled her ear, violently reining in his desire before he claimed more than her mouth.

"Jessalyn." She tightened her hold, and it took every ounce of his strength to pull back. He tugged her hair to pull her away from him. "Jessalyn, for both our sakes, please stop."

She was breathing hard, and he pushed her back to sit on the surface of the ring, prying her legs from around his torso. Once she was steady, he braced his hands on either side of her thighs, dropped his head, and focused on his breathing.

FORTY-FOUR

Jessi felt the heat of Alexander's long breath against her thighs. Achingly sweet and soft, the scent of his freedom was worth the pain her next actions would cause. Allowing them both a moment to enjoy the aftermath, she ran her fingers through the wet mass of red hair covering his head as she watched the tension seep from his body. The pain he lived with for most of his life was gone, and little by little, she sensed the reality of it relaxing him.

As she let it soak in, her stomach trembled with a desire for more. His strong body had held her fiercely but tenderly, and the taste of him filled her mouth with dark chocolate and oranges. It lingered on her tongue, and she licked her lips wanting more. Basking in the wonder of the moment and trying to memorize every piece of him, her fingers slid over the stiff hairs of the beard that left prickling scratches on her cheek. She wanted to draw this out as long as possible and brand every sensation into her memories, until a sudden shift in him caused her to draw her hands back.

"Alexander?" she whispered. There was no putting off the inevitable. "We need to talk."

"A little late for that, don't you think?" He huffed and pushed away from her, his hand brushing the length of her leg to soften his words. "This complicates things, Jessalyn."

"No. It doesn't. This needed to happen." She reached for his face and turned him to look at her. "It changes nothing but your pain."

Insult fired into his eyes, and his large hands braceleted her wrists. "This changes everything. Immediately." He let go and crossed over to the bench to pull a t-shirt from his bag. "We're bonded."

She swallowed when his intense eyes swung toward her as he slid the shirt over his head. It stuck heavily to his sweaty chest, and she watched in fascination as he tugged it into place.

"We can't ignore what this means just because we haven't had time to properly work through the implications of it."

Of course, Alexander would insist they be together, consequences be damned. She couldn't let that happen. She dropped less than gracefully from the edge where he set her. Alexander was there in an instant to catch hold of her when her knees buckled.

She shrugged him off and backed up a step. "We can still take that time, Alexander. There's no need to rush into..."

"You really don't get to make that argument." His eyes hardened, and she felt the hair on the back of her neck begin to rise. "I know you came here intending for this to happen. For what reason, I can't guess, but it's done. You don't get to tell me *now* that you want time."

Jessi's shoulders stiffened, his demanding tone cutting through the haze of bliss still surrounding them. Lifting her chin, she glared defiantly at him. "I came to tell you I'm going back to Arizona tomorrow. I'm taking Ulysse and Armani home." He didn't flinch. She touched her lips. "I never meant for this to happen."

Ignoring the last, Alexander stepped toward her. "Will you be coming back to California?"

"I don't know." Deep down she wanted to believe he would choose her. If she confessed that she knew about the prenuptial he had with Rebekka, he would say he wanted her and nothing else. Especially now, but she knew that would change in time. Eventually he would resent what she took from him. She glanced at the hard line of his mouth and shivered at the thought of never tasting him again.

He gripped her shoulders. "Do you want me to go with you?"

"You can't." She turned away. "You have responsibilities that don't include me."

"Everything I do includes you now." He was in front of her before she could draw a breath, and she flinched, expecting him to grab her. His hand reached out to cup her cheek as he lowered his forehead to hers. "I'm sorry for what I said last night. If that's why you're leaving..."

The warmth of his citrus filtered through her, and she tilted her chin to press her lips gently to his. The bond changed his scent further, and through it she knew he truly was sorry. But how did she know he wouldn't lose his temper again if Rebekka took everything?

"I'm the one who should be apologizing. I've interrupted your life, your plans. I disrupted everything." She wanted to take the words back. Why had she said that?

Before she could retract her statement, he pulled her against him, and she melted. Mixed with the sharp scent of him was the thick masculine smell of his sweat. She should have been disgusted, but the power in his gaze and the feel of his body made her press herself along the length of him. He groaned and kissed her with passion that stopped her words.

"You haven't disrupted anything. I'm so sorry I've hurt you." He buried his hands in her hair, and when he tilted her face to his again, she didn't want to analyze the desperate look in his eyes. His next kiss was thorough and exploring, and she responded eagerly. She wanted to get lost in him and believe she was his first choice, but she had written proof otherwise. When he finally drew back, she ducked her head and backed away.

She immediately regretted it when he let go. "We both have things we need to do." She tossed her hair back. "How long will you be in New York?"

"A week." He cocked his head, regarding her as she retreated another step. "There are meetings with the other Vampir representatives all week before the Gathering. You could meet me there after you take your horses home."

She inhaled and realized he knew she was running away again, and that he intended to let her. Anger and jealousy pinched her chest. "I will if I can. I have to make sure my mom is all right."

"Be careful, Jessalyn." He wrapped a towel behind his neck and gripped the ends hard enough to turn his knuckles white.

"I promise." Her throat closed up and was afraid to say anymore. Instead, she turned and walked out the door, pretending she didn't hear the sound of his fists against the wall as she climbed into her car.

FORTY-FIVE

ALEXANDER

She's lying again.

There was nothing in his instincts that felt right about what had just happened and letting her walk out the door was the hardest thing he'd ever done. When he heard the wheels of her truck spin in the loose gravel he swung again, this time tearing a large chunk of skin off the back of his hand.

She came here to say goodbye.

Everything in him wanted to run into the parking lot, yank her from the cab, and insist she tell him exactly what was going on. He was willing to bet next month's profits it had something to do with her father, but there was nothing he could do. The moment he challenged her she was ready to bolt. Letting her go and believing she would come back was the only logical solution. Now that they were bonded, she would eventually have no choice. She had to know they couldn't survive without each other.

He ground his teeth and shook out his hand. He looked down at the knuckles and grimaced. Reaching into his bag, he pulled out a clean wrap and bandaged his hand.

His eyes landed on the ring where he and Jessalyn had just

shared the most intimate moment of their lives. He was too tired to be frustrated anymore, and her constant running exhausted his patience. He needed help, and he needed it before Jessalyn got too far.

The pain in his hand almost made him laugh as he pulled his phone from the pocket of his bag. He was disappointed when his friend didn't answer. "Peter, I need your help." He lifted the duffel bag from the bench and switched the lights out as he exited the building. "Jessalyn was here, and I need you to find her."

He knew beyond a shadow of a doubt she wasn't planning to take the horses home. He heard the lie in her voice immediately. Underneath the lie, there was anger and betrayal he didn't understand. But confronting her would only drive her further away. Despite all they had worked through, she still didn't trust him. Part of him wanted to be angry, but Marcus had hurt her far more deeply than he ever realized. Even though he was unable to hurt anyone else, the damage he had done to his daughter continued to drive a wedge between Jessalyn and himself.

He'd intended all along to make sure for her sake that her past demons were at least exposed before they completed the Blood Exchange. He wanted to fight them with her, yet she insisted on keeping him in the dark. She'd dealt with them alone for so long, she didn't know how to let someone in.

Growling in frustration, he sank into the car and tossed the phone atop his bag. He had to go home and pack. The long cross-country flight was leaving in a couple hours, and as much as he wanted to stay, they needed him in New York.

Of course, Jessalyn knew that and timed her little stunt perfectly. There was nothing he could do about it now, but when he returned from the Gathering, he would make certain she never left his side again.

FORTY-SIX

Jessi's breath came in racking sobs as she drove down the highway away from Alexander. She had no idea where she was going. Her phone rang and rang, but she ignored it. She would need to get a new number.

Included with the copy of the lawsuit, she left the horses' papers signed over to Dennis. She trusted he would either keep them himself or find them new homes. Tucked inside, she left cash to cover the food and board for at least three months. In her pocket she had enough to last her a month and hopefully enough to put a deposit down on a new apartment.

The roads blurred past, and she didn't pay much attention to where she was going until she saw signs for Scottsdale. At the next stop light, she rested her head on the steering wheel and contemplated what to do.

Her exhaustion and emotional state had led her to automatically drive toward the only friend she knew she could count on. The light changed, and instead of pulling into a hotel, she wove her way through the back streets until she found herself in Alyssa and Curt's driveway.

The house was dark, though she knew they would be home. Unable to keep her eyes open any longer, she leaned her head back and let them fall shut. *What am I going to tell her?*

She startled with the tapping of Curt's knuckles against her window. Her wide eyes locked with his. His expression went from concerned to amused.

Bracing his hands on the roof of the truck, his muffled voice was annoyed. "Open the door, Lyn. Alyssa has breakfast on the table."

She rubbed her eyes and reached for her phone. Twelve missed calls and nine messages. Curt opened the door and stood aside as she stepped out. "What are you doing here?"

"It's a long story."

His eyes narrowed, and he called to Alyssa who stood watching from the front door. "Get her inside and wait for me."

Resolutely gathering her courage, Jessi made her way around the front of the truck as Curt slammed the door shut. Seeing the expression on her friend's face drew the tears Jessi thought she had cried out.

Alyssa folded her in her arms and led her inside to the couch. The warm yellows and oranges of her living room smeared together, and Jessi covered her face with her hands. She felt Alyssa lower herself on one side then sensed Curt seat himself on the coffee table in front of them.

"What happened, Lyn?" Alyssa brushed the hair back from her face and handed her a tissue.

Curt interrupted. "Where is he? Is he on his way?"

"I came alone. Who would be coming with me?" Jessi glared at him.

Curt grunted. "The one you're bonded to. Where is he, and why isn't he with you?"

Jessi's face blazed. "How can you know that?"

Alyssa shifted. "Alexander?"

Jessi kept her eyes on Curt. His gaze was fierce, and he asked again, "Does he know you are here?"

"How do you know that?" she ground out. Alyssa's gaze bounced between them and settled on her. Jessi dropped her head. "How can you possibly know that?"

"You forget what we males are able to hear in your voice." He cleared his throat. "When a bonding takes place, the blood changes your echo. So, I ask again, where is he?"

"Slow down, Curt." Alyssa put a hand on her knee. "Start at the beginning."

Jessi pressed the heels of her hands against her eyes. "Yes. Alexander and I are bonded. I couldn't let him live in pain anymore, no matter how I feel about him." Curt huffed, and Jessi looked up in challenge. "You have no idea what's going on."

He sat back. "I may not, but I'll tell you this—if Alexander Koch comes pounding on my front door, I am not going to hide you."

"I would never ask you to. And for what it's worth, he won't. He's in New York for the next seven days, and he thinks I'm taking the horses home." Jessi leaned back and pulled a pillow across her lap. "It wasn't meant to be, Alyssa." Her voice was raw, and the words came out choked. "He's in love with someone else."

Curt sucked in a breath. "He bonded to you. He *can't* love anyone else."

"When did this happen? And why on earth are you here?" Alyssa asked.

"Last night. We bonded last night." Jessi looked pleadingly at her friend. "But he's in love with an Ordinair. They had prenuptials drawn up." She closed her eyes. "The papers were signed the year I disappeared. He was only pursuing me to take away his pain." Anger flared as she allowed the reality of the situation to sink in. "He would have bonded to me, maybe even made it look like we were happy for a while, but he wants her."

"Jessalyn, I'm telling you that's not possible. We aren't made that way. After I bonded to Alyssa." Curt's scent was angry as he stood. "Just the thought of touching another female made my skin crawl."

Memories Jessi didn't want to remember pushed forward and

caught hold of her. Walking in on her mother trying to clean her bruised and scratched arms in the bathroom...the sounds of another woman's laughter in the bedroom, while Jessi helped her mother in the kitchen...long nights working in the barn and seeing her father's car drive away. All the memories of her father's betrayal and abuse washed over her as she glared defiantly at Curt.

"It *is* possible. My mother lived it. Then, five years ago, my father pledged me to Alexander. But he sent me away after refusing to even meet me. My father was furious. With *me*. He said Alexander rejected me because I wasn't good enough to be a Koch, and he was going to change their minds." Tears poured down her face, and she angrily swiped at them. "One night, he argued with Alexander's father until they had him removed from their property." Seeing Curt begin to understand, she pressed on. "I tried to refuse, and father took a riding crop to me. I left with Ulysse the next day." Alyssa wrapped an arm around her shoulder. "Gregor and Ona died three months later. Alyssa disguised me, and we both went to the funeral. We saw Alexander almost kill his brother over the inheritance. I made up my mind then I would *never* live with him."

The room was silent for a long moment until Curt stood. "It still doesn't change the fact that you *are* bonded to him."

Jessi shoved to her feet. "I'm not just bonded to him, Curt! I *love* him, and if I let him, he will tear my heart out just like my father did to my mother! I can't do it. I'm not her, and I won't watch him love someone else." Her body shook with the stress of the last few days. "I've given him the one thing he needs from me. But I can't let him hurt me anymore than he already has."

Curt glanced at Alyssa then spoke thoughtfully. "Have you talked to him about this?"

"About what? The fact that I have written proof he loves someone else? No. What would be the point?"

Curt's eyes were still on Alyssa. "A bonded male can never hurt his mate. We're not made that way." When Jessi tensed, he raised a hand. "I believe Alexander should be allowed to explain. You need to talk to him."

"Coming here was a mistake." She started toward the door.

Alyssa blocked her and gave Curt a hard look. "Relax for a minute, all right?"

He shook his head in frustration and left the room.

"I didn't just take his blood and leave." The ache of realization stole all the fight from Jessi, and she sagged. "I love him, Alyssa. I didn't want to love him because I *knew* he would break my heart. I only bonded to him so he wouldn't ever have to be in pain again. So, we could finally be done with each other and... he could have his life back."

"You're exhausted. Why don't you get some sleep, and we can figure out what to do once you've gotten some rest." Alyssa pulled her in for a hug. "If Alexander is in New York, you have at least a couple days."

"Thank you. A couple hours, and I'll be on my way." Jessi followed her friend down the hallway to the guest room. Alyssa closed the door behind her, and Jessi fell fully clothed onto the bed and almost immediately slipped to sleep.

Jessi rolled over and stretched flat on the tiny twin mattress. Her neck was cramped from the uncomfortable position she slept in, but the rest felt good. Swinging her feet to the floor, she pulled aside the curtains and was surprised to see it was dark. The house was quiet, and she padded down the short hallway to the bathroom. She splashed cool water on her face and ran the brush she found under the counter through her hair before sweeping it back up into a ponytail.

The reflection in the mirror made her wince. Her eyes were dark and puffy from crying, and the bruise on her face was splotchy and purpling fast. Splashing more water and holding the damp cloth to her eyes, she startled at a knock on the door.

"Lyn? Are you hungry?" Alyssa called.

Lowering the cloth back to the sink, she cleared her throat. "Yeah. Give me a minute, and I'll be right out."

"Curt just got home, so I'll have dinner on the table in a few minutes. Take your time." Alyssa's footsteps retreated down the hall.

Curt worked second shift, which meant she had slept for almost ten hours. Much longer than she had intended to. Bracing her hands on the counter, she searched her reflection.

"What am I going to do?" she whispered. Her hazel eyes gave no answer, and she blew out a breath. "I guess I can go home." The thought brought her some comfort, and she knew her mother would be glad to see her. She would go home and perhaps take over management of the barn. That was what she needed. A new purpose to help her forget about Alexander. Her throat burned, but she fought it back.

"He's free." She pushed her shoulders back. "And so am I." She no longer had to hide who she was. There was no need to be afraid. Her father was in the custody of the Clan, Alexander had freed her from the pledge, and the two of them could finally live their lives pain free. Jessi waited for those truths to bring her peace, but the ache she felt for Alexander persisted.

All I need is time and distance.

The smell of whatever Alyssa was making for dinner wafted into her awareness, and her stomach growled. She followed the smell, but when she rounded the corner and saw the dining table set for five, she froze. Her friend was at the stove with her back to her.

"Who else is eating with us?" Instead of waiting for an answer, she drew a deep breath and a chill shot through her when she picked out a familiar salty scent. Jessi turned slowly to see Peter leaning in the opposite doorway.

"I hope you don't mind if Hannah and I join you." Peter's smile was warm and sympathetic, just as it had been the day he challenged her to meet with Alexander.

"How?" Jessi's voice faded away.

"Alexander found you by tracking phone calls. You covered your tracks well until a week ago."

"What do you mean?"

Peter crossed his ankles and tilted his head while Alyssa set the food on the table. "One call. You called Alyssa's cell once, and though Alexander wasn't looking for you anymore, the report still went to him."

She met his stare. "And what do you plan to tell Alexander?"

"He already knows I'm here."

She backed out of the room. When Peter followed, she bolted to the living room.

"He's not here to force you to go back." Jessi paused at the foot of the couch and looked accusingly at Hannah, who was holding her bag.

"That's good. Because he doesn't want me. I had to trick him into bonding with me. And even after I did, he let me go." She gritted her teeth and glared at Peter and Curt in the doorway. "If you males are as faithful as you claim you are, he shouldn't have been able to let me leave, right?" Curt's conflicted expression said it all. "That's what I thought." She whirled on Peter. "Is his pain gone?"

"For now," he admitted.

"Then that's all that matters." She turned to Hannah and strode up to her, reaching for her bag. "I'm going home. Tell Alexander I hope he and Rebekka are happy."

Alyssa exhaled slowly and came around to stand between Jessi and Hannah. "I wish I could tell you it was that easy." She lowered her head to look her in the eyes. "What do you think is going to happen in a month? Six months? You're bonded to him. You *can't* stay away from one another. Didn't your mother teach you that?"

Jessi folded her arms defiantly. "The only thing my mother taught me was how to be a doormat. I *can* stay away from Alexander, and I will. Eventually, we'll get over it."

"It's not about love anymore, Jessi." Peter's voice was sad. "The pain will come back. Given a long enough time..." He paused and his jaw tightened. "This isn't how this conversation was supposed to happen." The first glimpse of real anger she had ever seen from him darkened Peter's expression. "Just like I wouldn't use his pain to guilt you into getting to know him, I won't use the reality of the bond to convince you to come back." He took the case from Hannah and held it out to her. "Ask your mother. She'll tell you the real truth about a bonding."

She narrowed her eyes as she took it from him. "That's it?"

"Yes." He held the front door open. "He told you. It's always been your choice. Even now. When you're finally ready to trust him, call Hannah."

FORTY-SEVEN

Despite Alyssa's pleas for her to stay, Jessi left. It was time to go home to her mother. They were both safe now, and it was long past time for them to have a conversation.

The simple ranch house looked no different when she pulled into the drive. She sat in the truck in front of the place that held so many memories and rested her head on the steering wheel. Going inside took more effort than she expected, but she couldn't put it off any longer. By now, the truck would be on the cameras, and Rosston would come out to see who parked in the drive. As much as she was dreading the talk with her mother, she was looking forward to seeing Rosston again.

Rosston James was a little bit of everything to the Vogts. He had been hired as a driver when she was a child but quickly established himself as much more. Her father relied on him for security, and her mother trusted him. Rosston had often taken time out of his day to spend with Jessi, and he had sheltered her from the worst of her father's wrath. He hadn't been able to protect her mother, but when things got tense between Jessi and her father, Rosston was always close by.

The night she fled, it was he who helped her hitch up the trailer and load Ulysse. He never asked about the marks on her arms, and he didn't try to talk her out of leaving. It was almost as if he'd been waiting for that night to come.

She looked up to see him come around the corner of the house, a dusty cowboy hat pulled low over his face, shielding his keen eyes. He paused at the edge of the drive, and when the brim of his hat rose, she was relieved to see his kind smile. She opened the door and stepped onto the concrete.

"I wondered when we would see you." His face creased into the grin she knew so well. "Mrs. Vogt has been worried sick since Marcus was taken to the Compound."

"How is Mom?"

He took in the new truck and swept his knowing gaze across her. "She'll be better once she sees you." He slapped a pair of gloves across his thigh. "It's good to have you home again. Is there anything I can take inside for you?"

"No. I only have one bag." He nodded and turned to head back to the stables. "Rosston?" The man's head swung back, but he didn't turn. "Can I ask you a question?"

His shoulders rose. "You can ask me anything." He ticked his head toward the barns. "I'm just shutting down for the night. Can we work and talk?"

She smiled. "Like old times?" She searched his eyes. "Did you know what my father was doing?"

He sighed and led the way down the stone path beside the house. The smell of horses and sweat made tears prick her eyes. The scene was so familiar she felt like she was sixteen and working side by side with him again.

"Marcus loves your mother very much, Lyn." He didn't look up, but his quiet words carried through the still evening air.

"What makes you say that? He was horrible to her!" She could scarcely believe her ears.

"There's more to their story than you know." He exhaled and

turned the corner toward the foaling corrals. "I never understood why they wouldn't tell you."

Jessi grabbed his arm to stop him. "Tell me what?"

"I've never been just an employee, Lyn." He met her gaze. "I came here to protect my granddaughter."

She stared at him as the truth hung between them. "But my grandparents are dead!"

He pulled the hat from his head, his gaze trailing across the barns ahead of them. His jaw sawed back and forth before he dropped his head. "Your mother was beautiful, and as the daughter of a baron, extremely wealthy. I resented her and her family for having the ability to escape. I called my son a coward when Marcus told me he was leaving Germany with her, and I disowned him. Called him a traitor for joining up with Res and Samuel." His eyes looked through her as his memories carried him away. "I blamed him for the loss of my grandsons and never took the time to realize he had lost his children. Your brothers and sister." He cleared his throat. "By the time I realized what a fool I'd been, your grandmother and I had nothing. The war cost us everything just to survive."

Jessi struggled to absorb it all. "Why didn't anyone tell me?"

"I wasn't allowed to tell you anything that didn't have to do with horses. I disowned him, Lyn." He replaced his hat. "Those aren't just words. If it hadn't been for your mother, your grandmother and I wouldn't be here at all." He resumed their walk back to the barns. "And if it wasn't for how much your father loves her..." He looked toward the sky and stopped. "That's not my story to tell. It's hers." Rosston shrugged. "I did my best to protect you. Marcus is impulsive and controlling, but he was almost always right even if he did things the wrong way." The horses caught sight of them, and their neighing made him smile. "My son knew two things. He could match mares and stallions and produce winners like no one I ever knew." They reached a paddock where a mare stood with a young foal teetering at her side. He reached out a hand and smoothed it up the mare's forehead. "He could take one look at them and know."

The tall horse shifted, and the foal slid his head under her belly to watch them. Jessi placed her hands on the fence, trying to grasp all this man was telling her. It was a side to her father she had never considered. A long silence stretched between them, and he turned to lean against the fence.

"Rosston, you said there were two things." She couldn't bring herself to call him grandfather. "What was the other?"

He huffed a sad laugh. "He was never wrong about a bonding." His eyes met hers.

"What do you mean?"

"Just like he could look at a pair of horses and know what kind of foal they would produce, he could look at a room full of Vampir males and females and know who was intended for who." His face softened. "The moment he met the man, he knew Alexander was meant for you, and he wasn't going to take no for an answer. He risked everything he and your mother owned to make sure it would happen." He watched her carefully. "When you left, he was sure the Kochs would get everything. He made finding you and that blasted horse his mission in life. When Alexander never came back to claim anything, he thought he was finally wrong." A light came on inside the house, and his eyes squinted. "He wasn't wrong though, was he? You and Alexander bonded?"

"We did."

He tipped his head back. "Then he got what he wanted. You and Alexander are a good match."

"Genetically, maybe, but Alexander is in love with someone else. If my father loved my mother so much, why did he bring other women here? Why did he hurt her?"

Her grandfather pushed away from the fence. "Don't judge someone's pain until you understand it, Lyn." The words rifled through her like a shot, but his back was already to her. "Go talk to your mother before you condemn him."

Rosston left her standing in shock on the stone walkway. She stared at his retreating back, wondering how she had ever missed how much he and her father looked alike. The light inside the house went out as another came on upstairs. Jessi turned away from the barns. She pushed open the mudroom door and stepped inside the tidy space. It was filled with white cabinets and a washer and dryer for all their horse related items.

The house was dark as she felt her way through the kitchen and into the dining room. The space widened into a great room that made up the main sitting room, dining area, and entryway of the place she once called home.

"Rosston? Is that you?" Her mother's voice floated down from the balcony, and she heard light footsteps as her mother came out of the master bedroom. "Whose truck is that?" She looked out the large arched window facing the front of the house.

"It's mine, Mom." Her mother froze before her eyes slowly lowered to where Jessi stood. Her mother silently shook her head in disbelief. "I'm home."

Tears ran down her cheeks as she gripped the railing and descended the stairs to embrace her. "Lyn. You're home!"

Jessi rested her head on her mother's shoulder and relished the comforting arms that wrapped her in the familiar smell of pine.

"I've missed you, Mom. I'm so sorry I left. I should have stayed to protect you. If he hurt you because of it, I am so sorry. He can't hurt us anymore, Mom. We're safe." Her voice cracked, and her mother stiffened as she spoke.

"You were always safe." Her mother leaned back. "Is that why you left? Because you didn't feel safe?"

Jessi moved out of her mother's arms. "Of course I didn't feel safe! He hit us, Mother!"

"Oh, Lyn." Jessi flinched when her mother reached out to touch her bruised cheek.

"I met Rosston on the way in." Sorrow flared in her eyes, and Jessi backed up another step. "Why didn't you tell me who he is?"

Behind the sadness, Jessi saw relief. "I'm glad he finally told you. He's wanted to since you were a little girl, but we wouldn't let him."

She gestured toward the patio doors. "Let's go outside and sit. It's time you knew the truth." When Jessi didn't move, she turned away. "It's why you came home, isn't it?"

The patio overlooked a pool surrounded by stone, and the soothing sound of the waterfall reminded her of all the evenings she had spent here talking to Rosston or reading a book. The calming effect the place once brought was absent tonight as doubt and bitterness washed over her. Jessi lowered herself into one of the large red cushioned chairs and waited for her mother to do the same.

Her mother folded her feet under her and regarded her daughter silently. "You and Alexander?"

Jessi threw her hands up. "Yes. We bonded. No, we're not together. He doesn't want me." Her mother's lips pressed together, and Jessi sighed. "He's in love with someone else, and I can't stand the thought of living with him the way you lived with Dad. Watching him be with someone else, always angry."

"It wasn't your father who was in love with someone else." Her mother's voice was so quiet Jessi had to watch her lips to hear what was being said. "He always loved me, Lyn. Don't blame him for what happened."

"He hit you! How can I not blame him?" Her mother's defense of him kept the full impact of what she'd said from sinking in.

"Jessalyn, your father's anger is justified though his actions are not. I never defended myself because..."

"Because why?"

"*I* never wanted *him*." Her mother's jaw hardened. "I was in love with someone else, but my father listened to Marcus when he said we were intended for one another. Obviously, Marcus was right, but I hated him for forcing the issue." She shook her head. "I was furious but had no choice. My father, being the baron, insisted I complete the bonding with Marcua immediately, and banished the male I loved. He didn't even let me say goodbye." She shivered. "When our sons were born, I turned them against your father. When the war broke out and they died, then our first daughter was killed during a bombing raid, he stayed away so long we barely survived."

Horrified, Jessi leaned back, and her mother softened. "I realized then what I had done, but it was too late." Her mother's gaze drifted across the pool. "I hoped that when my father agreed to send us to America with Res and Samuel, Marcus would forgive me, and we could start over." Another shiver raked her. "But then Marcus's father legally disowned him for taking advantage of my father's wealth. When we received the news, that was the end of his ability to care for me. He made it clear to everyone we were bonded in name and blood need only. He wanted another son; one he hoped he could turn against me. I refused to tell him we were having a daughter until the day you were born." Her tone went flat in defeat. "He took one look at you and left the room. I didn't see him for almost a week, all three of us nearly died with blood need."

"You keep saying that." Jessi felt cold all over. "What do you mean, blood need?" she whispered.

"I will always need your father's blood to survive, just as you will need Alexander's. Even now, with Marcus in custody we will have to make arrangements, or we will both die." She said it matter of factly, not noticing Jessi's reaction. "I hired Rosston to help me around the house, not knowing who he was. Your father was gone as often as possible when you were little, and I wanted someone around I could trust." She glanced toward the barns. "He never told me who he was, until Marcus came home one night and tried to kick him out. They spent the whole night out here in the barns, and the next morning it was agreed he could stay, but you couldn't be told who he was. Once you were old enough to ride and showed real talent, your father poured his heart and soul into you. But he was so broken and bitter from what I had done to him..." Her gaze dropped. "I'm sorry for what he did." When she looked up, there was hope in her eyes. "But it will be different for you. For you and Alexander."

She sucked in a breath as the weight of her situation crashed in on her. "It's different. He's the one in love with someone else." Jessi pressed her face into her hands. "What have I done?"

FORTY-EIGHT

Jessi felt the weight of her mother's stare. Peter's statement from earlier came crashing back into her thoughts. *"You can't stay away from him, or the pain will come back. Given enough time..."* She refocused on her mother.

"You said Dad always loved you. How is that possible? I saw the other women he brought here."

She shook her head sadly. "Did you ever see the same one twice?"

"No."

Her mother blushed. "He's a man, Lyn. I certainly don't condone what he did, but I also couldn't expect him to remain faithful to me when I refused to..." She pursed her lips.

Shock began to wear off, and anger rushed in to take its place. All her life, Jessi thought her mother was the victim. All her life she believed her mother was the one wronged by her father. She hardly knew the woman sitting across from her. Jessi looked up to see Rosston leaning against a post. "You knew all this?"

"It was always Natalie and Marcus's story to tell. I swore I wouldn't interfere, but I wish I had. Lies and deception destroy families. As if our Clan hadn't learned that lesson well enough." He slid the rim of his hat though his hands. "Marcus made his share of mistakes. Signing that contract with the Kochs was never supposed to happen. He swore to me he would let you make your own decision. That's why I helped you leave."

Jessi couldn't take much more, but there was something tingling at the edges of her mind. "What contract?"

"It's an old Vampir practice," her mother said. "When two family lines are about to end like ours and the Kochs, the families can agree to an arranged partnership. Gregor and Marcus signed one between you and Alexander. They never told the two of you because Marcus was sure you were intended for one another, and it wouldn't matter. But tradition is tradition he said." She shrugged. "Then, when Alexander sent you away without ever meeting you, Marcus lost it. He wanted so badly for things to be different for you."

Rosston crossed the patio and lowered himself into a chair beside her mother. "I told him not to push you. Tried to convince him to arrange a way for the two of you to meet and nature would take care of itself, but he wouldn't listen. He was convinced you were just like your mother, and you'd refuse him." His lips thinned. "You proved him right. Though you had no idea."

Nearly unable to breathe, Jessi looked from one to the other. Her mind worked overtime as details from the list of assets in the document Rebekka gave her scrolled through her mind. At the time she had only looked at the numbers, but words and addresses became clearer in her memory. "What did the contract say?"

"It made you and Alexander joint owners of both family assets within four years. When you disappeared, ninety-five percent of everything was supposed to go to Alexander, but he never came back to claim it. Your father got the bright idea he could sue Alexander for selling his architectural firm because of a clause preventing the sale of anything prior to the partnership." Her mother waved a dismissive hand. "But the contract was voided at the last meeting, or we would have lost everything instead. Alexander's attorney planned to countersue on the grounds of your disappearance."

Jessi felt the ground go out from under her. "Mom, when was the contract signed?"

"Four years ago. Just before you left. Why?"

Jessi's voice fell to a whisper. "Alexander never knew about it?"

"No," Rosston said. "They never told either of you."

Her mind raced to Peter's admonition to call Hannah if she wanted to know the truth. But there was still one question, "Rosston, how was Father able to be with those other women?" She choked on her words. "Everyone is telling me it's not possible. If it's not, how..."

Her grandfather's face paled then reddened. "Not a conversation I ever expected to have with you, but you deserve the truth."

Her mother's cough sounded suspiciously like a sob, but Jessi ignored her. "How, Rosston?"

"Your father would take an infusion of your mother's blood first." He reached out to cover her mother's hand with his. "Not all the bruises on her arms were from beatings, and most of the time when things got broken..."

"I was too weak to hold onto things." Her mother's eyes begged her to understand. "I gave him as much of my blood as I could, and it made me weak." Jessi stared at her in horror. "Most of the time he yelled, it was because I dropped and broke something he bought me. He thought I did it on purpose. At first I did. But by the time I realized how wrong I was, it was too late. He couldn't forgive me." Tears poured down her mother's cheeks. "I'm so sorry, sweetheart. We all did our best to hide the truth from you. All of us. We all wanted something so much better for you, Jessalyn." She curled into Rosston's chest, and his eyes filled with tears.

"Better would have been to tell me the truth! Better would have been letting me make my own decisions!" Jessi stood and escaped into the house. She couldn't look at her mother anymore. The echo of the slammed door resonated through the empty house. Standing in the familiar living room, Jessi titled her head back and screamed in frustration. She wanted to throw anything she could get her hands on, but her anger soon dissolved into a burning regret.

She glanced up and behind her. Was her old bedroom still the same? Her suitcase was resting at the bottom of the stairs, no doubt left there by Rosston before he'd joined them on the patio.

Jessi hefted the case and climbed the stairs. It was near midnight, and though she had no intention to stay any longer than she had to, she needed a good night's sleep. Her door was the third one on the left. She wished this felt like coming home, but it felt more like visiting a place she barely knew.

The door swung open silently, and she paused to drink in the smell before flipping on the light. Her breath caught when she realized the room was filled with the heavy scent of her father. Her hand shook, knowing he couldn't possibly be here, but the overwhelming layers of his rich leather scent saturated everything. Flipping on the light, Jessi's eyes swept a room that hadn't changed a bit.

Even the closet door she'd left half open in her rush to leave, still showed her the designer contents in brilliant colors and patterns. In the center of the far wall stood her four-poster bed. Once a ruffly canopy bed, it had been stripped of the pink and lace when she graduated high school to be replaced with rich mahogany posts and a gently curved frame.

She set the case near the matching dresser and rested her hands on the brown and pumpkin orange comforter. Her eyes flooded with tears when she realized this was where the scent was coming from. Her father had slept on her bed. In the heady scent laden fabric, she detected sorrow and regret. Looking closely at the neatly stacked pillowcases, she saw dried tearstains sprinkled the material. Lifting her eyes to the ceiling, Jessi vowed she would see her father. For so many years she hated him. Feared him. No way was she going to excuse his behavior, but she knew she needed to make peace with him. Though forgiveness would take time, he deserved to know she knew the truth.

But before she did anything else, she had to call Alyssa and Hannah. There were still four days until the Gathering, and she needed help.

The next afternoon, Curt held the front door open as Jessi and Alyssa stepped inside the foyer of the Compound. Natural light flooded the room, and he led the way into a richly furnished sitting room. The moment her feet touched the polished stone; she was assaulted by the scent of at least four other males. Hannah trailed behind in silent support as Jessi approached the man she came to see.

Her father sat on a narrow love seat facing a broad fireplace and sleek dark wood mantle. Even with the sharp bite of Curt's anger beside her, she instantly picked out the familiar leathery scent of her father. His eyes, nearly an exact match to hers, followed her as she crossed the space toward him. Her pulse pounded in her temples as she approached and studied his face. He looked exhausted, and a pinch of worry crept over her.

Alexander had beaten him within an inch of his life, and his face bore the evidence. Stitches lined his cheek and forehead, and his left eye was nearly swollen shut. With the yellow and purple bruising across his chin, he was frightening to look at.

She looked to each of the men surrounding him, but all their gazes were fixed on the wall behind her. When she refocused on her father, anger washed away the worry.

"I don't think I can ever forgive you," she said.

His lips thinned, and his shoulders stiffened.

"I know it isn't all your fault, but you hurt me. You hurt my mother." The words she had rehearsed so carefully evaporated. "You lied to me. You both lied to me!" Clenching her fist and reminding herself yelling wouldn't change anything, she sucked in a deep breath and tried again. "I don't understand, and I don't want to. Not now. Maybe not ever."

His chin dropped. "If you'll let me explain - "

"No. You had twenty-four years to explain." Jessi took a step forward, and Curt laid a hand on her arm. She shrugged it away. "I know what Mom did. I know who Rosston is, and I know all about the contract you signed with the Kochs. I don't need *you* to explain anything!" She smelled the anger rising and laughed. "You got what you wanted by the way."

He looked up in surprise. "What? What do you think I wanted, Jessalyn?" He started to push up from the couch, but four hands landed on his shoulders. He grimaced in pain. "All I wanted was for you to have a chance at a real bonding. But you threw it away, because of what? A couple blows? A little bit of anger? I raised you stronger than that, Jessalyn."

"You didn't raise me strong. You raised me to be afraid." She felt hysteria rising, and Curt laid a hand on her shoulder. "Well, I'm not afraid anymore! Not afraid of you, and not afraid of my mate." Seeing her father's eyes widen, she pressed on. "Oh, yes. You were right about that. And you know what's sad? He is the greatest, strongest, most giving man I've ever met, and because of you, I left him in pain because I thought he was just like you." Her father's eyes hardened. "Mother said you both wanted better for me. Well, Alexander *is* better, but because of you I lied to him. And you know what? In spite of it all, he never gave up on me." Jessi laughed at the irony. "He's not just my mate because of what we are. He's the man I love! And to think you almost caused me to walk away from him."

Jessi sagged against Curt. "But do you know what's harder for me to understand? I still love you." Tears slipped down her cheeks. "I still love you and Mother. I don't know why, but I do." She pulled her shoulders back. "I don't know if I'll be back, and I already told you I don't know if I can ever forgive you, but I couldn't leave without telling you the truth. And the truth is, I love you."

Alyssa wrapped an arm around her shoulders and pulled her away from Curt, heading toward the door. All Jessi could think about now was getting to New York and Alexander.

Curt and Alyssa drove her back to her mother's house.

"Are you packed?" Alyssa walked her to the front door.

"Mostly." Jessi pushed it open and leaned heavily against the frame. "Thank you for coming with me."

Alyssa hugged her tightly. "Anytime. When does your flight to New York leave? I wish Curt and I could go with you."

"First thing in the morning." Jessi's stomach turned. "Do you think he'll forgive me?"

"Alexander?" Alyssa rested her hands on Jessi's shoulders.

"He was so angry." She wrapped her arms around her middle. "What if..."

"Lyn!" Alyssa caught her face between her hands. "Listen to me." Her friend's eyes shimmered with tears. "He loves you, and you love him. You were made for each other. All of this," she said, waving a hand, "is in the past, and none of it matters anymore. What matters is what you do from here forward. Alexander Koch of all people should understand that. Stop worrying! For heaven's sake, he sent his best friends to come get you because he couldn't."

Jessi sighed and pulled her in for another hug. "You're right. I love you, Al."

"I love you, too." She stepped back. "Now get some sleep, then go make that tall hunk of muscle and Gucci suits yours."

"It's Tom Ford, actually." Jessi grinned at Alyssa. "I'll be wearing the Gucci."

"Not for long!" Alyssa sang as she walked away.

Jessi blushed then pushed the door shut. Despite the truth of Alyssa's words, she couldn't stop wondering how Alexander would react to seeing her tomorrow.

FORTY-NINE

ALEXANDER

Alexander stood to the side of the podium, waiting for Emerick to introduce him, and slipped a finger under the collar of his shirt. For the first time ever the perfect fit of his tuxedo chafed him. After spending nearly a week in Jessalyn's world, he had grown used to the feel of less confining clothing.

The last four days had consisted of endless meetings, filled with suits, ties, businessmen and women, and planning committees had worn him thin. Doing it all with Jessalyn so far away was torture. Last night, Peter called to tell him Jessalyn and her mother were safe. He itched to go to Jessalyn. He would follow her anywhere until she trusted him again.

Though his pain was gone, it had been replaced by an ache in his chest that wasn't physical. He'd spent the last four days trying to forgive himself for losing it so badly he'd actually intended to kill someone. Marcus survived, but Alexander wasn't sure his daughter would ever forgive him.

He tried to contact Jessalyn, but she blocked his calls, and his emails bounced back. It felt like he was living in the dark, operating blindly and trying to be what all these people needed him to be, while the one person he needed most remained out of his reach. Frustrated, he pulled at his collar again.

Ellen whispered, "You aren't nervous are you?"

He dropped his hand as Emerick wrapped up his speech. "No. But my mind isn't exactly focused on the Gathering." Alexander glanced down at the grey-haired woman beside him and smiled into her warm brown eyes. "Thank you for being here."

Applause rang through the room and with a last brush of a hand down his jacket, Alexander stepped forward to stand next to Emerick. "Ladies and gentlemen, it is my honor to introduce you to Alexander Koch."

"Thank you, Mr. Tate." Pushing thoughts of Jessalyn aside until his duties were done, Alexander adjusted the microphone. "You and Ellen have gone above and beyond to ensure our people survive for centuries to come. For your service, we would like to present you a token of our appreciation." Alexander waited as Koen and Leisel Lockton came forward, followed by Baden Dietrich.

Baden approached the Elder couple first and handed them an envelope. He kissed each of their cheeks, then paused in front of the microphone.

"In honor of all you've done and sacrificed for the Vampir, we want to send you on an extended vacation." He raised an eyebrow toward the crowd. "I will not tell you where they are going, so don't ask." The crowd mock groaned. "The service they have done for all of us is more than we ever could have asked of them. In light of this, we, as a united race once again, insist they be relieved of the official position as Elders." Emerick and Ellen both gasped in surprise. He turned toward Koen and nodded.

Koen gestured for Leisel to precede him. In her arms she carried a large bouquet of flowers, and as she gingerly placed them in Ellen's arms, she leaned forward to place a kiss on the woman's cheek. Everyone watched as Ellen laid the flowers in her lap, caught the younger woman's face in her hands, and spoke quietly to her. The whole room held its breath as Leisel's shoulders shook.

Ellen held her close for a moment then Leisel took Koen's hand and stepped up to the podium with him close behind. Alexander remembered with shame the way he had once pursued her. They had long since forgiven him, but Alexander wondered if he would ever be able to forgive himself. As though sensing the direction of his thoughts, she reached for his hand.

Unsure what she was about to do or say, he looked to Koen, who was grinning widely. Alexander allowed Leisel to draw him to her side and looked down in puzzlement. She didn't look up, instead leaning forward to speak into the microphone. "I'm not very good at this sort of thing, so I'm just going to tell you that if it weren't for the integrity of Alexander Koch, none of this would be possible. In light of his dedication to making sure our people continue not just to survive as a species, but also making sure we guard the responsibilities we have through our wealth and the knowledge we gain," Leisel's soft green eyes looked up as she continued, "it is our decision, and the decision of the Council to offer the position Emerick and Ellen are vacating—to him and his intended."

It took a moment for the applause and the words Leisel said to sink in. *They want me to be Elder?* When he looked across the faces of those standing beside him, he was overwhelmed that they thought enough of him to ask. His jaw tightened, and his heart pinched, wishing Jessalyn were here beside him to accept the honor. Would she ever stand beside him?

Koen narrowed his eyes. "Alexander?"

He shook himself back to the moment and looked across the crowd. All eyes were on him. Was this what he wanted? Jessalyn's face swam into his thoughts. Would she want this? The responsibility weighed heavy for a moment, but he knew he couldn't turn it down.

"I would be honored. I certainly didn't expect this." Regaining his composure, he smirked. "You keep secrets well."

The crowd laughed, and he kissed Leisel's cheek lightly. "If it weren't for your boldness, Leisel, I would still be the angry, arrogant man I used to be."

Baden chuckled. "Oh, you're still arrogant, Alexander, but your intended will correct that."

His face reddened, and he laughed with the crowd. "I'm sure she will." He swept his eyes across the Gathering of four hundred of his people, and pride welled up in him.

Setting aside the ache of not having his intended with him to share in the moment, he squared his shoulders. "We are Vampir, the Lasting Ones. The last year has been an exciting one for us. By focusing on what unites us rather than the things that have tried to divide us, we are once more a united people, ready to move on and make our world a better place for our children. A world that allows them to find their own way and provides the means for them to become successful." The crowd clapped, and he paused.

Until this moment, having children was never anything he wanted, but the vision of Jessalyn carrying his child flooded him with longing.

"Last year, we confronted the rift that nearly destroyed us, and learned the devastating consequences of our division." Though he tried not to let it, his tone hardened. "This year, we dismantled a twisted system of control and greed that divided not only the Vampir but threatened the very foundation of who we are. I am ashamed to say that the actions of my Clan have caused many of you to question the wisdom of complete disclosure among the Vampir of the world. It may seem safer to remain separate, but if we do, the choices of one Vampir could once again leave us vulnerable. If we truly wish to survive and become the leaders, teachers, and influencers we once were, we must unify. There will be difficulties. We have held one another at arm's length for centuries. Blending cultures, customs, and traditions that have formed and become part of us will not be easy. But the end result will be worth it."

To the left of the podium stood Winston Parchell with a beautiful young blond female next to him. The girl's arm was wrapped around the waist of a tall dark-haired male. They looked happy.

"No matter how well-intentioned our ancestors may have been, we are living in a vastly different world now. A world that is opening new possibilities and new relationships. While we are navigating these new relationships, old traditions will surface. Some are wise and necessary. We will always have a responsibility to guard the purity and integrity of those who have yet to meet their intended, but we must temper that responsibility with wisdom and grace. We have to allow this generation to find their own way." Winston nodded in agreement. "The fear of our ancestors was that we would be driven by our instincts."

Alexander smiled and glanced around the room. Aware there were many in the room who had met their intended that day, he quipped, "Unlike them, the new Council is not convinced following our instincts is such a bad thing." Amid the light laughter, he caught movement at the double doors across the room.

Peter and Hannah entered the ballroom, and Alexander's next words died on his lips at the smiles on his friends' faces. The smirk on Peter's face could only mean one thing. *Jessalyn was on her way.* Shaking himself back on task, he straightened his jacket.

"Currently, the Council consists of nine members and one Elder. In addition to myself, we currently have Council members from Arizona, the US East Coast, Ireland, Germany, Australia, South Africa, Asia, Greenland, and Italy. It is our desire to add more as we locate and integrate other Clans. I see no need to bore you with the details of the Council's day-to-day operations, but you should know who your representative is, and how to contact them."

Alexander gestured to Baden, eager to turn the microphone over to him. "Mr. Dietrich developed and oversees the new communication network that enables us to coordinate meetings such as this one. He and his team are the primary contact for both of the US Clans."

Alexander leaned into the podium. "Before I turn the microphone over to Mr. Dietrich, I want to leave you with this. Never give up hope. Our numbers are diminished, and they may remain so for years to come. What we lost in decades will not be rebuilt overnight. Those who have left us in fear may return. Those who are among us may still leave. But those of us who remain, those who believe we are stronger united, will never give up hope. As long as your heart beats, there is always hope." Applause erupted, and he turned, nodding to Baden.

Congratulations swirled around him, but he barely heard it. Alexander's only thought was finding out where Jessalyn was. Peter and Hannah waited at the back of the room, and the story they told put all the pieces together. After a quick call to Thomas, he requested they do him one more favor and handed Peter his credit card.

His friend took it and laughed. "You're going to burn the place down."

"It will be worth it, and I can afford to rebuild it later," Alexander replied dryly.

He re-entered the ballroom and was immediately surrounded by Baden, Koen, and Emerick.

He sighed, explaining. "Peter said Hannah found copies of the lawsuit at Jessalyn's apartment, and Thomas found evidence in Ms. Wellington's office of her alterations. Apparently she led Jessalyn to believe the Clan contract was a prenuptial agreement." Alexander's voice was tight. "Rebekka was the CFO for my company. She and I had a relationship that did not end well, but I have no idea why she would go after Jessalyn."

Emerick shook his head. "And you never told Jessalyn anything about the contract. That was a mistake."

Alexander's shoulders tensed at the accusation, but the Elder was right. He pinched the bridge of his nose. "At the time I was angry and never did."

Leisel's face creased into a confused smile at someone behind him. "Hello."

Koen followed her gaze. "Can we help you?"

"I just arrived and came to say hello to Mr. Koch." Chills ran across Alexander's scalp at the familiar voice.

Alexander slowly turned to face Rebekka. When his piercing eyes met hers, she took a step back.

"Is something wrong?" He stared down at the hand Rebekka laid on his arm as though it were a snake. "Alexander? Are you all right?"

"Would you all please excuse us for a moment?" The group of friends reluctantly moved a few paces away. "This is a private engagement. How did you get in here?"

Scoffing, she blinked innocently. "You left the invitations on your desk." She stepped closer and rested her other hand on his chest, sliding her fingers inside the lapel of his jacket with a familiarity that made his skin crawl. "When I heard Ms. Vogt wasn't willing to come with you, I didn't want you to be alone."

Alexander removed her hand and held it tightly. He kept his voice low enough no one else could hear. "How did you know she wasn't coming?"

"Does it matter? Now that she's moved on, I thought you would be glad to see me."

He looked across the room, and with her hand still firmly in his, led her toward a second set of doors near the back. Pushing them open, he waited for her to exit the room. The hallway was dimly lit and cold, obviously a service entrance. He knew anger rolled off him in waves, and he hoped leaving the ballroom would take his scent with him, otherwise security would soon follow. She took a step toward him, then gasped when he trapped her against the wall. He leaned down to growl in her ear.

"Let me make this very clear, Ms. Wellington." Her head fell back, and his voice came out rough. "I don't know how you got here or why, but if I find out that you have threatened Ms. Vogt in any way, I will press charges, and you will find your job will be cleaning the boardroom rather than running it." Her eyes widened. "If you answer my next questions truthfully, things will go much easier for you." He backed off, and she swallowed.

"I know Jessalyn received a copy of the lawsuit. Did you give it to her?"

Rebekka crossed her arms. "Only when I found out she didn't know about it."

He didn't move. "Did you tell her the suit had been dropped?"

"No," she whispered.

"Last question, Ms. Wellington, and I suggest you think very carefully before you answer." He gripped her chin and tilted her face toward his. "Why did you alter the document before you gave it to her?"

She pressed her lips together. "Why do you think?"

His fingers tightened on her chin before he pushed away and ran a hand down his beard. "I'm not sure." He regarded her for a moment. A dawning realization darkened his eyes at her tears, and regret softened his anger. "You actually thought I would come back to you if she was gone."

Rebekka's pride caused her to lash out in anger. "She's nothing but a waitress, Alexander! She doesn't even *want* to be with you, but you *chase* her. You spend huge amounts of money on her. *I* waited for you. Can't you see I love you? I've loved you from the first time I saw you." She stepped closer to him. "Do you even remember that day? We were nineteen when your father brought you into the boardroom to introduce you to the staff. I saw the way you resented him for forcing you to take his place, and he saw how I reacted to you. That's why he asked me to..." Her voice cracked.

"He asked you to what?"

"Spy on you! He told me to keep track of everything you did. Everywhere you went. I watched and hoped one day I would get to tell you how I felt." Her tears fell freely. "And when you walked into the boardroom alone that day, and we...I knew you felt it too." Alexander's shoulders collapsed, and she wrapped her arms around him. "I know you were only with her because of the contract. Now it's over and we can be together!"

Alexander held himself still as Rebekka clung to him. He wanted to shove her away but knew he couldn't. Her hurt and anger were justified even if her actions weren't. Taking a deep breath, he disengaged her arms and set her gently away from him.

Behind her, the door to the ballroom cracked open, and Koen's concerned gaze met his. Alexander shook his head. Rebekka didn't need the humiliation of security removing her from the premises.

He looked back at the woman he had taken so much from, and regret pooled in his stomach. "Rebekka." Dragging a hand through his hair, he turned his back so he wouldn't have to look at her tear-stained face. "There is more going on between Ms. Vogt and myself than you can ever understand." He drew a deep breath and admitted something to her he wished he'd had the courage to say to Jessalyn. "I love her, Rebekka, and I intend to spend the rest of my life with her."

More sobs came just before her fists impacted his back. Tensing, he let her release her anger on him. When she slowed, he turned.

"I will forgive what you've done because of the hurt I've caused you." Her fist rested against his chest, and he moved it away. "I *am* sorry I hurt you, but it doesn't change the way I feel nor what I intend to do about it." When her eyes brightened with challenge, he lifted a finger in warning. "You falsified legal documents. Do you really want to continue your argument?"

Her face tightened in anger, but this time he didn't care. He reached inside his coat pocket and withdrew his phone. He dialed quickly and watched as she shifted from one foot to the other, unsure what he was doing. "Thomas?"

"Alexander, is everything all right?"

"It's fine." Alexander smoothed a hand over his shirt. "Rebekka has confessed. What I need you to do is contact security at the office building and let them know she will be in the office within the next three days to empty her personal belongings. After that, she is not permitted in the building."

Thomas sighed in relief. "I am truly sorry, Alexander. I will make sure there is someone with her at all times."

"I know you will. Hold on one moment if you don't mind." When Thomas agreed, he looked back at Rebekka and flicked his eyes toward the hallway leading out of the building. "I think it best if you go now."

She squared her shoulders and turned away, heels clicking on the concrete floor. She stopped as he was about to return to his call. "Your father would be proud of who you've become, Alexander. He always believed in you."

The air left his lungs in surprise, and he nodded his thanks mutely. She pushed the door open and disappeared into the night.

"Thomas?" His voice broke, and he cleared his throat.

"Are you okay?"

"I'm fine." He re-entered the ballroom. Baden, Koen, and Emerick were across the room talking with Ellen. The three men watched him as a petite woman in a cream gown with shiny black hair flowing down her bare back shook hands with Ellen.

"Thomas, I'll call you tomorrow." He barely remembered to end the call as Jessalyn turned toward him.

FIFTY

J essi's heart skittered when she slowly turned and caught sight of Alexander. Even from across the room the electricity between them hummed. Sensing something was about to happen, the room hushed, and all eyes turned toward them.

Jessi blushed as Alexander's eyes glided from hers to her shoulders to her chest and down to her feet. When he started his upward journey, Jessi followed suit. His broad shoulders were perfectly framed by the black material stretched across them, and the buttoned tuxedo coat skimmed his tapered abs and lay flat against his narrow hips. His feet were planted apart with one hand tucked into the pocket of his pants. Alexander never broke eye contact as he gracefully lifted two champagne glasses from a passing server.

The moment the glasses were in his hands, he crossed the room with the intent to claim. His green eyes lit with a glow of fire that raced through her veins and threatened to force her fangs to drop.

But his steps never hurried. In true Alexander fashion, he played the moment up, letting the tension build until the room could barely contain it. The bergamot smell of his desire made her blush. He was making no attempt to hide his thoughts.

The room buzzed with excitement, and the crowd shifted back from where she and Alexander faced each other. Feeling dizzy under the weight of his gaze, Jessi gripped the back of a chair and sucked in a lungful of air as his steps slowed even further. The guitar continued to play softly in the background, making it all feel like a dream sequence.

After what seemed like an eternity, her mate came close enough to touch. Anticipation raced through her, and she resisted the urge to disregard all pretense and throw herself into his arms. Though the burning in his gaze shot through her, Alexander remained perfectly poised. With only the tick of his jaw to betray his tight control, he held one of the crystal flutes out to her, and his green eyes raked over her again.

Afraid she would drop the glass; she took it and lowered it to the table beside her. When she looked up, his feline-like eyes peered down from inches away, locking her in place. A near whimper escaped her when his free hand tenderly cupped her face.

"Never leave me again, Jessalyn."

Her breath hitched, and she gripped the lapels of his jacket, making him lean toward her. "Never again. I promise."

His thumb caressed her cheek, and a throat cleared beside them. Alexander's lips curved, and he broke their stare to meet the eyes of the one beside her.

Peter brushed invisible lint from his sleeve. "So. Are you two finally going to make this thing official?" He gestured around. "I mean, everyone is already here." The crowd chuckled and began to clap. "Just doesn't seem right to have a Gathering without cele-brating at least one Bonding."

Keeping one hand on her cheek, Alexander set his glass aside and lifted her hand from his jacket. Chills coursed through her when he pressed his lips to the inside of her wrist. "What do you think, Ms. Vogt? Are you ready for me?"

Those standing closest cheered, and Jessi ducked her head to hide the blush. Alexander lifted her chin. "No more hiding." His grin was teasing, but his beautiful eyes begged her. "I love you, Jessalyn, and I'm offering you everything I have. You've already tasted my blood. We're already bonded, but I'm asking you, here in front of all our people—Will you have me, Jessalyn?"

It felt like her heart exploded. "Yes, Alexander. Yes."

The room erupted in a chorus of congratulations and applause as Alexander tenderly lowered his lips to hers. The slightest brush of his mouth made them both tremble from head to toe, and her upper jaw ached.

"A promise." He leaned closer, and his breath tickled her ear. "You are mine, Mrs. Koch."

Barely breathing, Jessi leaned her forehead against his chest, and he cradled her to him. She felt his next words rumble against her cheek. "If you would please excuse us, I think we have a little cele-brating to do."

They both straightened, and she had to laugh as Peter and Hannah stood holding fire extinguishers.

"Safety first!" Peter hefted one over his shoulder and winked at her. "Spontaneous combustion is a thing you know." He slipped a card into Alexander's hand. "Just like you asked."

Curious, Jessi looked up, but Alexander gave nothing away. Instead, he clapped his friend on the shoulder and led Jessi through the center of the ballroom and out the main doors to the cheers of the crowd.

On the way, she and Alexander shook hands and accepted the kind words of everyone they passed, but her hand tightened on his when the hallway widened and the elevator doors slid open.

A young man in a black suit and white gloves stepped from the gleaming box, one hand holding the doors open. "Going up?"

Alexander gestured for her to enter, then turned to the man and slipped something into his hand with a quiet whisper. Grinning, the bellboy pressed a button and stepped out of the elevator. Alexander's back was to her as the door slid closed.

Her stomach dropped as the elevator lifted, and she gripped

Alexander's arm for support. But her knees still almost failed when once again, he flexed his bicep under her palm. Rock hard muscle slid under her hand as he faced her, pressing her against the shiny steel wall. He reached behind him and paused the elevator.

The roar of blood in her ears was nothing compared to the flood of heat filling her belly when Alexander rested a hand above her head and sank gentle fingers through her hair. Shaking with need, she looked up to see a steely composure on his face that belied the raging desire of his eyes. A thread of fear wormed its way up her neck. "Alexander?"

"Do you trust me, Jessalyn?" His body rested lightly against her, and she felt the drumming of his heart. He searched her face and asked again, softer. "Do you trust me, Jessi?"

Somehow, she was still holding her clutch, and with trembling fingers, she reached inside and turned her palm over. Alexander's breath caught when he saw what she was holding.

"You said I was the fulfillment of your hope, Alexander." His glorious eyes shimmered in tears along with hers. "You said you didn't know what I was hoping for, but you wanted me to find it in you." His forehead rested against hers as their tears blended together on her face. "I didn't know what hope was until I met you, Mufasa."

His head fell back, and a huff of laughter escaped him. "Do you know half my staff calls me that now?"

Still holding the pendant in the palm of her hand, she dropped the purse to the floor and pulled his face back to hers. "King. Mufasa means king. And good kings give their people hope." His breathing stilled. "Alexander means defender. You gave me hope, and you make a practice of defending those you love, even teaching them to defend themselves." She clenched her hand around the anatomical heart and threaded her fingers into the length of red hair that slipped over his shoulder, tugging slightly. "You are more than I ever dared to hope for." She rose on her toes as her fangs swept down. "I love you, Alexander."

The arm that had been braced against the wall drug her against him as he crushed his mouth to hers with a growl she felt to her toes. Clinging to him with every ounce of her strength and raking her fangs across his searching tongue, Jessi once again took a deep swallow of the rich chocolate and orange flavor of the blood that flooded their mouths. Alexander swept her into his arms, sucking her lower lip and reaching behind him to start the elevator moving again. His warm hand sent shivers through her as he stroked her bare back from the nape of her neck to the base of her spine.

The doors opened, and he carried her across the hallway, slipping the key card into a door and pushing it open. The smell of lilies assaulted her, and when he switched on the light, vase after vase of stargazers filled the room with their brilliant pink and white blooms. He set her on her feet and braced his hands on her shoulders until her legs supported her.

"You knew I was coming!" Jessi laughed breathlessly. "Hannah can't keep a secret!"

She crossed the room, trying not to stare at the huge bed. The crisp sheets and white comforter were already turned down and waiting for them. Visions of Alexander's bare back flitted through her memories, and her palms itched to smooth through the light dusting of red hair on his sculpted chest.

Alexander lifted a bottle of champagne from a bucket and poured each of them a glass. Amusement danced in his eyes. "It's not that she can't keep a secret." He set the glasses on the nightstand and reached for her hand. "But the king knows everything." He nodded toward the window. "He even knows how to give appropriate gifts."

Jessi followed his gaze and covered her mouth. "Alexander!" she whispered. The bed and lilies had distracted her from noticing the simple white crib with a pale pink and blue blanket draped over the rail. Nothing fancy, nothing ornate, but the baby bed was the most precious gift he'd given her yet. Taking a deep breath, she turned to face him.

The amusement in his eyes flared into desire when she reached for the buttons of his suit coat and pushed it from his shoulders. It slipped to the floor, and her fingers traced the lines of muscle outlined under the starched white shirt. She looped a finger through the bow tie and tugged. "I love you, Mufasa."

His fingers traced down her spine, and she felt the zipper of her dress slide open. "I love you, Jessi." His voice roughened as his hand caressed the newly bared skin of her hip. "But you didn't answer me. Do you trust me?"

Feeling brazen, Jessi stepped back and let the dress fall from her shoulders in a puddle of beads and silk. "With my life."

THE END

ABOUT THE AUTHOR

Michelle Bolanger is a Christian author of contemporary and speculative fiction. She also writes non-fiction articles that share the hope of Christ through daily life lessons as a wife, author, and child of God. In addition to her writing, she is also a talented vocalist and enjoys painting. She lives in small town Ohio with her husband. Together, they enjoy going on long cruises, motorcycle rides along side roads and back roads, and cheering for their favorite professional hockey teams.

After 30+ years of mid-level management in banking and finance, Michelle left the corporate life to pursue her creative passions. She has co-lead Biblical courses on personal finance and budgeting, and served as the women's ministry co-ordinator for her local church where she crafted Bible studies and taught women how to apply Biblical principles to their daily lives. As a vocalist, she has served as a member of her church's worship team, leading the congregation into a deeper connection with God through song.

She began her publishing journey in 2015 with her urban fantasy debut novel, *"The Kiss"* the first book in a young adult series now titled *"The Divided Hearts Series."* She also published the first two stand alone contemporary novels in a collection of gritty, hot button stories that follow characters who come to faith in Christ after walking through some topics most Christian novelists won't write about. She tackles topics like LGBTQ, human trafficking, abortion, and adultery.

Michelle and her husband host a small group Bible study in their home once a week, and she has plans to expand her teaching and encouraging opportunities in the future by organizing an in person writer's group for writers of all levels in her local area. Her greatest desire is to demonstrate the hope of faith in Christ by sharing the lessons God is teaching her as she continues to publish new stories, grow her business, and encourage other writers and women in their giftings and callings.

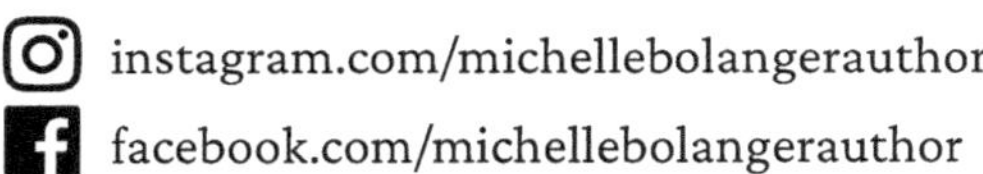

Connect with Michelle

Find me online:
Website: michellebolanger.com
Socials: @michellebolangerauthor
Email: Michelle@risenfiction.com